Mary Higgins Clark's bestselling novels have sold more than three million copies in the UK alone. She is the author of thirty-seven suspense novels as well as three collections of short stories and a memoir.

Alafair Burke is the bestselling author of ten novels, including Long Gone, If You Were Here, and the latest in the Ellie Hatcher series, All Day and a Night. A former prosecutor, she now teaches criminal law and lives in Manhattan.

MARY HIGGINS CLARK
& ALAFAIR BURKE

THE SLEEPING BEAUTY KILLER

SIMON &
SCHUSTER

London · New York · Sydney · Toronto · New Delhi

A CBS COMPANY

First published in the US by Simon & Schuster, Inc., 2016
First published in Great Britain by Simon & Schuster UK Ltd, 2016
A CBS COMPANY

This paperback edition, 2017

1 3 5 7 9 10 8 6 4 2

Simon & Schuster UK Ltd
1st Floor
222 Gray's Inn Road
London WC1X 8HB

Simon & Schuster Australia, Sydney
Simon & Schuster India, New Delhi

www.simonandschuster.co.uk
www.simonandschuster.com.au
www.simonandschuster.co.in

A CIP catalogue record for this book
is available from the British Library

Paperback ISBN: 978-1-4711-5421-8
Export Paperback ISBN: 978-1-4711-5422-5
eBook ISBN: 978-1-4711-5423-2

This book is a work of fiction. Names, characters, places and
incidents are either a product of the author's imagination or are
used fictitiously. Any resemblance to actual people living or
dead, events or locales is entirely coincidental.

Printed and bound by CPI Group (UK) Ltd, Croydon, CR0 4YY

MIX
Paper from
responsible sources
FSC® C020471

Simon & Schuster UK Ltd are committed to sourcing paper
that is made from wood grown in sustainable forests and support the Forest
Stewardship Council, the leading international forest certification organisation.
Our books displaying the FSC logo are printed on FSC certified paper.

For Agnes Partel Newton
With love
—Mary

For Chris Mascal and Carrie Blank
To another 20 + 20 years of friendship
—Alafair

1

Fifteen Years Later

Casey Carter stepped forward once she heard the click, then heard the loud, familiar *clank* behind her. The *clank* was the sound of her cell doors. She'd heard them close every morning when she stepped out for breakfast, every night after dinner, and usually twice in between. Four times a day for fifteen years. Roughly 21,900 clanks, not including leap years.

But this particular sound was different from all the rest. Today, instead of her usual orange prison attire, she wore the black slacks and crisp white cotton shirt her mother had brought to the warden's office yesterday—both a size too large. Today, when she walked out, her books and photographs would be leaving with her.

It was the very last time, God willing, that she'd hear that stifling metallic echo. After this, she was done. No parole. No restrictions. Once she stepped from this building, she would be completely free.

The building in question was the York Correctional Institution. When she'd first arrived here, she'd felt sorry for herself every morning and every night. The papers called her Crazy Casey. More like *Cursed* Casey. Over time, however, she trained herself to feel grateful for small blessings. Fried chicken on Wednesdays. A cellmate with a lovely singing voice and a fondness for the songs of Joni Mitchell. New books in the library. Over the years, Casey had earned the privilege of teaching art appreciation to a small group of fellow inmates.

York wasn't a place where Casey had ever pictured herself, but York had been her home for a decade and a half.

As she walked the tiled halls—one guard in front of her, one behind—fellow inmates called out to her. "You go, Casey." "Don't forget about us." "Show them what you can do!" She heard whistles and claps. She wouldn't miss this place, but she would remember so many of these women and the lessons they had taught her.

She was excited to leave, but she hadn't been this scared since she first arrived. She'd spent 21,900 clanks counting down her days. Now she had finally earned her freedom, and she was terrified.

As she heard an entirely new sound—the prison's outside doors swinging open—she wondered, What will my life be like tomorrow?

A wave of relief washed over her when she saw her mother and cousin waiting outside. Her mother's hair was gray now, and she was at least an inch shorter than when Casey began serving her sentence. But when her mother wrapped her arms around her, Casey felt like a small child again.

Her cousin Angela was as gorgeous as ever. She pulled Casey into a tight hug. Casey tried not to think about the absence of her father, or the fact that the prison hadn't allowed her to attend his funeral three years earlier.

"Thank you so much for coming all the way up from the city," Casey said to Angela. Most of Casey's friends had stopped talking to her once she was arrested. The few that pretended to remain neutral during her trial disappeared from her life once she was convicted. The only support Casey had received beyond the prison walls was from her mother and Angela.

"I wouldn't miss it for the world," Angela said. "But I owe you an apology: I was so excited this morning that I left the city without the clothes your mom asked me to bring. But no worries. We can stop by the mall on the way home for some basics."

"Leave it to you to find any excuse to go shopping," Casey joked. Angela, a former model, was now the head of marketing for a women's sportswear company called Ladyform.

Once they were in the car, Casey asked Angela how well she knew the Pierce family, which founded Ladyform.

"I've met the parents, but their daughter, Charlotte, runs the New York operations. She's one of my best friends. Why do you ask?"

"The disappearance of Amanda Pierce, your friend's younger sister, was featured on last month's episode of a show called *Under Suspicion*. It re-investigates cold cases. Maybe Charlotte can help me get a meeting. I want them to find out who really killed Hunter."

Casey's mother sighed wearily. "Can't you just enjoy one peaceful day before starting up with all this?"

"With all due respect, Mom, I'd say fifteen years is a long enough wait for the truth."

2

That evening, Paula Carter was sitting in bed, her back against the headboard, an iPad mini on her lap. She found comfort in the muffled voices of Casey and Angela from the living room, backed by a television laugh track. She'd read several books about the "re-entry" transition for prisoners returning to the outside world. Based on Casey's free-spiritedness in her younger years, Paula had initially been worried that her daughter might immediately try jumping back into a busy life in New York City. Instead, she'd learned that, more often than not, people in Casey's position had a hard time realizing the extent of their freedom.

Paula was self-confined to her room to give Casey a chance to move around the house without her mother hovering over her. It pained Paula to think that a trip from the bedroom to the living room, with full use of the TV remote control, was the most independence her smart, talented, strong-willed daughter had enjoyed for fifteen years.

She was so grateful to Angela for taking the day off to meet Casey when she was released. By blood, the two girls were cousins, but Paula and her sister, Robin, had raised their daughters as if they were siblings. Angela's father had never been in the picture, so Frank had been a father-figure to Angela. Then when Angela was only fifteen years old, Robin was gone, too, so Paula and Frank finished raising her.

Angela and Casey were as close as sisters, but couldn't be more different. They were both beautiful and shared the same bright blue eyes, but Angela was blonde, and Casey was brunette. Angela had the height and frame of the very successful model she had been in her twenties. Casey's build had always been more athletic, and she had played competitive tennis in college at Tufts. While Angela skipped college to work on her modeling career and a busy social life in New York, Casey had been a serious student, dedicated to multiple political causes. Angela was a Republican, Casey was a Democrat. The list went on and on, and yet the two of them remained as thick as thieves.

Now Paula looked down at the news she'd been reading on her iPad. Only ten hours after leaving her cell, Casey was back in the headlines. Would the attention drive her into her room, never to venture out again?

Or even worse, would it send her straight before the public eye? Paula had always admired her daughter's willingness to fight—often loudly—for what she thought was right. But if it were up to Paula, Casey would change her name, start a new life, and never speak of Hunter Raleigh again.

She had been so relieved today when Angela sided with her against Casey's idea of contacting the producers of *Under Suspicion*. Casey had dropped the subject once they were at the mall, but Paula knew her daughter. That wouldn't be the end of the conversation.

She heard another burst of canned laughter from the television. Casey and Angela were watching a sit-com for now, but with one click, they could stumble onto the news. She was surprised that word had leaked so quickly. Did reporters monitor the names of prisoners released each day? she wondered. Or maybe one of the prison guards had made a phone call. Or perhaps Hunter's family had put out a press release. Lord knows they thought Casey should have gone to prison for the rest of her natural life.

Or maybe someone had simply recognized Casey at the shopping mall. Paula kicked herself again for delegating to Angela the task of pulling together a wardrobe for her cousin. She knew how busy her niece was.

Paula had made such an effort to have everything Casey would need waiting for her at home. Magazines on the nightstand. New towels and a bathrobe. A medicine cabinet filled with the very best spa products. The whole point of preparing was to keep her out of the public eye, but instead they'd ended up at the mall.

She looked again at her iPad screen. CRAZY CASEY'S SPENDING SPREE! There were no photographs, but the so-called reporter knew which mall Casey had been to and which stores. The hit piece concluded, "Apparently prison food was kind to the sleeping beauty's figure. According to our source, Casey is slim and fit from all the hours she spent exercising in the prison yard. Will the accused gold digger be wearing her new wardrobe to find a new boyfriend? Only time will tell."

The blogger was Mindy Sampson. It had been a long time since Paula had seen that name in print, but she was up to her same old tricks. The reason Casey was in excellent shape was because she had always been the worker-bee type, constantly on the go between her job, volunteer work, political groups, and art showings. In prison, she had nothing to do but exercise and obsess over finding someone to help her clear her name. But a tabloid hack like Mindy Sampson made it sound like she'd been preparing for a red carpet.

Whether Paula wanted to or not, she had to alert Casey. As she walked down the hallway, she could no longer hear the sounds of canned laughter. When she turned the corner, Casey and Angela were staring at the television screen. The cable news host's face was filled with pious indignation. "It has been reported that Casey Carter was released from prison today and headed for a shopping mall. That's right, folks, Crazy Casey, Killer Casey, the so-called

Sleeping Beauty Killer is back among us, and the first thing on her mind was a closet full of new clothes."

Casey clicked off the television. "Now do you see why I'm so desperate about *Under Suspicion*? Please, Angela, I've written to defense lawyers and law clinics across the country, and no one will help me. That television show could be my best shot, my *only* shot. And your friend Charlotte has direct access to the producers. Please, I just need one meeting."

"Casey," Paula interrupted, "we already talked about this. It's a terrible idea."

"I'm sorry, but I have to agree with Paula," Angela said. "I hate to say this, but some people think you got off with a slap on the wrist."

Paula and Frank had been devastated when their only daughter was convicted of manslaughter. But the media reported the verdict as a loss for the prosecution, which had depicted Casey as a cold-blooded murderer.

"Let one of those people spend a week in a cell," Casey protested. "Fifteen years is an eternity."

Paula placed a hand on Casey's shoulder. "The Raleighs are a powerful family. Hunter's father could pull strings with the producers. That show could paint you in a very negative light."

"A negative light?" Casey scoffed. "I'd say I'm already there, Mom. You don't think I saw all those people staring at me when we went shopping today? I can't even walk into a store without feeling like a zoo animal. What kind of life is that? Angela, will you call your friend for me or not?"

Paula could feel Angela beginning to cave. The two of them had always been so close, and Casey was as persuasive as ever. Paula looked to her niece with pleading eyes. Please, she thought, don't let her make this mistake.

She felt so relieved when Angela tactfully responded, "Why don't you wait a few days and see how you feel then?"

Casey shook her head, clearly disappointed, but then reached silently for the remote control and turned off the television. "I'm tired," she said abruptly. "I'm going to bed."

Paula fell asleep that night praying that the media would move on to something else so Casey could start adapting to a new life. When she woke up in the morning, she realized she should have known that her daughter never waited for anyone's approval to do anything she believed was important.

Casey's room was empty. There was a note on the dining room table. *Took the train into the city. Be home tonight.*

Paula knew that Casey must have walked the mile to the train station. She didn't need to wonder why Casey had left while she was sleeping. She was going to see the producer of *Under Suspicion*, no matter what it took.

3

Laurie Moran smiled politely to the waiter and declined another refill on her coffee. She stole a glance at her watch. Two hours. She had been at this table at 21 Club for two full hours. It was one of her favorite restaurants, but she needed to get back to work.

"Mmmm, this soufflé is absolute heaven. You're sure you don't want a bite?"

Her companion at what was turning out to be a painfully long meal was a woman named Lydia Harper. By some accounts, she was the brave widow from Houston who'd been raising two boys on her own since a deranged stranger killed their father, an esteemed medical school professor at Baylor, after a road rage incident. By others, she was the manipulative woman who'd hired a hit man to kill her husband because she desperately feared that he was going to divorce her and sue for custody.

The case was perfect for Laurie's show, *Under Suspicion*, a series of true crime–based "news specials" focusing on cold cases. It had been two weeks since Lydia agreed on the phone to participate in a reinvestigation of her husband's murder, but she still hadn't signed the paperwork. After telling Laurie repeatedly that she "kept meaning to go to the post office," she suddenly declared two days ago that she wanted to meet in person—in New York, with a first-class airline ticket and two nights at the Ritz-Carlton—before signing on the dotted line.

Laurie had assumed that Lydia was looking for a free five-star trip on the show's dime, and was willing to oblige if that's what it took to get her to sign her participation agreement. But each time Laurie tried to broach the issue over lunch, Lydia had changed the subject to the Broadway show she'd seen the previous night, her shopping trip to Barneys that morning, or the excellence of 21's classic turkey hash she'd ordered from the lunch menu.

Laurie heard her cell phone buzz from the outside pocket of her handbag once again.

"Why don't you answer it?" Lydia suggested. "I understand. Work work work. It never stops."

Laurie had ignored several other calls and texts, but was afraid to ignore this one. It might be from her boss.

She felt a pit in her stomach as soon as she saw her phone screen. Four missed calls: two from her assistant, Grace Garcia, and two from her assistant producer, Jerry Klein. She also saw a string of text messages from both of them.

Brett is looking for you. ETA?

OMG. Crazy Casey is here about her case. She says she knows Charlotte Pierce. You're going to want to talk to her. Call me!

Where are you? Are you still at lunch?

CC is still here. And Brett is still looking for you.

What do you want us to tell Brett? Call ASAP. Brett's head might explode if you don't get back soon.

And then a final message from Grace, sent just now: *If that man comes back to your office one more time, we might need an ambulance on the 16th floor. What part of "she's not here" does he not understand?*

Laurie rolled her eyes, picturing Brett pacing the hallways. Her boss was a brilliant and renowned producer, but he was impatient and petulant. Last year, a Photoshopped image of his face pasted onto the body of a swaddled baby with a rattle in hand had made the rounds among studio employees. Laurie always suspected that Jerry was the guilty party, but she was confident that he'd covered his electronic tracks so as not to get caught.

The truth was that Laurie had been avoiding Brett. It had been a month since their last special aired, and she knew he was eager for her to start production on the next.

Lord knew she should be thankful. It wasn't that long ago that Laurie had been losing sleep wondering if she still had a career. First, she'd taken time off from work after her husband, Greg, was killed. Then when she returned, her track record was bumpy at best. With each flop of a show, she heard ambitious, young production assistants—each of them eager to take her place—wondering aloud whether she was "in a funk" or had "lost her touch."

Under Suspicion had changed all that. Laurie started toying with the idea before Greg died. People loved mysteries, and telling the stories from the perspective of the suspects was a fresh take on cold cases. But after Greg was killed, she sat on the idea for years. In retrospect, she realized she didn't want to look like a widow obsessed with her husband's own unsolved murder. But, as they say, necessity is the mother of invention. With her career at stake, she finally pitched what she knew was her best idea. They'd had three successful specials, with ratings and "viral trending" increasing each time. But, as they also say, the reward for good work is more work.

A month ago, Laurie had been convinced that she was well ahead of schedule. She had what she thought was the perfect case. Students from the criminal law clinic at Brooklyn Law School had contacted her about a young woman who was convicted of murdering her college roommate three years earlier. They had proof that one of the prosecution's key witnesses had lied. It didn't fit her show's typical model, which looked at unsolved cases from the perspective of the people who'd lived for years under a cloud of suspicion. But the possibility of freeing a woman who had been wrongly convicted tapped into the sense of justice that had drawn Laurie to journalism in the first place.

She fought like the dickens to get Brett to approve the idea, selling him on the concept of wrongful convictions as a hot narrative trend. Then three days after Brett gave her an enthusiastic green light, the prosecution announced at a joint press conference with the law students that they were so convinced by the new evidence that they had agreed to release the defendant and reopen the case on their own initiative. Justice was served, but Laurie's show was dead before arrival.

And so Laurie had moved on to her second choice: the murder of Dr. Conrad Harper, whose widow was now seated across from her, almost done with her dessert. "I'm terribly sorry, Lydia, but there's an urgent matter at my office. I need to get back, but you said you wanted to speak in person about the show."

Lydia surprised Laurie by setting down her spoon and signaling for the check.

"Laurie, I did want to meet in person," she said. "I felt it was only fair. I won't be participating after all."

"What—"

Lydia held up a palm. "I've talked to two different lawyers. They both say I have too much to lose. I'd rather live with the dirty looks from the neighbors than put myself in legal jeopardy."

"We already talked about that, Lydia. This is your chance to help find out who really killed Conrad. I know you have deep suspicions about his former student." Her husband had been stalked by a student he'd failed the previous semester.

"And by all means, if you want to investigate him, be my guest. But I won't be submitting to any interviews."

Laurie opened her mouth to speak, but Lydia immediately interrupted. "Please, I know you need to get back to work. There's nothing you can say to change my mind. My decision is final. I just felt that I should tell you the news in person."

At that exact moment, the waiter arrived with the check, which Lydia promptly handed to Laurie. "It was very nice to have crossed paths with you, Laurie. I wish you all the best."

Laurie felt a chill run up her spine as Lydia rose from the table and left her there, alone. She did it, Laurie thought, and no one will ever be able to prove it.

As she waited for the server to return with her credit card, Laurie sent a joint text message to Grace and Jerry: *Tell Brett I'm ten minutes away.*

What was she going to say once she got there? Her murdered-professor case was down the drain.

She was about to hit enter when she remembered Jerry's earlier text about Crazy Casey. Was it possible? She revised her message. *Did Casey Carter really ask to see me?*

Grace immediately responded. *YES! She's in conference room A. A convicted killer is in our building! I nearly called 911.*

As a journalist, Laurie had interviewed several people accused and even convicted of murder. Grace, however, still flinched at the thought. Jerry's response arrived immediately after Grace's. *I was worried she'd leave but when I thanked her for waiting, she said we wouldn't be able to get rid of her until she saw you!*

Laurie found herself smiling as she signed the bill for lunch. Lydia Harper's pulling out of the show may have been a blessing in disguise. Casey's release had been the lead story on every network last night, and now she was asking for Laurie. She typed a new message from the cab. *Buy me as much time as possible with Brett. Tell him I have a lead on a promising new case. I want to talk to Casey first.*

4

When Laurie exited the elevator on the sixteenth floor of the Fisher Blake Studios offices in Rockefeller Center, she headed directly to the conference room. Grace had managed to learn from Brett's secretary, Dana, that Brett would be on a conference call for the next fifteen or twenty minutes, but that he'd be continuing his hunt for Laurie once he was finished.

She was wondering why Brett was so eager to speak to her. She knew he was pushing her to lock down her next case, but that was nothing new. Was it possible he had somehow figured out in advance that the professor's widow was going to cancel on her? She shook off the thought. Her boss might want people to think he was clairvoyant, but he wasn't.

The woman waiting for her in the conference room sprang to her feet when Laurie opened the door. Laurie recognized Katherine "Casey" Carter immediately. Laurie was just out of college, beginning her journalism career, when the Sleeping Beauty case hit the headlines. The start of her "career" meant fetching coffee in the newsroom of a regional paper in Pennsylvania, but at the time, Laurie was in heaven, soaking up every ounce of training.

As an aspiring journalist, she'd been riveted by the trial. When she'd heard the news last night of Casey's release, Laurie couldn't believe it had been fifteen years already. Time flew so fast, though probably not for Casey.

When her trial had occupied the headlines, Casey had been absolutely stunning, with long, shiny dark brown hair, alabaster skin, and almond-shaped blue eyes that sparkled as if she was thinking of a joke. Right out of college, she had landed a coveted job as an assistant in the contemporary art department at Sotheby's. She was pursuing a master's degree and dreamt of having her own gallery when she met Hunter Raleigh III at an art auction. It wasn't just because of her fiancé's prominence that the nation had been riveted by the case. Casey was captivating in her own right.

Even after fifteen years, she was still beautiful. Her hair was shorter now, bobbed at the shoulders like Laurie's own style. She was thinner, but looked strong. And her eyes still sparked with intelligence as she shook Laurie's hand firmly.

"Ms. Moran, thank you so much for seeing me. I'm sorry I didn't call for an appointment, but I imagine you get flooded by requests."

"True," Laurie said, gesturing that they should both take a seat at the conference table. "But not from people with names as well known as yours."

Casey let out a sad laugh. "And which name are we talking about? Crazy Casey? The Sleeping Beauty Killer? That's why I'm here. I'm innocent. I did not kill Hunter, and I want my name—my *good* name—back."

For those who weren't on a first-name basis with him, *Hunter* was Hunter Raleigh III. His grandfather, Hunter the first, had been a senator. Both of Hunter the first's sons, Hunter Junior and James, joined the military after graduating from Harvard. After Hunter Junior was an early casualty of the Vietnam War, his younger brother, James, committed himself to a lifelong army career, and named his first-born son Hunter the Third. James ascended to the level of a three-star general. Even in retirement, he continued to serve as an ambassador. The Raleighs were a smaller version of the Kennedys, a political dynasty.

And then Casey killed the heir to the throne.

At first, the papers called Casey the Sleeping Beauty. She claimed to have been sleeping soundly while an unknown person or persons broke into her fiancé's country house and shot him to death. The couple had attended a gala for the Raleigh family's foundation in the city that night, but left early after Casey said she felt sick. According to her, she fell asleep in the car and did not even remember arriving at Hunter's house. She woke up hours later on the living room sofa, wandered into the bedroom, and found him covered in blood. She was a young, beautiful up-and-comer in the art world. Hunter was a beloved member of a treasured American political family. It was the kind of tragedy that captivated the nation.

And then, within a few news cycles, the police arrested poor Sleeping Beauty. The prosecution's case was strong. The papers started calling her the Sleeping Beauty Killer and, eventually, Crazy Casey. According to most theories, she'd flown into a drunken, jealous rage when Hunter broke off the engagement.

Now she was in a conference room with Laurie, claiming still— after all these years—to be innocent.

Laurie was aware of the seconds ticking away before she'd need to speak to her boss. Normally, she would have wanted to walk methodically through Casey's side of the story, but she needed to cut to the chase.

"I'm sorry to be blunt, Casey, but the evidence against you would be hard to set aside."

Even though Casey denied ever having fired the handgun that

was determined to be the murder weapon, her fingerprints were found on the gun. And her hands tested positive for the presence of gunshot residue. Laurie asked her if she was denying those facts.

"I assume the tests were done correctly, but all that means is that the real killer pressed my hand to the weapon and let off a shot. Think about it: Why would I have said I never fired the gun if I had shot Hunter with it? I could have easily explained my prints by saying I fired it at the range. Not to mention, whoever shot Hunter apparently missed twice, based on the bullet holes found at the house. I was a very good shot. If I had wanted to kill someone—which I never would—trust me, I would not have missed. And if I had fired his gun, why would I consent to GSR, gunshot residue, testing?"

"What about the drugs the police found in your purse?"

Casey described her illness that night as so severe that the police had tested her blood for intoxicants. But by the time the results confirmed that she had both alcohol and a type of sedative in her system, a search of Hunter's home had turned up that very same drug in Casey's own evening bag.

"Again, if I went through all the trouble of drugging myself, why would I keep three extra Rohypnol tablets in my own purse? It was one thing to accuse me of being a murderer, but I never thought anyone would believe I'd be that stupid."

Laurie was aware of Rohypnol, a drug commonly used in date rapes.

So far, what Casey was saying was all a rehash of the arguments that her lawyer tried to raise at the trial. She was claiming that someone drugged her at the gala, went back to Hunter's house, shot him, and then framed her while she was sleeping. The jury hadn't bought it.

"I followed your trial at the time," Laurie said. "Forgive me for saying this, but I think one of the problems was that your lawyer never seemed to suggest a concrete alternative explanation. She hinted that police may have planted evidence, but never really explained a motive for them to do so. And most importantly, she never gave the jury an alternative suspect. So tell me, Casey: If you didn't kill Hunter, who did?"

5

"I've had a long time to think about who might have killed Hunter," Casey said as she handed Laurie a sheet of paper with five names on it. "I don't think it was a random break-in or failed robbery while I was knocked out on the couch."

"I wouldn't have thought so either," Laurie agreed.

"But when I found out there was a sedative in my system, I realized that whoever killed Hunter must have been at Cipriani for the Raleigh Foundation gala that night. I felt fine earlier in the day. It wasn't until an hour or so into the event that I began to feel sick. Someone must have slipped the drug into my drink when I wasn't looking, which means they had to have access. I can't imagine anyone wanting to hurt Hunter, but I know it wasn't me. These people all arguably had motive and opportunity."

Laurie recognized three of the five names, but they were all a surprise to her as possible suspects. "Jason Gardner and Gabrielle Lawson were at the gala?"

Jason Gardner was Casey's ex-boyfriend and the author of a tell-all memoir that ingrained the nickname *Crazy Casey* into the cultural lexicon. Laurie couldn't recall all the details about Gabrielle Lawson's connection, but the woman was one of the city's famed socialites. As Laurie recalled, there was tabloid chatter that Hunter was purportedly still interested in her, despite his engagement to

Casey. Laurie hadn't realized that either Jason or Gabrielle had been at Cipriani the night of the murder.

"Yes. Gabrielle always seemed to turn up wherever Hunter went. I remember her coming over to our table and throwing her arms around him in typical fashion. She could easily have slipped something into my drink. And Jason—well, supposedly he was there to fill one of the seats at his employer's corporate table, but it seemed far too coincidental for me. Sure enough, he pulled me aside at one point and told me he still loved me. I of course told him that he needed to move on. I was marrying Hunter. So both of them were clearly jealous of what Hunter and I had together," Casey argued.

"Jealous enough to kill?"

"If a jury believed it about me, I don't see why it couldn't be true about one of them."

The third familiar name on the list was especially shocking. "Andrew Raleigh?" Laurie said, arching an eyebrow. Andrew was Hunter's younger brother. "You can't be serious."

"Look, I don't enjoy accusing anyone. But like you said, if I didn't do it—and I know I didn't—someone else did. And Andrew was drinking a lot that night."

"As were you," Laurie added, "according to many witnesses."

"No, that's not true. I had a glass of wine, two at most, but stopped when I began feeling ill. When Andrew drinks, it's . . . well, he becomes a different person. Hunter's father never made it a secret that he loved Hunter more than Andrew. I know the man has an outstanding reputation, but he could be cruel as a parent. Andrew was incredibly jealous of Hunter."

It sounded like a stretch to Laurie. "What about these other two names: Mark Templeton and Mary Jane Finder?" Neither rang a bell.

"Those take a little more explanation. Mark, in addition to being one of Hunter's closest friends, was also the chief financial officer

of the Raleigh Foundation. And, if you ask me, he's the most likely
suspect."

"Even though he and Hunter were friends?"

"Hear me out. Hunter hadn't said anything publicly, but he
was preparing to run for elected office, either as the New York City
mayor or potentially for a seat in the U.S. Senate. Either way, he was
determined to shift from the private sector to public service."

He may not have declared his political intentions, but the public
certainly had speculated. Hunter was a regular on the lists of the
country's most eligible bachelors. When he suddenly announced
his engagement to a woman he'd been dating less than a year, many
wondered if it was the first step toward becoming a candidate. Others viewed Casey as a risky choice for a political wife. The Raleigh
family was well known for its conservative views, while Casey was an
outspoken liberal. They were a political odd couple.

"In advance of any political race," Casey explained, "Hunter had
been inspecting the foundation's books to be absolutely certain that
there were no donations or fundraising practices that could prove
embarrassing or controversial under public scrutiny. The night of
the gala his chauffeur drove him down from Connecticut, and they
picked me up at my apartment. In the car he mentioned that he
was going to hire a forensic accountant to conduct a more thorough
investigation because of what he called some 'irregularities.' Hunter
quickly assured me that he was being abundantly cautious and was
certain there was nothing to worry about. I never thought about it
again until four years after I was convicted, when Mark suddenly
resigned without notice."

This was the first Laurie had ever heard of the subject. "Is that
unusual?" Laurie asked. She was not well-versed in the workings of
private foundations.

"The finance reporters apparently thought so," Casey said. "The
prison law library allowed us to search online media outlets. Appar-

ently, the foundation's assets were low enough to trigger speculation. You have to understand, when Hunter poured himself into that
foundation, he tripled fundraising results. It's one thing for revenue
to fall off without Hunter at the helm. But the media reports said
that total assets were actually down, raising questions about whether
they were mismanaging the funds or perhaps worse."

"How did the foundation deal with the speculation?"

She shrugged. "All I know is what I could glean from my media
searches, and the assets of a nonprofit foundation aren't quite as
newsworthy as, say, a high-profile murder trial. But from what I can
tell, once reporters started talking about Mark's sudden resignation,
Hunter's dad appointed a new CFO while praising Mark at length.
The story went away. But the fact remains, the foundation's assets
were mysteriously low. I think Hunter detected the problem years
earlier. Plus, I can tell you this: Mark Templeton was seated right
next to me at the gala. He could easily have slipped a drug into my
drink."

Laurie had only agreed to see Casey out of curiosity and to tell
Brett she had a lead on a possible story, but she could already picture
putting each of these alternative suspects in front of the camera. She
realized that when she envisioned the show, she still pictured Alex as
the show's host. Once their last case was finished, he had announced
that he needed to focus full-time on his criminal defense practice.
His departure from the show left the status of what had been a deepening personal relationship between them unclear. She shook the
thought from her mind and pressed on.

"And Mary Jane Finder? Who is she?"

"General Raleigh's personal assistant."

Laurie felt her eyes widen. "What's the connection there?"

"She began working for him a few years before I met Hunter.
Hunter did not like Mary Jane from the very beginning, but was especially concerned about the authority she seemed to wield after

Hunter's mother passed away. He thought she was trying to take advantage of his father, or perhaps even marry him now that he was a widower."

"The boss's son didn't like her? That doesn't seem like a strong motive for murder."

"It's not just that he didn't like her. He thought she was scheming and manipulative. He was certain she was hiding something and was determined to get her fired. And here's the thing: when we were on our way to the gala, I heard him call a lawyer friend for a referral for a private investigator, saying he needed a background check on someone. Then I heard him say, 'It's a sensitive matter.' When he hung up, I asked him if it was related to the audit he was planning of the foundation."

A knock at the conference room door interrupted them. Jerry popped his head in. "I'm very sorry, but Brett's off his conference call. He's with Grace now, demanding to know where you are."

Laurie didn't dare give Brett an exact location or he'd barge in here and take over the discussion. But she also didn't want to put Grace in a position where she was directly lying to her boss's boss.

"Can you please tell him you spoke to me and that I will be in his office in no more than five minutes?" Brett would assume that the conversation was a phone call. It would get him off Grace's back, but Laurie needed to hurry.

"Okay, so the private investigator was for the foundation," Laurie said, getting back on track.

"No, it wasn't. Or at least, I don't think it was. I asked Hunter if it was related to the audit. He looked sort of warily toward his driver, Raphael, as if to say, *Not now*. It made me think that he didn't want Raphael to hear the name of the person he was checking on."

"Maybe it was Raphael," Laurie speculated.

"Absolutely not," she said. "Raphael was one of the kindest, most gentle men I have ever met, and he and Hunter adored each other.

He was almost an honorary uncle. But he was also extremely trusting and wanted to believe the best about everyone, including Mary Jane. Hunter had stopped complaining about her in Raphael's presence to avoid putting him in an awkward position with a woman who was exercising more and more influence on the family staff. If Hunter was right about Mary Jane hiding something, she may have found a way to stop him from finding out the truth."

"But was she at the gala?" Laurie asked.

"Oh, she certainly was, in the seat right next to General Raleigh. There was a reason Hunter was worried about her agenda."

Laurie could almost picture Brett starting to look at his watch, counting the minutes until her arrival. "Casey, this list is a great start. Let me do some preliminary research and get back—"

"No please, I have so much more to say. You're my only hope."

"I'm not saying no. In fact, I'm very intrigued."

Casey's lower lip started to shake. "Oh my gosh, I'm so sorry." She fanned her eyes. "I swore I was not going to cry. But you have no idea how many letters I've written to lawyers and law clinics and reporters. So many of them wrote back saying the same kind of thing—*I'm intrigued,* or *let me look into it.* And then I'd never hear from them again."

"That's not what's happening here, Casey. If anything, I should be the one worried that I'll pour a lot of resources into investigating these claims, only to find out that you've taken your story to the nearest website that will hit the publish button."

She shook her head adamantly. "No, absolutely not. I've seen the hatchet jobs these so-called journalists come up with. But I know your show, and I know that Alex Buckley is one of the best defense attorneys in the city. I won't talk to any other media until you make up your mind."

The mention of Alex's name grabbed Laurie in the heart.

Casey implored her. "When can we meet again?"

Laurie remembered Jerry's text message from earlier. *She said we wouldn't be able to get rid of her until she saw you.* Right now, she needed to get rid of her.

"Friday," Laurie blurted. That was two days from now. She was about to backtrack when she realized it would be a good idea to meet Casey and her family outside the office before making any final decisions about whether to proceed. "In fact, I can come to you. Maybe meet your parents?"

"My father passed," Casey said sadly, "but I'm staying with my mother. We're in Connecticut, though."

I guess I'm going to Connecticut, Laurie thought.

They were at the conference room door when Laurie realized she'd forgotten to follow up on one part of the earlier string of text messages. "My assistant producer mentioned that you know Charlotte Pierce?"

Three months ago, Laurie had had no sense of Charlotte Pierce as a person. She thought of Charlotte as "the sister"—as in "the sister" of Amanda Pierce, the missing bride whose disappearance was the subject of Laurie's most recent special. But, to Laurie's surprise, once the production was over, Charlotte had invited her to lunch. Several meals later, Laurie now thought of Charlotte as a friend, the first one she'd made in a very long time.

Casey grinned sheepishly. "I may have overstated our connection," she confessed. "My cousin, Angela Hart, works with her. They're super-good friends, but I've never actually met her."

Laurie watched as Casey put on large dark sunglasses, twisted her hair up, and pulled a Yankees cap low over her forehead. "It was bad enough being recognized at the mall," she said bitterly.

As Laurie rushed to Brett's office, she dictated a reminder to herself to call Charlotte to see if she had any insider information. She also made a mental note: Casey Carter was willing to stretch the truth if it served her purposes.

6

Brett's secretary, Dana Licameli, gave Laurie a sympathetic look as she waved her into what felt in that moment like the gallows. "Beware," she warned. "I haven't seen him on a tear like this since his daughter came back from Europe with a pierced nose."

Brett immediately swiveled in his chair to face her. "I thought with your extended sojourn from the office, you might return with a tan, smelling of rum and sunscreen." He glanced at his watch. "Nearly three hours at 21 Club? We should all be so lucky. Don't blame your staff, either. They did their best to cover for you, but I made Dana sneak a peek at your calendar on your assistant's computer."

Laurie opened her mouth to speak but nothing came out. She hated the idea that she had subjected Jerry and Grace to Brett's abuse during her absence. If she said what was truly on her mind, all three of them would be out of their jobs. She finally found words she was able to force herself to mutter. "My apologies, Brett. I obviously forgot we had a meeting scheduled for this afternoon."

Her dry delivery seemed to calm him down. He even gave her a half smile. At sixty-one by her last count, Brett was still quite handsome. With a full head of iron-gray hair and a strong jaw, he had the look of one of the many news anchors he'd hired over the years.

"Don't be so snarky. You know there was no meeting. But you've been avoiding me, and we both know why."

"I haven't been avoiding you," Laurie fibbed, tucking a long strand of light brown hair behind one ear. She had just been waiting for that darned release from the Texas widow, so she could tell Brett they were officially ready to roll. "I really thought we had our ducks in a row on the medical-professor case. The widow was dragging her feet, but I was sure she'd come around."

"You mean she didn't? You told me she was just too busy with those rug rats of hers to get to the post office."

Laurie was positive she had not referred to Lydia's boys as rug rats. Instead she said mildly, "She apparently had second thoughts or was leading me on the whole time."

"I bet she's afraid to do it," Brett said. "Maybe she's guilty."

One of the hardest parts of Laurie's job was convincing all of the key players to participate in the show. Normally, she tried to appear so gentle and nice that it was difficult for people to say no, but tougher tactics were sometimes called for. She wasn't always proud of the maneuvers she had to use, but a single missing piece of the puzzle pulled the entire production apart.

"I think so, too. She said she consulted two lawyers and has too much to lose."

"Well, that makes her guilty in my book."

"I happen to agree in this instance," Laurie said, "but her mind was definitely made up. And a special about her husband's unsolved murder wouldn't be compelling without her on camera."

"You really are trying to ruin my day, aren't you?" Brett's tone had become sarcastic.

"Not intentionally, no. But the good news is that my sojourn, as you called it, has paid off with a new lead. I just met with Casey Carter."

"Crazy Casey? I heard about her on the news last night. Was she wearing one of the outfits she bought at the mall?"

"I didn't ask. I was too busy listening to her claims that she's innocent. And she laid out five alternative suspects. It could be great for *Under Suspicion*. Wrongful conviction stories are all the rage."

"But only when they're wrongful."

"I know. It was just a first meeting. I still have a lot of work to do, but at least she's talking to me and not anyone else."

"Honestly, in this case, I don't care whether the gal is a murderer or not. Her name alone will be a ratings bonanza." Laurie expected Brett to give her the third degree over details she didn't have yet. But instead of pressing her for information about the case, he simply said, "Well, I hope this one actually sticks. Fisher Blake Studios hasn't survived all these years by funding false starts."

"Message received," Laurie said, trying to conceal her relief. "Was an update on the next special the only reason you wanted to see me?"

"Of course not. We need to talk about the elephant in the room: whether we like it or not, Alex is gone, and you need a new host." Brett reached across the desk and handed her a piece of paper. "Lucky for you, I've got the perfect man for the job."

As Laurie stared at the sheet of ivory stock paper in her hand, all she could think about was Alex. The way she knew, the first time she saw his blue-green eyes look into the camera behind black-rimmed glasses, that he was the perfect host for *Under Suspicion*. How he had jumped into the car with her without hesitation after her father was admitted to the hospital with heart palpitations. Their first dinner alone at Marea. How he had run on instinct to her and Timmy when the man who killed Greg tried to murder them, too. All those hours spent bouncing case theories around over a bottle of red wine. The feeling of his lips against hers.

She realized in that instant that Brett was right. She had been avoiding her boss, and it wasn't because she was waiting for a piece of paper from some woman in Texas. Just as she had kept hoping that the widow would come around, she realized that part of her had been hoping that Alex might, too. Maybe his law practice would settle down temporarily. Or maybe once she had a case in hand, he'd be too intrigued to resist. Or maybe he would just miss working with her.

But now the idea of Alex leaving the show was real. She was looking at a résumé that belonged to an actual person with an actual name: Ryan Nichols. Magna cum laude from Harvard Law School. A Supreme Court clerkship. Courtroom experience as a federal prosecutor. It wasn't until she got to the entry about his talking head experience that she connected Ryan's name to the face she'd seen all over the cable news circuit lately.

In her mind, she previewed a recording that didn't exist yet. *Under Suspicion, featuring Ryan Nichols.* No, she thought, that doesn't sound right. The name should be Alex Buckley.

Her thoughts were interrupted by the sound of Brett's gruff voice. "I know, Ryan's perfect. He'll be here Friday at four to make it official. You can thank me later."

As she turned to leave, Laurie didn't think the knot in her stomach could feel any thicker. Then she heard Brett's voice again behind her. "And we'll talk about Crazy Casey then, too. Can't wait to hear the details."

Great. She had two days to come up with a detailed pitch of Casey Carter's wrongful conviction claim, even though she had no idea whether the woman was innocent or a killer. She needed to call Charlotte.

7

Laurie had just taken a seat on the wine-colored velvet sofa in Ladyform's luxurious lobby when Charlotte appeared through a set of white double doors. She rose and gave Charlotte a quick hug.

"We're the same height today," Charlotte observed cheerfully.

"Thanks to my three-inch heels and your flats," Laurie said. Charlotte was just shy of five-ten. She was slightly stocky but seemed confident in her own skin. Her chin-length light brown hair neatly framed her round, makeup-free face. Laurie thought of her as the perfect representative of her family's company.

"Thank you so much for seeing me on such short notice," Laurie said, as Charlotte led the way to her office.

"No problem. I could use the distraction. My mom's flight from Seattle lands in an hour. And big news: Dad decided to come up from North Carolina. So as soon as we're done here, I may need to break out the vodka."

"Oh dear. Is it that bad? They seemed to be getting along so well the last time I saw them." More than getting along, Laurie thought. If the disappearance of Charlotte's sister was what broke the couple apart, finding out the truth about what happened to their daughter seemed to have brought them back together again.

"I'm kidding. Mostly. It's almost like they're dating each other. It's very sweet. I just wish they'd get back together again, so they'd stop using visits to me as an excuse to see each other. Dad's gotten better about trusting me with the company, but I still feel him looking over my shoulder when he's here. Speaking of possible couples, how are things with Alex?"

"Fine. Last I heard, he was fine."

In theory, Alex's departure from the show had been strictly business, as he needed to return full-time to his law practice. But she'd only seen him once in the last month, and their "date" this Thursday was to watch the Giants game at his apartment with her father and son. It would be a late night, but Timmy's school was off the next day for teachers' meetings.

"Message received," Charlotte said. "When you called, you said it was about the show?"

"Do you work with a woman named Angela Hart?"

"Sure. She's my marketing director, also one of my closest friends. Oh, I know why you're here," she said excitedly. "It must be about her cousin."

"So you know she's related to Casey Carter?"

"Of course. She has kept her connection to Casey quiet at work, but I knew that the reason she left early every other Friday wasn't to go to the Hamptons as she claimed. She visited Casey faithfully. A few years ago, after too many martinis, I asked Angela point-blank: Did your cousin do it? She swore on her very life, with no hesitation, that Casey is innocent."

"Did she mention that Casey came to see me today? She wants to be featured on *Under Suspicion*. She even gave me a list of five alternative suspects that her defense attorney never really explored."

"I had no idea," Charlotte said. "I'm not an expert on the case, but I was under the impression the evidence was compelling. I make a point never to share that observation with Angela, of course, but everyone in prison claims they didn't do it."

"I know, but I can't help being intrigued. It's one thing to say you're innocent, but she showed up in my office the very first day after she got out of prison. To tell you the truth, it reminded me of how I felt when your mother showed up asking for help. I couldn't turn her away."

"Obviously, Angela might have a blind spot when it comes to her cousin, but would you like to speak to her?"

"I was hoping you'd introduce us."

8

The woman who arrived at Charlotte's office two minutes later was stunningly beautiful. Her long, honey-colored hair fell in perfect waves, and when she smiled, her teeth literally sparkled behind strawberry-colored full lips. She was even taller than Charlotte, maybe six feet tall, and was trim and graceful. She had the same blue, almond-shaped eyes as her cousin Casey.

She was juggling an armful of files and papers. "I drew up some tentative plans for the show, and I've got the warehouse lease. I negotiated a better rate, but we have to get the papers in by tomorrow morning."

She stopped suddenly when she saw that Charlotte had a visitor in her office. She freed one hand for a quick shake. "Angela Hart," she said.

Laurie introduced herself as the producer of *Under Suspicion*.

Angela seemed to realize the connection to her cousin immediately. "I should have known she'd go charging forward. Once Casey puts her mind to something, she's like a dog with a bone."

"She mentioned her interest in our show?"

"We were barely in the car at the prison."

"You don't sound particularly enthusiastic about the idea."

"I'm sorry. I don't mean to sound so negative. I just wanted her to take a few days to think about it. Obviously, I know Charlotte's family had a positive experience, so I was going to ask you about it today, Charlotte, and pass that on to Casey. But this lease situation got complicated—"

"The space we normally use for our fall show had an electrical fire last week," Charlotte explained. "We had to find an alternative on short notice. Complete nightmare."

"Charlotte said you're in marketing here?" Laurie asked, realizing that she had jumped too abruptly into a discussion of the case.

"Ever since Ladyform opened a New York office," Angela said brightly. "Gosh, that's more than twelve years. If it weren't for Charlotte, I'd probably be wandering the streets, scrounging for cans and bottles."

"Stop it," Charlotte said. "Any company would have been crazy not to hire you."

"Charlotte's too kind," Angela said. "The truth is, I was a washed-up model when she hired me. You hit thirty, and suddenly your best gigs are for girdles and wrinkle cream. I blanketed the entire city with résumés, searching for some other job in fashion, and couldn't even get an interview. No degree. No job experience besides posing for a camera. Now I'm a forty-four-year-old woman with an actual career, all because Charlotte gave me a chance."

"Are you kidding?" Charlotte said. "You gave *us* a chance. I can't imagine what you thought when you showed up for an interview to meet Amanda and me. We were just kids!"

Laurie knew that Charlotte and her younger sister, Amanda, had been the ones to push Ladyform in a new direction with offices in New York City. What had once been a small, family-owned business manufacturing "foundational garments" became a go-to brand for women's fashionable athletic attire.

"Anyway," Angela continued, "we had an hour-long interview and then wound up going next door to continue the conversation over wine. We've been pals ever since."

"I know the feeling," Laurie said. "Charlotte and I met when my show handled her sister's case, but she's the one who made sure we stayed friends afterwards."

"For what it's worth," Charlotte said, "my family spent more than five years in a living hell, with no idea what happened to Amanda. *Under Suspicion* brought us out of that hell. Laurie could do the same for Casey."

"I know your show can unearth new evidence," Angela said, "but my aunt and I are worried about adding to Casey's notoriety. It would be one thing if this were ten years ago when she was still in prison. But she's free now. She did her time. I understand Casey's desire to convince people that she would never hurt a fly, let alone Hunter. She loved him dearly. But I don't think she has any idea of how much the world has changed in the last fifteen years. If she thought the tabloid headlines were bad, wait until she sees what Twitter and Facebook will do to her. There's something to be said about leaving the past behind her."

"I take it that your aunt is Casey's mother?" Laurie asked.

Angela nodded. "Aunt Paula is Casey's mother and my mom's sister. But Casey and I were both only children, so we were very close growing up. I was probably five when I realized her full name was Katherine Carter, which meant we had different last names. I remember my mom having to explain that she wasn't actually my baby sister."

"It must have been hard on you when she was convicted."

Angela sighed. "Absolutely devastating. I was so sure the jury would see the truth. I realize now how naive I was. She was only twenty-five years old then, barely out of college. Now she's forty years old and has no idea how different things are now. She had a flip cell phone before she went to prison, and had no idea how to use my iPhone to look up something."

"Paula's opposed to Casey doing my show?"

"*Extremely* opposed. To be frank, I think Casey's conviction killed her father prematurely. I worry about what the stress of the renewed attention will do to Paula."

Charlotte patted her friend's hand supportively. "I had the same concerns about my parents when my mother convinced Laurie to look into Amanda's disappearance. I thought it was time for them to move on. But now that they know what happened, they're finally free from the limbo they lived in for five years."

Laurie had felt the same way after she learned the truth about Greg's murder a year ago. *Limbo* was a perfect word to describe the state she'd been in until recently.

"Were you at all involved in the case?" Laurie asked, shifting direction. "Did you know Hunter?"

"Obviously I wasn't there when he was killed," Angela said. "But I saw both of them earlier that night at the gala for his foundation. And I was the first person she called from the country house when she found his body—after 911, of course. I had a photo shoot scheduled the next morning, but I hopped straight into my car. Even by the time I drove up to New Canaan, Connecticut, she was still completely out of it. It was obvious to me she had been drugged. In fact, I was the one who insisted that the police run a test on her blood. Sure enough, it turned up positive for both alcohol and Rohypnol. Would any sane person take Rohypnol on her own? Absolutely not. It's not a recreational drug. It turns you into a zombie from what I'm told."

Laurie found herself thinking of her friend, Margaret, who had been convinced that someone had dropped a drug in her drink while they were at a bar together shortly after graduating from college. She remembered how Margaret described feeling like she was watching everything from outside her own body.

"So you still believe Casey is innocent?"

"Of course. That's why she turned down a plea deal that would have had her out of prison with a six-year sentence."

"And if Casey and I wind up deciding to go forward with the show, will you help? As I understand it, you and her mother are the only people who have kept contact with her."

"Is there any way I can convince you to give her some time to adjust before she makes a final decision? This entire thing feels rushed."

"No, I'm afraid not. I have deadlines to meet."

"Be honest: You don't really need Paula and me, do you? You'll go forward regardless of what we think."

"Yes, as long as we have Casey and at least some of the alternative suspects."

"Then what can I say? I'll continue to support Casey because that's what I've always done. But I can tell you right now: Paula will be in your way at every step. She's convinced Casey is making a terrible mistake."

"Well, I hope that isn't true," Laurie said. "And I'll consider myself warned."

9

Two days later, Laurie examined her face in the mirror of her bedroom vanity. She swore the crease between her eyebrows hadn't been there yesterday. Was that possible? Could wrinkles literally appear overnight? She started to reach for concealer, but stopped. She preferred to look like herself, and if that meant a few more lines, she'd take them—not happily, but accepting nonetheless.

In the mirror's reflection she saw Timmy bound into her room, iPad in hand. "Mom, you're going to get caught in traffic both ways. You need to leave Connecticut by three o'clock at the latest if you're going to make it to Alex's in time for kickoff. You'll be stop-and-go all the way down the Bruckner."

She couldn't believe how quickly her son was growing up. He had mastered all the online traffic apps while serving as backseat "navigator" during last month's trip to Florida.

She saw no need to tell him that she actually needed to hit the road even earlier. She had her meeting with Brett and his choice for her new host at four.

She gave Timmy a quick hug before guiding him into the living room. "I'm the one who taught you never to be late, including to school," she reminded him. "Get your shoes on and your backpack. And don't forget your math assignment. It was on the coffee table last night."

While Timmy trudged back to his room, her father came in and handed her a mug of coffee. "I even remembered to use that horrible almond milk you're so enamored with."

The truth was that she'd originally bought it hoping her father would take to it. Ever since he had two stents inserted in his right ventricle last year, he was following a heart-healthy diet, but still insisted on using pure cream in his coffee. Oh well, she thought, if anyone deserves a small vice, it's my father. Six years ago, her father was NYPD First Deputy Police Commissioner Leo Farley, a potential contender to be the next commissioner. Then one late afternoon, while pushing Timmy on a swing, Laurie's husband, Greg, was killed by a gunshot to the forehead. Laurie was suddenly a single mother with no idea who murdered her husband. Leo walked away from the job he loved, all for her and Timmy.

Now he was about to walk Timmy to school, as he did every single day after walking the few blocks from his own apartment to pick up his grandson here. If he wanted cream in his coffee, he could have it.

"I can tell Timmy's excited to see Alex tonight," he said.

"Of course he is," she said. "He adores Alex."

"We all do," her father said. "Sorry," he immediately added, "I wasn't trying to make a point."

"I know, Dad, it's fine."

It was an open secret that Leo wanted Laurie to find her happily-ever-after with Alex. Part of her desperately wanted that, too. But every time she thought she might be ready, she would picture Greg, and could feel herself pull back from Alex. Her husband still filled her heart to the point that she wondered whether there'd ever be room for someone else.

Since leaving her show, Alex said he'd been keeping a busy travel schedule on a major case, but she knew why he hadn't been picking up the phone. He had fallen in love with her and was keeping his distance until she was ready to feel the same way. She had to give him some space and hope he'd still be there if and when she could make a commitment.

"Timmy said something about you going to a prison?" Leo asked. "What's that about?"

Timmy had a way of hearing only the most exciting words to escape his mother's mouth. "I'm not literally visiting a prison, but I am seeing someone who was released on Tuesday. Dad, what do you remember about the Sleeping Beauty Killer?"

"That she murdered a damn fine man and then tried to blame the police for railroading her. She should've gone to prison for life, but that jury got suckered into feeling sorry for her." A worried look passed over his face. "Oh, Laurie, please tell me she's not the one you're meeting with."

10

The screen of Laurie's cell phone notified her that her car had arrived and was waiting on 94th Street, but Leo was still trying to persuade Laurie that the drive was a waste of time. "She'll look you right in the eye, then lie to your face, just like she did to the police when she was arrested."

She was starting to regret mentioning the reason for her trip to Connecticut. She gulped down the final sip of her coffee, needing every ounce of caffeine.

"I haven't made a decision yet," she said.

"I can already predict what Casey will tell you. She was drugged at the fundraiser by some unidentified stranger."

"I know, I know," she said, checking her briefcase to make sure she had everything she needed for the day. "Her blood tests proved that she had consumed not only alcohol, but Rohypnol. She'll tell me it's what people call a *roofie*, used to incapacitate a victim, not as a recreational drug."

"Except she wasn't drugged by a stranger, Laurie. She drugged herself so she could blame the crime on someone else." Leo shook his head in disgust.

"Dad, I have to go, okay? I *promised* Casey I would at least consider her case. You're the one who taught me: Once you give your word—"

"Well, why do you have to go today? Take some time and consider some other cases."

She wanted to say, *Because Brett is breathing down my neck,* but she didn't want to give her father another reason to despise her boss. Her father was supportive to a fault. How many times had he told her that she could join any television team in the country? If you asked Leo, she should have had a cabinet filled with Emmy Awards and *60 Minutes* was pining to recruit her.

"Apparently Casey's mother doesn't want her going on my show."

"Smart woman," he said emphatically. "She probably knows her daughter's guilty."

"In any event, I'd prefer the chance to get to know her sooner rather than later, in the event I do decide to cover the case."

"Which I hope you absolutely won't do."

Timmy and Leo walked Laurie to the black SUV waiting outside their building. Laurie gave Timmy a final hug, and then watched as he and Leo began their daily walk to Saint David's school.

As she watched the city roll past her through the window of the SUV, she was grateful that she was making the long trip to Connecticut and back today. Her son was not the only one who was excited to see Alex tonight. A busy schedule between now and then would make the time fly by.

11

Paula Carter stood in the doorway of the guest room, watching her daughter sort through the makeshift office she had created. Casey had left the prison with two boxes. From what Paula could see, most of the contents were files and notebooks, now stacked on the top of the dresser and both nightstands. With the exception of her trip into the city two days ago, Casey had spent all of her time in here, poring over these documents.

"Oh dear, the room is quite small, isn't it?" she asked.

"It's a palace compared to what I'm used to," Casey said with a sad smile. "Seriously, Mom, thank you for everything you've done for me. I know it must have been hard to move up here."

Up here was Old Saybrook, Connecticut, only ten and a half miles from the prison that had been Casey's home for the last fifteen years.

Paula had never thought she'd leave Washington, D.C. She moved there when she was only twenty-six years old to marry Frank, twelve years her senior. They had met in Kansas City. He was a partner at one of the nation's largest law firms. She was a paralegal for one of his corporate client's local counsel. A massive product defect that originated in the client's Missouri plant meant months of depositions. By the time the case was settled, Frank had proposed and anxiously asked her if she would consider moving to Washington, D.C. She had told him that the only downside was that she would desperately miss her twin sister, Robin, and her little niece, Angela, who had just learned to call her Aunt Paw-Paw. Robin was a single mother; Angela's father had never been in the picture. Paula had gotten Robin a job as a secretary at her firm and was helping to raise the little girl. Growing up, Paula and Robin had both dreamed of going to law school.

Within three days, Frank had a solution. Robin and her daughter, Angela, would move to D.C., too. His firm would hire Robin as a secretary and would give her a flexible schedule if she wanted to pursue a paralegal license or even law school. All three of them—Paula, Robin, and little Angela—headed to D.C. together.

And what an adventure it had been. Paula and Frank were married within a year, and Casey came along before their second anniversary. Paula never followed through on her dream of becoming a lawyer, but Robin did, while Paula had a wonderful life with Frank. They had a beautiful home in Georgetown with a small yard where the girls could play outside. The White House, the National Mall, and the Supreme Court stood just outside their door. Whoever thought, she and Robin would say, that our daughters would grow up with all of this at their fingertips?

The capital became a member of her family.

Then, just two years after graduating from law school at the age of thirty-six, Robin got her cancer diagnosis. She did all the treatments, lost her hair, felt sick around the clock. But it didn't work. Angela was still in high school when they buried her mother. She lived with the Carters in the Georgetown house until she graduated and then moved to New York City with dreams of being a model. Four years after that, Casey also left, at first to attend college at Tufts, then to pursue a career in art in New York.

It was just Frank and Paula in D.C. At least the girls had each other in New York—at first, before the trouble with Hunter.

Then three years ago, as Paula and Frank walked up the steps of the Lincoln Memorial, Frank collapsed. The doctor at Sibley Memorial Hospital told her that he didn't suffer. "It would have felt like the lights turned off." In her mind, her husband died of a broken heart. It broke the day Casey was convicted.

Without Frank, the house in Georgetown felt much too large. Paula would go for a walk and see all of the sights she used to visit with people she desperately missed. Robin and Frank were gone. Angela was still in New York. And Casey lived in a six- by eight-foot cell in Connecticut. No, the nation's capital was not her family. Casey, Frank, Angela, and Robin were. So she sold the house and bought this townhouse in Old Saybrook for no other reason than its proximity to her daughter. Truth be told, she would have paid a million dollars to move into the cell next door to Casey's if they had let her.

But now her daughter was here, so it felt a little more like home. She wiped a tear forming in the corner of her eye, hoping Casey hadn't noticed. Frank begged you to take that plea deal, she thought. *I'm old*, he had said, *and I'm only getting older.* Casey, you could have been out nine years ago. Frank would have had at least six years—maybe more—to spend with you.

Her thoughts were interrupted by the sound of a knock at the door.

"That must be Laurie Moran," Paula said. "I don't know why you want to put yourself through this, but Lord knows you never take my advice." Just like you refused to take your father's, she thought.

12

"Are you sure I can't get you some tea?"

It was the third time that Paula had offered. In between, she had repeatedly straightened the hem of her skirt, stood to adjust a painting on the wall, and shifted constantly in her corner of the sofa.

"Actually, that would be lovely." Laurie had no interest in tea, but was willing to drink sour milk if it would give her a break from the woman's nervous energy.

Once Paula had left the room, Casey said, "I'm having flashbacks to the last time I was under the same roof with my parents, right after Hunter was killed. They came up from D.C. and insisted on staying in my apartment because they didn't want me to be alone. I wasn't sure I wanted that, either. But for two straight days, my mother offered me fruit, cheese, juice, tea. She'd stand up in the middle of a conversation and start scrubbing the kitchen counters. The floors were so clean, you could see your reflection."

By the time Paula returned with a sterling silver tea tray, Laurie had shifted the discussion to the night of Hunter Raleigh's murder.

"What time did you leave the gala at Cipriani?" she asked.

"It was shortly after nine o'clock. I felt horrible causing Hunter to leave his own party. The waiters were only beginning to serve dessert. I offered to take a cab, but he insisted on coming with me. I was terribly ill, barely able to stand up, and I think he could see that something was very wrong. It was only later that I realized that some-one had drugged me."

We will definitely get to that subject, Laurie thought. But she wanted to hear the big picture first, from beginning to end.

"So Hunter's driver took you both back to Hunter's house?"

"Yes, Raphael. He was waiting outside with the car."

"You didn't want to just stay in the city since you weren't feeling well?" In addition to Hunter's country home in New Canaan, both Casey and Hunter had apartments in Manhattan.

Casey shook her head. "That house was magical. I really thought I'd feel better once we got there. I was in and out of sleep during the drive. I should have known immediately that something was wrong no matter what the hour. Normally, I am a very difficult sleeper. I could never sleep in a car or on a plane."

Even the prosecution conceded that Casey had Rohypnol in her system. The only question was whether she had taken the drug her-self after shooting Hunter, to create an alibi, or if someone else had drugged her earlier in the night.

Laurie knew from reviewing the case that the police had pulled a photograph of Hunter's car passing through the toll lane on the Henry Hudson Parkway. Casey was sitting upright in the backseat, next to Hunter. At trial, the prosecutor offered the image into evi-dence to disprove Casey's claim of being drugged at the gala, rather than after the murder, by her own hand.

"Was fatigue the only symptom you were experiencing?" When Laurie's friend Margaret was convinced she'd been drugged, she said the feeling was very different from simply being tired.

"No, it was awful. I was dizzy and confused and nauseated. I felt hot and cold at the same time. I was having a hard time speaking, like I couldn't remember any words. I just remember feeling like I had absolutely no control over my mind or body. I remember pray-ing to God to help me stop feeling that way."

It was the exact same feeling that Margaret had described.

"You called 911 after midnight," Laurie noted. "Twelve-seventeen A.M. to be exact. What happened between the time you got home and that emergency call?"

Casey blew her long bangs out of her eyes. "It's so weird to be talking about this again. For years, I've replayed that night over and over in my head, but no one has wanted to hear my side of the story ever since I was first arrested."

Laurie heard her father's voice in her head: *If she's so innocent, why didn't she testify?* "I have to correct you, Casey. People desperately wanted to hear your version, but you didn't take the stand."

"My lawyer told me not to. She said they had found a couple of people who heard Hunter and me having some intense fights. Yes, that would look bad for me on trial. The prosecution would tear me to pieces by confronting me with every time I ever lost my temper. Just because I speak my mind doesn't make me a murderer."

"If you do our show, we'd be asking you the same tough questions. Do you understand that?" Laurie asked.

"Absolutely," Casey said. "I'll answer anything."

"With a polygraph?"

Casey agreed without hesitation. Laurie would not actually use the technology because it was unreliable, but Casey's willingness to undergo lie detection weighed in her favor. Laurie decided to throw in another test of her openness by asking whether she would be willing to waive attorney-client privilege so her attorney could speak to Laurie directly. Once again, she agreed.

"Please, go on with your story," Laurie urged.

"I barely remember going into the house. As I said, I was floating in and out of sleep. Hunter woke me when we pulled into the drive. Raphael offered to help when I had trouble getting out of the car, but then I managed to get inside, holding on to Hunter's hand. I must have gone straight to the couch and passed out. I was still wearing my evening gown when I woke up."

"And what happened when you woke up on the sofa?"

"I stumbled to the bedroom. I still felt woozy, but I was able to make it down the hall. Hunter was on the bed, but not in it—not like he was sleeping, but as if he'd fallen backwards onto it. I know from photographs that the blood was actually on his shirt and the duvet, but at the time, it seemed like he was absolutely covered in blood. I ran to him and shook him, begging him to wake up. When I checked his pulse, I thought I felt something, then realized it was my own hand trembling. He was already cold. He was gone."

13

Casey's mother, Paula, was fidgeting on the sofa again. "I knew this was too much for you to handle so soon after you came home. Maybe we can continue this conversation later, Ms. Moran."

The flash of irritation in Casey's previously flat eyes was unmistakable. "Mom, I've been waiting nearly half my life to say this. Please stay out of it. After I called 911, I called my cousin Angela. Thank God for her. I'm not sure I would have made it through prison without her." Casey immediately looked at Paula, then added, "And my mother, of course. The police found me on the bed, clinging to Hunter. My gown was strapless, so my hands, arms, and shoulders were all smeared with blood. Hunter was still in his white shirt and tuxedo pants. His jacket was tossed on the bench at the foot of the bed."

"How did the police get in?" Laurie asked.

"They said they found the front door slightly ajar, which I didn't notice when I woke up on the sofa."

"Isn't that unusual that the door would be open?"

"Of course, but we often left the door unlocked out there until we went to bed. Hunter had an alarm system, too, but we usually only set it when we left for the city. Hunter would have had his hands full helping me inside and probably didn't lock the door behind him. My best guess is that whoever killed him slipped through the door before he had a chance to lock it, then left it open."

In addition to the two bullet wounds that had killed Hunter, police had found two bullet holes in the walls between the living room and the master bedroom. "Then once the police were there," Laurie said, "they found Hunter's gun in the living room?"

Casey nodded. "As I said, I was on the bed, holding Hunter, when I heard the police come in. They were yelling at me to get away from the body. It felt as though I was in a dreamlike state again. Whether it was shock or the drugs, I didn't immediately obey. I was still so groggy. Part of me wonders whether everything would have been different if I had followed their instructions more quickly. They were rushing through the house, checking the bathrooms and closets. They were being very confrontational with me, insisting that I go to the foyer. They had to pull me away from Hunter. Then once I was in the foyer, I heard a female officer yell, 'GUN!' I was terrified, thinking they'd discovered an intruder hiding in the house. But then the officer held up a gun she'd found beneath the living room sofa. She asked me if I'd seen it before. It looked like Hunter's new Walther P99. A nine-millimeter," she clarified. "It was his most recent purchase."

"Hunter was an avid sportsman and collector," Paula explained. "I thought surely Casey would persuade him to change his ways, but instead, the next thing I know, she's running off to the shooting range with him. Frank and I were appalled."

Laurie made a mental note that certain political views might run in Casey's family.

"He enjoyed it as a hobby," Casey explained, "the way other men play golf."

"What was your reaction when the police found a handgun under the sofa where you claimed to have been sleeping?" Laurie asked.

"I was surprised. Hunter generally kept all the guns locked in a safe, except for one that he kept in his nightstand. When I told the police it was Hunter's newest gun, it never dawned on me that they would think I was the one who used it to kill him."

According to the trial summaries Laurie had reviewed yesterday, Casey told the police she had never had a chance to fire the new weapon. She thought Hunter might have taken it to the range when he first bought it, but she swore that she had "definitely" never touched it herself. But then police found her fingerprints on the gun, and gunshot residue on her hands.

Paula jumped in again. "When the police asked to test for GSR, they told Casey it was to eliminate her as a suspect. You tell me: Is that fair? They led her to believe they were on her side, but they were after her the whole time."

"Of course I agreed to the test. I was willing to do anything to help. You have no idea how horrifying it is to know that I was there that night. I was *right there* while someone chased him from the living room to the bedroom, firing shots. I was on the sofa, asleep, while someone murdered the only man I ever loved. I will always wonder whether he yelled to me for help." Her voice broke again.

Paula let out an exasperated sigh. "I don't know why we have to dredge this all up again. We can't turn back time. If we could, I'd force you to take that plea bargain. Instead, you went with the jury. And then your incompetent lawyer basically locked you up herself by arguing that you were out of your mind that night. If Casey wanted to be convicted of manslaughter, she could have pled guilty in the first place and gotten a better sentence."

Casey held up a palm. "Mom, of all people, I'm the one who knows what price I paid for going to trial."

Laurie ran through the five names of alternative suspects Casey had given her: her ex-boyfriend, Jason Gardner; Gabrielle Lawson, the socialite who'd been pursuing Hunter; Andrew Raleigh, who was jealous of his older brother; Mark Templeton, the foundation's chief financial officer; and Mary Jane Finder, the personal assistant

Hunter may have been investigating. "Is there anyone we're missing?" she asked.

"That's everyone I could think of," Casey confirmed. "Any one of them could have slipped a drug into my drink, then left the gala after we did and driven up to Connecticut, confident that I'd be passed out by the time they arrived."

"But what if you hadn't been?" Laurie asked. From what she had heard about Rohypnol, its effects varied widely. The killer could not have known with any certainty that Casey would be completely unconscious.

"I've thought about that," Casey said. "On the one hand, I hate the fact that I wasn't awake to help Hunter. But I have to assume that whoever shot him would have done the same to me if I'd shown any sign of consciousness."

Paula looked at her daughter imploringly. She begged her. "You're jumping into this much too fast. Naming names on a television show? Have you thought about how these people will respond? They'll try to destroy you. Any hope you have of turning over a new leaf will be over."

"Mom, I'm already destroyed, and I don't need a *new leaf*. I don't want to start over as some other person. I want my life back. I want to walk through a mall without you looking around at every other customer, wondering if they recognize me."

Without explanation, Casey suddenly rose from the sofa, disappeared momentarily down the hallway, and returned with a photograph. "I've spent two days poring over every piece of my file in a new light. I can't believe I never saw it before, but I think being out of that cell, in a new place, opened my eyes. I've had fifteen years to figure out a way to prove someone else came into the house that night, and I think I finally have it."

14

Four hours later, Laurie checked her watch once again from the backseat of the SUV. Usually, she loved the fact that Fisher Blake Studios was located in Rockefeller Center with a view of the iconic skating rink. But today, midtown traffic was at an absolute standstill. Livid at the thought of keeping Brett waiting, she finally hopped out three blocks from the building and practically jogged to it. It was three fifty-five when she stepped from the elevator on the sixteenth floor. She was out of breath, but she was here.

She spotted Jerry and Grace lurking outside her office door. Grace, as usual, had a full face of expertly applied makeup. She wore a V-neck purple sweater dress that hugged her curves but was long enough to skim the top of her thigh-high black boots. For Grace, the outfit was practically demure. Tall, thin Jerry towered over her, looking dapper in what Laurie knew he liked to call his "skinny suit."

They both perked up at the sight of her.

"What are you two conspiring about?"

"I was about to ask you the same thing," Jerry said wryly.

"The only conspiracy I know about was the traffic that tried to keep me from my four o'clock with Brett."

"Not only with Brett," Grace said teasingly.

"Will you please just tell me what's going on?" Laurie demanded.

Jerry spoke first. "We saw Brett's secretary meet Ryan Nichols at reception fifteen minutes ago. He's our new host, isn't he? His résumé is perfect."

Grace pretended to fan herself. "Not just his résumé. I mean, we'll all miss Alex, but that man is fine."

Great. Laurie hadn't even met Ryan Nichols, but he already had the support of not only Brett, but now Grace and Jerry. And he had arrived fifteen minutes before their meeting was scheduled to begin.

She entered Brett's office and found him seated next to Ryan Nichols on the sofa. She noticed a bottle of champagne on the coffee table and three glasses. Brett never asked her to sit on the couch for meetings, and the only time he'd offered her champagne was after their first special had dominated its time slot in the ratings. She resisted the urge to apologize for interrupting their "bromance."

Ryan stood to greet her. Grace hadn't been exaggerating about his good looks. He had sandy blond hair and wide green eyes. His smile revealed perfect teeth. His handshake was so firm that it was almost painful. "It's great to finally meet you, Laurie. I'm so excited to be joining the team. Brett was just telling me that you're in the process of choosing our next case. I'm so grateful to be jumping in on the ground floor."

The team? Jumping in? More like jumping the gun, she thought.

She tried to sound equally enthusiastic, but knew she was never a good liar. "Yes, Brett and I have a lot of decisions to make about the show's direction, both the next case and the new host. But I'm so appreciative that you're interested. With your background, your time must be in very high demand."

Ryan looked to Brett with a confused expression.

"Laurie, I'm sorry if I wasn't clearer when we spoke earlier. Ryan *is* your new host, so you can cross that off your to-do list."

She opened her mouth, but no words came out.

"You know," Ryan said, "I need to find the men's room. Do you think Dana would mind pointing the way? I'll learn my way around in no time."

Brett nodded, and Ryan shut the door on his way out.

"Are you trying to sabotage this?" Brett sneered. "That was embarrassing."

"I didn't mean to create a situation, Brett, but I had no idea that you'd already made this decision without any input from me. I thought *Under Suspicion* was my show."

"Every show made by this studio is *my* show. And I gave you Ryan's résumé and heard no objection."

"I didn't realize it was 'speak now, or forever hold my peace.' "

"Well, this is my call, and I've made it. We were lucky to have Alex, but Ryan's even better. He'll connect more with younger viewers. And frankly, with his credentials, he could be on a fast track to be the next attorney general. Fortunately, he wants to be a celebrity instead."

"And that's a good thing in a journalist?"

"Oh, enough with the high-horse rhetoric. You make a reality TV show, Laurie. Embrace it."

She shook her head. "We're more than that, Brett, and you know it."

"Fine, you've done some good work. And you've helped people. But that's only possible because of your ratings. You had a month to propose another host, and you kept dragging your feet. So you can thank me later for finding you someone as good as Ryan."

She heard a tap at the door, and then Ryan walked in again.

She mustered her best smile. "Welcome to *Under Suspicion*," she said, as Brett popped the champagne cork.

● ● ●

She had barely finished her first sip of champagne when Brett asked about her progress on the Casey Carter story.

She began summarizing her meeting with Casey when Ryan interrupted. "It's not an unsolved case. The entire premise of the show is to revisit unsolved cases from the perspective of people who have lived—quote, unquote—*under suspicion*."

Thanks for telling me the premise of my own show, Laurie thought.

"Hunter Raleigh's murder is solved," he continued, "and the only person under suspicion was convicted and sent to prison. Case closed. What am I missing?"

Laurie started to explain that she and Brett had already decided that a wrongful conviction case would be a good next move for the series.

This time, it was Brett who interrupted. "Ryan has a point. That case was a slam dunk. The girl had too much to drink at that gala and embarrassed him in public. They probably had a fight at home. He was going to break things off, and she pulled a gun on him. As I recall, the evidence was overwhelming. The only issue, it seems, was whether she did it in cold blood or in the heat of the moment. I guess the jury gave her the benefit of the doubt on that score."

"With all due respect, Brett, the last time we spoke, you said you didn't care whether she was innocent or not. Her name alone means viewers will tune in."

Ryan did not even wait for Brett to respond. "That's an old media model," he argued. "Fifteen minutes of fame is now more like fifteen *seconds*. By the time we air, she could be old news. And ratings are driven by young audiences. We need viewers who buzz about the show on social media. They've never even heard of Casey Carter."

Brett pointed his champagne flute in Ryan's direction. "Again, he's got a point. Do we have a fresh angle here, or is this just a rehash of her defense from fifteen years ago?"

Laurie felt the urge to down the rest of her champagne in one gulp, but she set down her glass instead. She wanted to be clear-headed.

She reached into her briefcase, pulled out the photograph she'd gotten from Casey, and handed it to Brett. "That's our angle."

"What am I looking at?" he asked.

"Casey has had fifteen years to study the evidence in her case. She can recite every word of every police report from memory. But after we spoke on Wednesday, she went home and started looking through everything with a new eye, including the old crime scene photographs. She thinks being out of prison let her see the images in a different light. She let herself remember what it was like to be with Hunter in that house."

"Oh, please," Ryan said sarcastically.

"That's when she noticed this," Laurie said, gesturing toward the photograph.

"It's a nightstand," Brett said. "So what?"

"It's not a matter of what's there, but what *isn't* there. Hunter's favorite memento—a framed picture of himself with the President at a White House function recognizing the Raleigh Foundation—is missing. According to Casey, it was always there. And she studied all the other crime scene photos. The police photographed every *inch* of that house. And Hunter's picture with the President doesn't ap-pear anywhere. Where did it go?"

"So you're taking a killer's word that there used to be a picture on that nightstand," Ryan said.

"Our show works because we give every participant's version of events a fair shake," she snapped. "It's what we call research."

"Time out," Brett said, forming his hands in a capital T. "So *as-suming* she's right about the missing picture, what's the theory?"

"That the real killer took it as a memento. Nothing else was miss-ing from the house."

Laurie was relieved to see Brett nodding. "So whoever took it would have had to know how much it meant to Hunter," he said.

"Exactly." Laurie was thinking again about the alternative suspects, especially Hunter's friend, Mark Templeton. Hunter had trusted him to run the finances of his most important initiative—a foundation named for his mother. To embezzle money from that particular fund seemed personal. Hunter was wealthy, handsome, powerful, and beloved. She imagined years of resentment building within a man who worked in his shadow, capped off by an accusation of financial wrongdoing and the threat of exposure. Two shots in the bedroom. The photograph on the nightstand of Hunter and the President, as if mocking him.

"Think of the ratings," she said, nudging, knowing Brett's bottom line. *"The return of Sleeping Beauty: Casey Carter speaks on camera for the first time ever."*

She was infuriated when Brett's gaze shifted to Ryan for approval.

"How do we know that picture frame even existed?" Ryan asked.

"We don't," Laurie said, "not yet. But what if that changes?"

"Then you might just have a story to tell, so get on it." Brett suddenly set down his glass and stood up. "We better get going, Ryan. Don't want to be late to the book signing."

"What's that?" Laurie asked.

"You know my historian friend, Jed?"

"Of course." Laurie knew him because every time Jed Nichols published a book, Brett pressured the news division to find time slots for him to promote it. She also knew that Jed was Brett's best friend and college roommate from Northwestern. And then she made the connection. Nichols, as in Ryan Nichols.

"Jed's Ryan's uncle," Brett explained. "I thought I mentioned that."

No, she thought. I would definitely remember.

• • •

Laurie stood on a stoop in front of a walk-up building on Ridge Street and Delancey, her index finger against one ear to block out the sound of traffic on the Williamsburg Bridge. She could barely hear her father on the other end of the line.

"Dad, I'm going to be late to Alex's." She felt like she'd run late more times in the past week than in the last five years put together. "Can you please take Timmy, and I'll meet you there."

"Where are you? You sound like you're in the middle of the freeway. You're not still with Casey Carter, are you? I'm telling you, Laurie: the woman is guilty."

"No, I'm downtown. But I need to talk to a witness."

"Right now? You're still working?"

"Yes, but it shouldn't take long. I'll be there by the kickoff."

When she hung up, there was a new text message on her screen. It was from Charlotte. *Angela just got off the phone with Casey, who said you were there for hours. Angela told her not to get her hopes up. How'd it go from your end?*

She tapped a quick answer on the screen. *Cautiously optimistic. Still much to do.* She hit send and tucked her phone in her pocket.

She didn't want to think about how her father would feel if she wound up believing Casey was wrongly convicted. And she didn't want to disappoint Charlotte by concluding her friend's cousin was guilty of murder. But she did need to nail down a case for their next episode.

As she pressed the buzzer for the apartment, she thought: I'll go wherever the evidence leads me. That's the only right answer.

15

The apartment was modest but sparkling clean. Not surprising, perhaps, given that its owner had spent decades as the Raleigh family's most beloved housekeeper, Elaine Jenson.

"Thank you for seeing me on such short notice, Mrs. Jenson."

"Please, call me Elaine." The woman was just as tidy as her apartment, with a perfectly pressed turquoise blouse and black pants. She was five feet tall at most. "But I have to admit I'm not sure I would have agreed to this if I had known the nature of your television program. I assume it's no coincidence that you called me with questions about Hunter shortly after the release of Casey Carter."

When Laurie had called while riding back from Connecticut, she had simply said that she worked for Fisher Blake Studios and wanted to speak to her about her former employer. "Not a coincidence. In fact, I got your name from Casey." Elaine's pursed lips made clear that she wasn't happy about the connection. "I take it you're not a fan."

"A *fan*? No. At one point, yes, but no longer."

"You believe she's guilty."

"Of course. I didn't want to, not at first. I adored Casey. She was young, but she was formidable, and I believed she was a fine choice to be Hunter's wife, despite his father's concerns. I'm glad I never spoke up, because it turned out the General was right about her. Not that he ever predicted murder, of course."

"Hunter's father didn't approve?"

"Oh dear, see? I just assumed as a reporter you must have known. I don't speak about the family. I think you should go, Ms. Moran."

"I'm not here to dig up old gossip," Laurie said. "If the family disapproved of Casey before Hunter's death, Casey didn't mention that to me."

Elaine's eyes dropped to her lap. "That's because Hunter never told her," she said quietly. "Now, please, that's all I will say. I'm retired now, but the Raleighs have been wonderful to me. It's not right for me to talk about this."

"I understand." Laurie rose from her chair. "This is a lovely apartment," she said, changing subjects. "Have you always lived in the city?"

Elaine still had the same phone number listed in police reports after Hunter's murder. Finding her had taken one phone call.

"This has been my home since I married my husband twenty-six years ago, but Hunter knew how much my children loved the outdoors. I'd take them up to the country house for weeks at a time in the summer. We'd stay in the guest house and help out up there, but usually I worked for the family in the city."

"What about Mary Jane Finder? Did she ever go to the country house?"

"Not to work per se, but she was at the General's side more often than not," she said, a slight edge in her voice. "She'd been to the house, of course."

Detecting disapproval, Laurie decided to press further. "I believe she even attended the foundation gala with him the night Hunter was killed. That seems unusual for an assistant."

"I thought so, too. Many of us did, but who am I to say?"

Elaine might be protective of the Raleigh family, but not of the General's assistant. "I've heard that Hunter didn't approve."

Laurie could tell that Elaine was choosing her words carefully. "He was wary. His father was a widower. Powerful, moneyed. It's not unheard of for outsiders to step in and take advantage."

"What about Hunter's driver, Raphael? I've heard he and Mary Jane were friends. Are you still in contact with him?" Laurie had him on her list of people to interview. At the very least, he could describe Casey's condition on the ride home from the gala.

Elaine's face saddened. "Such a lovely man. He passed away about five years ago. Raphael was a friend to all. Most of the staff I knew are gone now. But not Mary Jane. If it were up to that woman, she'd be there until her last breath. Now I think I've said enough."

Laurie thanked Elaine for her time once again. As she neared the apartment door, Laurie offered one more observation. "Hunter sounds like he was a wonderful man."

Elaine's eyes brightened. "A true gentleman. Not only generous and honorable, but a visionary. He would have made an excellent mayor, or even the President of the United States."

"I believe he even met the President, didn't he?" Laurie asked.

"Oh, he certainly did," Elaine boasted. "At the White House. The Raleigh Foundation was one of five charities chosen to exemplify the value of private giving. That was all Hunter's doing. The foundation had been around for years, but it was Hunter who decided to focus its mission on breast cancer prevention and treatment after his mother passed from the disease. Poor Miss Betsy. Oh, that was so horrible," she said, her voice drifting off.

"I've heard that Hunter was quite moved to be recognized by the White House."

"Very proud," she said, sounding proud herself. "He even kept a picture from that night, right on his nightstand."

Bingo, Laurie thought. "At the country house?"

She nodded. "Most people would keep something like that front and center on the office wall. But Hunter wasn't one to brag. I think he kept it in a special place because it meant something to him personally."

"I know this seems like a strange question, but would the picture have been on the nightstand the night he was killed?"

"That's a strange question, indeed. But the answer is yes."

"Because that's where it always was?"

"No, I'm more certain than that. You see, I used to go to Hunter's Connecticut house one day a week to clean. Raphael would drive me back and forth. But that night a car service took me home because Raphael was driving Hunter to the gala. I was dusting the picture of him and the President when he came into the bedroom. As he was about to leave for the gala, I asked Hunter whether he'd be getting another picture with the President there. He laughed and said, 'No, the President will not be attending.' I thought about that conversation after he left. I had no idea it would be the last thing I ever said to him."

"And was anyone else in the house after that?"

"No, just me. I locked up when I left. And then of course Hunter and Casey came back to New Canaan . . ." Her voice trailed off.

Laurie could picture the scene as if it were happening today, right in front of her. It felt absolutely real. She believed Elaine that the picture frame had been on that nightstand when Hunter left for the gala, which meant that Laurie was beginning to believe that Casey just might be telling the truth.

Someone else was with them in the house that night.

16

They were in Alex's apartment waiting for the kickoff. The football game hadn't started, but game snacks were in full force. An array of chips, dips, and crackers was spread across the top of a sideboard in Alex's living room. "I assume Timmy is responsible for the nearly empty bowl of cheese popcorn," Laurie said.

"I ate some, too," Alex volunteered. He was sitting on the couch, his arm around her.

"Ramon, if it were up to Timmy, he'd eat nothing but macaroni and cheese, and cheese popcorn," Laurie said.

Ramon's official (and self-selected) title was butler, but he was also Alex's assistant, chef, and trusted friend. And fortunately for Alex and anyone he invited into his home, he was a natural party planner, always able to pull together the perfect menu for an event.

"Don't worry, it's not all junk," Ramon responded with a smile. "I made a healthy turkey chili for dinner. Can I pour you a glass of Chardonnay?"

Alex had greeted Laurie with a warm kiss. "I'd say Ramon knows you pretty well, Laurie," he now said matter-of-factly. "I'm glad you made it. I know how heartbroken you'd have been if you missed a single play."

Laurie enjoyed watching football, but she was not an avid fan. But she loved watching her son and father enjoy sports together, so she cheered for all their favorite teams. And when Alex had settled next to her on the sofa for the kickoff and placed his arm around her shoulder, she liked that, too.

At halftime, Timmy eagerly followed Ramon into the kitchen to make his own sundae for dessert. Laurie's father immediately asked how things had gone in Connecticut. "At least Casey didn't take another shopping trip," he said disapprovingly. "Hitting the mall straight from the prison? Not the best PR move if she wants people to feel sorry for her."

"It wasn't like that, Dad. She literally didn't have any clothes."

Laurie started to bring Alex up to speed, but Alex cut her off. "Your father mentioned she had come to see you." There was something odd in his voice.

"Based on that reaction, I'd say Dad also made it clear that he doesn't want me touching the case with a ten-foot pole. And I suspect you don't either."

"Sorry," Alex said, "I didn't mean to sound so negative."

"So now that you've had more time with her, what's your opinion?" Leo asked. "Is she as crazy as they say?"

"Not at all." She paused, searching for the right adjectives. "She's straightforward. Very matter-of-fact. She spoke very clearly and openly about her own case, but without emotion. Almost as if she were a reporter or a lawyer."

"That's because she's lying," Leo said.

"I don't know about that, Dad. Her description of her mental state that night seemed very credible. And there's evidence that one of Hunter's most treasured possessions was missing from the house. From what I can tell, the police never looked into it."

"See? She's got you blaming the police, just like she did during her trial."

"That's not what I meant. No one ever realized it was gone. She figured it out herself from old crime scene photos. I confirmed it with Hunter's housekeeper. That's where I was after work tonight. Alex, you're being awfully quiet. Did you follow that case during the trial?"

"Sorry, I figured now that I'm no longer on the show . . ."

"Nothing official. I'm just curious about your take," she urged.

Leo shook his head. "Please talk some sense into her."

"Look, the evidence against her was very strong," Alex noted. "I'm sure you know that. Some of the jurors said after the trial that the overwhelming majority wanted to convict her of murder. There were two holdouts who felt sorry for her and convinced everyone to go with manslaughter to avoid a hung jury."

"Do you know anything about her lawyer, Janice Marwood? Casey and her mother made it sound like she was a disaster."

"Not personally, but at the time, I thought she wasn't very good. Her defense was all over the place. On the one hand, she tried to suggest that the police may have tampered with evidence to get a quick arrest in a high-profile case. But toward the end of the case, she suggested that even if Casey were guilty, she'd killed Hunter in a heat of passion. Meanwhile, Casey didn't testify, and the jury had no clear narrative to guide them. Basically, I'd give it a C-minus."

"Dad, for what it's worth, if I do look into Casey's claims, I wouldn't be giving her a free pass. You know how our show works. We put everyone under a microscope. She could come out of this looking very, very bad."

"But not going to prison," he said. "She already served her time. And if it turns out that she killed him in cold blood, they can't send her back for murder. She was acquitted. Double jeopardy, right, Alex?"

"That's correct. Laurie, she would be the first person to appear on your show without fear of being charged and convicted if you found additional evidence against her."

It was a good point, but Laurie wasn't sure it should be a deal breaker. "I'll need to decide soon. Brett is breathing down my neck."

Alex looked troubled.

"You look as though you want to say something."

He shook his head, but still seemed distant. "I just wouldn't rush into something because Brett is pressuring you."

"Not to mention the pain in the butt he hired as my host without consulting me."

Leo immediately began protesting on her behalf, threatening to call Brett to lecture him about leadership.

"Dad, I'm a grown woman. I can't have my father calling my boss."

"Any chance I know this particular guy?" Alex asked.

"Maybe. His name's Ryan Nichols."

Alex let out a whistle. "Serious up-and-comer. I've got to say, you could do far worse."

"I know. On paper, he's perfect in every way. He's got a big reputation, but with an ego to match. He strikes me as the kind of person who kisses the mirror every morning, and I'm just not sure he has the goods. Plus, he's the nephew of Brett's best friend, so there's major nepotism at work. You should have seen the way Brett kept looking to Ryan for his opinion. It's as though I'm losing my own show." She noticed Alex's gaze shift toward his view of the East River. Talking about Casey was one thing, but she shouldn't have started complaining about Ryan.

Timmy arrived in the living room with a banana split. "Mom, Ramon bought five different flavors of ice cream. Isn't that great?"

For the rest of the night, she didn't mention work because she didn't want Alex to feel responsible for the problems she was having. But she realized how much she was missing him already.

17

Casey found herself pressing the tiny button to lock the door of her new bedroom and then stopped. She forced herself to leave the door a little open instead.

Now that she was on the outside, what would she do? Where could a convicted felon find work? Surely not art auction houses. She could try her hand at writing, but that would bring her the publicity she wanted to avoid. Would a court allow her to legally change her name? Lots of questions, very few answers.

She had heard stories from women who left the prison, only to come back again, that it was difficult to adjust to freedom on the outside. Never once did she think that would apply to her. But, here she was, afraid to sleep with the door open in her own mother's house.

Nothing had been as awful as that trip to buy clothes. It didn't dawn on Casey until they walked into the shopping center how strange it would feel to be among strangers in public. No uniforms. No unwritten rules of conduct. On the train ride to and from the city the following day, she had hid behind the pages of a newspaper.

Maybe her mother and Angela were right. She could forget the past and try to start a new life. But where, and doing what? Was she supposed to change her name, move to the middle of nowhere, and live like a hermit? What kind of life was that? Besides, if she'd learned anything in the first few days, it was that she couldn't even go to a mall in suburban Connecticut without the past finding her.

And not her entire past. No one remembered her as a top student at Tufts, the star of the college tennis team, or the president of the local chapter of the Young Democrats. Or as one of the few people to get a job at Sotheby's straight out of college. Or the way she made Hunter laugh the first time she met him by reciting Picasso's full baptismal name from memory: *Pablo Diego José Francisco de Paula Juan Nepomuceno María de los Remedios Cipriano de la Santísima Trinidad Martyr Patricio Clito Ruíz y Picasso*. Or the night he held her and sobbed while describing the pain of watching his mother die from breast cancer, the same disease that stole her aunt Robin at such a young age.

No one will ever recall one kind thing about me, Casey thought, as she began to undress. She was a persona, a caricature, a punch line.

Unwillingly, she thought about Mindy Sampson. She was the one who had coined most of those nasty nicknames for Casey.

She would have thought Mindy would be retired by now. She knew Mindy had been fired by the *New York Post*. She hadn't realized until tonight that Mindy had taken her column online instead, to a blog called *The Chatter*.

The medium may have changed, but her garbage remained the same. Even before I was arrested, Casey thought, Mindy was out to get me. She was the one who ran that awful photograph of Hunter standing next to that miserable Gabrielle Lawson. The day it ran, I could hear the other women at Sotheby's whispering I-told-you-so's and I-knew-it's. *I told you she couldn't hold on to him. I knew they'd never make it to the vows.* So many people were jealous of what she'd had with Hunter, and Mindy had cashed in on that jealousy to sell papers.

Now Mindy was at it again to get more publicity at my expense for her website, Casey thought.

Casey put on her new pajamas, then picked up her new cell phone, which she'd been using to read *The Chatter*'s posts about her release. She used her fingertip to refresh the screen the way her mother had shown her and scrolled down to the comments. She felt an old, familiar chill run down her spine when she saw a new message in the comment section. *No surprise. Everyone who knows Casey can tell you she's a narcissist. In between shooting Hunter and drugging herself, she probably freshened her makeup to be ready for the cameras.* The user had signed the comment with a nickname: RIP_Hunter.

The room was quiet, but Casey could almost hear her heart thumping in her chest. The top of the little screen told her it was a little after ten o'clock. Thank heavens she still had one person who'd take her phone calls, no matter the hour.

Her cousin answered after two rings.

"Angela," she said, her voice breaking. "Go to Chatter.com and put in my name. There's another horrible comment about me from RIP_Hunter. I swear it must be Mindy Sampson getting dirt from Gabrielle Lawson. They're throwing knives at me again." She began to sob. "Dear God, haven't I gone through enough?"

18

The following Monday, Laurie's thoughts were interrupted by the sounds of Grace and Jerry outside her office, comparing notes about their weekend. From what she could make out, Jerry had binge-watched an entire season of a show she'd never heard of, Grace had had a third date with someone named Bradley, and Jerry was now pressing for all the details.

It was rare that Laurie beat Grace into the office, let alone early-bird Jerry, but today she planned to tell Brett that she wanted to use Casey's innocence claim for their next special. She needed to be prepared.

"So have you and Bradley picked out the china pattern yet?" she asked, popping open her office door.

"Sorry," Grace said, "I didn't realize you were here. You need coffee?"

Laurie held up the Starbucks Venti Latte she'd picked up on her way in.

"There will be no wedding," Grace announced, "nor any more Bradley for that matter."

"Oh boy," Jerry quipped, "what's wrong with this one?"

Grace had no difficulty finding fans among the opposite sex, but the reverse was not always true. "He asked me to be his date at a company party next weekend. And before I had a chance to accept, he said, 'And of course I'd pay for an outfit that would be appropriate for the setting.' "

"And is Bradley still breathing?" Laurie asked with a laugh.

Grace smiled. "I let him live. I wouldn't want to wind up featured in our next special, would I? But I blocked him from all my social media. He's a ghost as far as I'm concerned."

Laurie admired Grace's talent in the sometimes cutthroat world of modern dating. Before Laurie met Greg, she had never felt comfortable navigating romantic relationships. She found nothing more miserable than a disastrous date. Grace, on the other hand, always found a silver lining. Even a bad date was worth a good story down the road. And, above all else, she loved herself just the way she was, and that was all that mattered.

"Speaking of our next special," Laurie said, "I want to run my pitch past you before I roll it out for Brett. And tell me if you think it's okay."

They both pulled up chairs. "We're all ears," Grace assured her.

She had spent so much time preparing that she seamlessly laid out the core evidence against Casey, along with the new information she'd gathered since meeting her.

Jerry gave a quick round of applause when she finished speaking. "That was amazing. I'm not sure we need a new host after all."

Grace held up a stern index finger. "Don't you get between me and that Ryan Nichols. That could be a very dangerous place, Mr. Klein."

Having met Ryan, Laurie had a feeling he might not find Grace's banter quite as humorous as Alex had. "Please try to refrain from sexually harassing our new host, Grace. Besides, you may not be so fond of him once you meet him."

"Uh-oh. Sounds like someone's on your bad side already," Grace remarked.

"Do tell," Jerry urged, leaning forward for the details.

"Forget it. I shouldn't have said anything. So what do you think? Is this case good for the show?"

When Laurie had first met Jerry, he was a socially awkward college intern fetching sandwiches at lunch for production crews. Over the years, he had grown, not just figuratively but literally, as he no longer slouched to hide his tall, lanky frame. *Under Suspicion* had begun as Laurie's baby, but it was now a team project. Jerry had an eye for taking a reporter's story and transforming it into a visually compelling television show. And Grace had become their most valued test audience, able to pinpoint in an instant how viewers would respond.

Jerry spoke up first. "You know me, I always think first about setting. I love the idea of recreating the gala at Cipriani. Very ritzy and elegant. Then the transition to the pastoral Connecticut setting of the country house will be very dramatic. So it works from a production perspective. The Raleigh family and Casey herself are major audience draws. I'm less confident about how to present the financial stuff with the foundation, but I'm sure we can find a way to spell it out in compelling terms. What else do we know about the former CFO of the foundation?"

"His name's Mark Templeton," Laurie said. "I did a news search. When he first resigned, a reporter looked at the foundation's public filings and noticed that the assets had decreased substantially over the last few years, suggesting a possible link between his departure and the dwindling finances. But Hunter's father, James, quickly put the speculation to rest by saying that fundraising had decreased since Hunter's murder. He hired a new, full-time fundraiser and CFO, and since then, the foundation looks like it's been on sturdy footing. As for Templeton, he's now the director of Holly's Kids."

"What's that?" Jerry asked.

"A nonprofit dedicated to shelters for homeless teenagers. Sounds like a solid group, but he had an eight-month gap after leaving the Raleigh Foundation. Could be time off, or a sign that those rumors took their toll on his employability. I left a message for him late Friday, but haven't heard back."

Grace was being uncharacteristically quiet.

"You look concerned," Laurie told her.

"Don't ever let me play poker. I can't hide my thoughts with a blanket. Fine: I'll say it. Casey Carter's a nut. You can see it in her eyes. Even back then, I told my mom, 'Mommy, that girl's got crazy eyes.'"

Jerry was laughing. "Grace, we were kids when this happened."

"Maybe so, but I knew how to spot a mean girl, believe me. She had a good thing going. She was going to be Mrs. Hunter Raleigh the Third. She probably had a gown all picked out for his presidential inauguration. And then she was a big sloppy mess at that gala, and he dumped her when they got home. Case closed."

"And the missing picture frame?" Laurie inquired. "You didn't find that convincing?"

"She probably threw it at him when they were fighting, cleaned up the shards, and buried the picture in the woods before calling 911, or she took it with her as a souvenir after she wasted him."

Jerry wasn't convinced. "Then why wait until now to mention the missing picture? Her lawyer could have used it back then to create reasonable doubt at trial."

They were interrupted by the sound of Laurie's desk phone. Grace answered, "Ms. Moran's office." As she hung up, she said, "Speak of the devil. Reception says there's a Katherine Carter and an Angela Hart here to see you."

19

"Laurie, are you following all of this?"

The question was coming from Angela. Laurie found herself looking at Casey, remembering Grace's "crazy eyes" comment. Laurie had noticed a spark in Casey's eyes that she attributed to intelligence and humor. But now she could imagine a fire smoldering behind them.

"Sorry," she said. "I'm following. It's a lot to take in."

Casey and Angela had arrived at Laurie's office with printouts of online comments made over the weekend on stories covering Casey's release from prison. As far as they could tell, the first one had appeared on a gossip website called *The Chatter*. It was signed, "RIP_Hunter." "I found four other RIP_Hunter comments posted on other sites," Casey said. "They all say essentially the same thing: I'm a narcissist who killed Hunter so no one would know that he was going to break up with me."

Angela placed a protective hand on Casey's knee. "Nothing good ever comes from reading the comments section on the Internet."

"How can I not read it?" Casey asked. "Look what they're saying about me. I feel like it's fifteen years ago, all over again."

"Except you're not on trial," Angela reminded her. "You're free. Who cares what some Internet troll thinks of you?"

"I do. I do, Angela."

Unfortunately, Laurie knew a thing or two about the "trolling" that took place on the Web. A few years after Greg died, she made the mistake of going to a message board where armchair detectives opined about unsolved murders. She couldn't sleep for a week after reading the comments of strangers who were convinced that she had hired a hit man to execute her husband in front of their three-year-old son. Laurie flipped again through the comments that Casey had printed out for her.

Anyone who knows Casey . . . We're all afraid to talk to reporters in case she comes after us, too . . .

"He—or I guess she—talks as if they know you personally," Laurie observed.

"Exactly," Casey agreed. "And this happened back then, too."

"What do you mean?"

"During my trial, Internet news coverage was still fairly new. Most people still got their information from papers and television. But there were message boards to talk about my case. You can guess the tone of most of it. But here's the thing: someone kept posting, pretending they knew me, offering supposedly firsthand information that made me seem guilty. And they were all signed 'RIP_Hunter.' "

"Why do you assume it's a stranger?" Laurie asked.

"Because no one who knew me would say anything like that, because it's not true."

"Not even an acquaintance who didn't like you?"

Casey shrugged at the idea. "I suppose it's possible. Or it's someone who was obsessed with Hunter. The comments would go on and on about how wonderful he was, what a good mayor or even president he would have been. That I had stolen not just his future, but all the good things he would have done for the rest of society. I tried to find the old posts online last night, but didn't get anywhere. If Hunter had a stalker, he or she could easily have purchased a ticket for the gala that night. Maybe that's who drugged me, then followed us home. Maybe Hunter got the gun in self-defense and something went wrong."

"Is there a way for us to prove that someone using that same exact user name was trolling you during the trial?" Laurie asked.

"I'm not sure," Casey said. "I told my lawyer about it. And one of the jurors even saw one of the worst comments. He sent a note to the judge about it."

This was the first Laurie had heard of any juror note. "What did the note say?"

"The juror said his daughter was reading about the case on the Internet and tried to talk to him about it. He told her he wasn't allowed to speak to anyone about the trial until it was over, but then his daughter blurted out that someone on the Internet was saying I had confessed to them. The comment said something like, 'Casey Carter's guilty. She told me so. That's why she's not testifying.' And of course it was posted by RIP_Hunter."

Laurie wasn't a lawyer, but she was fairly certain that exposure to a comment like that would be grounds for getting the juror dismissed. It could even be the basis for a mistrial. "That's terribly prejudicial," Laurie said. "Jurors aren't supposed to read outside information about the case or speculate about the reasons a defendant doesn't testify. Not to mention that the author claimed you confessed."

"Which I absolutely didn't," Casey exclaimed.

"I didn't see anything about a juror note in the documents you gave me." She certainly would have remembered a note like the one Casey was describing. "Did the juror get excused? And did your lawyer ask for a mistrial?"

Angela jumped in, sounding outraged. "You mean that *excuse* of a lawyer, Janice Marwood? She didn't do anything. The judge read a blanket statement to the entire jury, reminding them to avoid any outside influences and to focus only on the evidence admitted in the courtroom. And when Casey asked Janice about it, Janice told her she needed to start trusting her more and not second-guess every strategic decision she made. What kind of strategy is that?"

Laurie remembered Alex describing Janice Marwood as a C-minus lawyer. The conversation reminded her that Casey had offered to sign a waiver of attorney-client privilege so Laurie could contact Marwood directly and have access to the case file. She opened the office door momentarily and asked Grace to work with Jerry to draft the relevant paperwork for Casey's signature while she was here.

Given the circus atmosphere surrounding Casey's trial, it didn't surprise her that crackpots would make outlandish allegations under the Internet's cover of anonymity, but it seemed to Laurie that she was more troubled by the return of whoever was calling himself or herself RIP_Hunter. The continued use of the same pseudonym was likely intended to rattle Casey psychologically. If so, the move appeared to be working.

Laurie closed the door again.

"Casey, do you know if your lawyer looked into the Internet posts?"

"Who knows?" Casey asked wistfully. "I look back on it now and realize I was much too deferential to her. Sometimes I wonder if I would have been better off representing myself."

Laurie assumed that there had to be a way to track down the original posts that were written during the trial. As they say, the Internet never forgets. She was jotting down a reminder to call the studio's tech people for help, when she noticed the time.

"I'm sorry to run out on you like this, but I have a meeting with the head of the studio. If you have time to wait, Grace will have some paperwork for you to sign. One's the waiver of attorney-client privilege that we talked about. And the other one's our standard participation agreement. There will be one for you, too, Angela, since you saw Hunter and your cousin just hours before the murder."

An awkward pause fell between Casey and Angela. "I thought—" Angela began.

"Angela," Casey said, "I need you to support me for this. You asked me to wait a few days, and I have. I'm more certain than ever. Please."

Angela grabbed Casey's hand and gave it a quick squeeze. "Of course. It's not the decision I would make, but I'll do whatever I can to help."

"Fantastic," Laurie said. "I'd also like to get a list of people who knew you and Hunter as a couple, Casey."

"Well, there's Angela, of course. And Hunter's brother, Andrew, but I can only imagine the horrible things he'll say about me now. There was a time when I felt like I knew anyone and everyone in New York City, but I lost my friends one by one. When you get arrested for murder, you're pretty much a pariah." Casey's eyes suddenly brightened with a new idea. She turned toward Angela. "What about Sean? The four of us used to double-date all the time. Boy, that was awkward at first."

The giggle told the story of an inside joke that Laurie wasn't privy to, but she could feel the camaraderie between these two women. Casey might have been in prison for fifteen years, but Casey and Angela were bonded as if they'd never been apart. Casey leaned forward as if she were telling a secret. "Angela and Hunter were an item before I met him."

Angela laughed. "To call us an 'item' is a gross exaggeration. It was a few dates. Not even—more like platonic plus-ones. If I wasn't going out with anybody but wanted to bring a date to an event, if he was free, he'd come. I used to do the same for him."

"Really?" Laurie asked. "Were those dates before or after Hunter met Casey?"

"Oh wow, *long* before. Casey had just moved to the city after graduating from Tufts. Then a couple years later, she told me she was seeing an amazing man she met at Sotheby's. When she said it was Hunter Raleigh, I probably threw her for a loop when I told her we'd gone out a few times. Anyway, it was no big deal. It became a running joke that Hunter and I would have made the worst couple. But Sean, that one was serious. I thought we might actually get married," Angela said wistfully. "But I have no idea how to get hold of him now."

"Don't worry about that," Laurie said. "We're very good at finding people. What's Sean's last name?"

"Murray," Angela replied. "So do all these questions mean that you will consider using Casey in your next *Under Suspicion* special?"

"I can't make any promises until I talk to my boss. But, Casey, I am happy to tell you I'm officially pitching your story as our next special."

"Really?" She leapt from the sofa and nearly knocked Laurie over with a hug. "Thank you. And thank you, Angela, for making this happen. This is the first piece of hope I've had in fifteen years."

As tears formed in them, Casey's eyes did not look the least bit crazy to Laurie.

20

Laurie should not have been surprised to see Ryan Nichols waiting on Brett's office sofa when she arrived for the meeting. He seemed to be getting more comfortable by the day. Maybe by next week he'd have a bed and nightstand in the corner. She still couldn't believe that Brett had hired his best friend's nephew for the job.

"Ryan, how are you managing to juggle your schedule to make time for the show? As Brett may have mentioned, we lost our previous host, Alex Buckley, because the pressures of a law practice were too much to balance with our production needs."

"Didn't Brett tell you? I'm taking a break from practice. I've got a full-time exclusive contract here at Fisher Blake Studios. In addition to hosting *Under Suspicion*, I'll be pitching in on the other news programs, giving legal opinions on the entertainment shows when celebrities get into court trouble, that kind of thing. If it works out, I may produce a show of my own."

He said it as if creating a television show was a little hobby. *If I take to playing in the sand, I may even build my own castle.*

Brett gestured for her to take a seat next to Ryan. "I've got to tell you, Laurie, I give you a hard time about putting journalistic principles over television ratings, but you hit the jackpot this time around. The Sleeping Beauty is back in the headlines, and as far as I can tell, she hasn't spoken to anyone but you."

"Not other reporters. Just her family."

"Are you sure?" he asked. "I can't count the number of times we've been burned by sources who told us we were their one and only."

"I'm quite sure, Brett. In fact, Casey just left my office with her cousin, and I have her word that she's on board if we decide to run with her case."

"Her word?" Ryan said skeptically. The annoyed glance between the two men was unmistakable. "Did she sign an agreement?"

"Actually, Ryan, she's signing it right now. Do you need me to show you a copy? One of the biggest challenges of our format is getting participants to trust us enough to cooperate. I build that trust from the very beginning. Getting her to sign that piece of paper is a big deal to me."

"Don't get so emotional," Brett said. "I know you have your *bonding thing* with the subjects. What did you find out about that missing picture?"

She told them about her meeting Friday evening with Elaine Jenson, who had a detailed recollection of the frame being on Hunter's nightstand before he left for the gala.

Brett seemed satisfied, but then Ryan interrupted. "That doesn't mean anything. Police didn't respond to the 911 call until after midnight. For all we know, the frame got broken during an argument and Casey managed to clean it up before calling the police. She's using it now as a red herring."

It was the same counterpoint Grace had raised.

"Then why didn't she use it when her trial started to go south?" Laurie asked rhetorically. "Because it's not a red herring. When Casey contacted me she said that at the time of the trial, she wasn't even aware that the picture was missing."

Seeing Brett look at Ryan, Laurie feared the worst until her boss said, "I agree with Laurie. It's possible to explain away the missing picture, but it's enough of a mystery to hook an audience. It's new evidence. So is the financial gobbledygook with the friend at the foundation. It keeps the show from being a rehash of a fifteen-year-old trial, and that's all that matters. But here's the thing, Laurie: Mindy Sampson is blogging 24/7 about Casey's every move. Casey's the flavor of the moment, and news cycles die fast. She'll be old news before long, so we'll need to film quickly."

With each *Under Suspicion* special, Brett's ratings expectations went up, while his time line shortened. Unlike Laurie's previous episodes, this case had already gone to trial, so she'd have the court record to work with, giving her a head start. "I'll go into production as soon as feasible," she said.

"Where's the Raleigh family on this?" Brett asked. "It's hard to imagine the show without them."

Laurie was proud to have secured the participation of the victim's family for every single episode so far. "I don't know. I've left messages for Hunter's father, but haven't heard back. It doesn't help matters that his assistant, Mary Jane, is on Casey's list of alternative suspects. But I have an appointment to see his brother, Andrew, this afternoon."

"Very well then. You get someone from the family on board, and it's a go."

As Laurie walked out of Brett's office, she heard Ryan say, "I tried a major fraud trial on a week's notice. We should be able to handle this."

She was beginning to wonder when the other half of the "we" was going to start earning his paycheck.

21

Andrew Raleigh had asked Laurie to meet him at three forty-five at an address on East 78th Street, just west of Park Avenue. She arrived to find a townhouse three times the width of the others on the block. The entrance was secured by a heavy black metal gate, overseen by a security camera. She rang the buzzer, and within moments the gate sprang open.

She was less than a mile from her own apartment on 94th, but in a completely different world in some respects. This was one of the most prestigious blocks in all of Manhattan, occupied by the families whose names were on university buildings, theater lobbies, and museum walls.

The woman who answered the ornate mahogany door wore an impeccably tailored navy suit and white silk blouse. Her long black hair was pulled into a tidy ponytail at the nape of her neck. Laurie introduced herself, and said she was there to meet with Andrew Raleigh.

"I'm Mary Jane Finder, General James Raleigh's assistant. Andrew is on the second floor, in the Kennedy Library. He's expecting you. I'll escort you up."

This house not only had a library, but a library with its own name. A different world, indeed.

Laurie paused at the bottom of the staircase and let the silence fill the foyer. She had learned that most people continued to speak when faced with silence. But this woman was not most people. Laurie's calls to the General, both on Friday afternoon and this morning, had been answered by Mary Jane. On both occasions, the woman had been all business, saying she'd relay the message, but with no reassurance of a return call. Now Laurie was standing beside her, and still Mary Jane said nothing about Laurie's prior attempts to reach the elder Raleigh.

She appeared to be in her fifties now, and was still very attractive, but she would have been around Hunter's age when she first began working for the family. Laurie wondered if the woman had always been so stony.

Over the weekend, Laurie had read a profile that described Hunter Raleigh's younger brother, Andrew, as a "big personality." When he greeted her in the Kennedy Library, she could see why that phrase was fitting. She estimated his height at six-foot-three. Unlike his lean, athletic brother, he had a barrel chest and thick neck. Each of his hands was the size of Timmy's baseball glove. His loose, brightly colored, tropical patterned shirt and khakis seemed out of place in this house.

Even his voice was big. "Thank you much for meeting me here, Ms. Moran," he boomed. "Is it all right if I call you Laurie?"

"Of course."

She looked around at the paneled bookcases, the Persian rug, and the draperies on the windows. "This room is magnificent," she said sincerely.

"This old mausoleum? This is Dad's place. Personally, I prefer downtown, but my loft's being renovated. I probably should have waited it out in East Hampton, but it's starting to get chilly out there already. Or I guess I could have gone to the house in Palm Springs, or my condo in Austin. Anyway, you don't need to hear about the Raleigh real estate."

Laurie detected a slight southern accent that was unexpected in a member of such a quintessentially New York family, but Andrew's mention of a condo in Austin reminded her that he had attended the University of Texas. He must have adopted the state as a second—or third or fourth—home.

Mary Jane had left them at the door of the library. "Ms. Finder said she is your father's assistant. Has she been with him long?"

"About twenty years. Just between you and me, the lady scares the dickens out of me. Not sure the blood's warm if you know what I mean."

"I spoke to her on the phone when I tried reaching your father. It's odd that when we just met she didn't say anything about the messages I left."

"Mary Jane's as locked as a vault, but Dad keeps her a whole lot busier than I am. He's consulting political candidates, serving on a dozen boards, working on his memoirs. Me? I like to fish and drink beer. You want a beverage by the way? It's five o'clock somewhere."

Laurie declined and Andrew took a seat in the chair across from her. "Your show is seriously thinking about jumping into the story of my brother's death? I have to tell you, I can't say I see the point, Laurie."

"As you probably noticed from the news coverage over the weekend, your brother's case is still of great interest to the public. The jury convicted his fiancée of manslaughter, while many courtroom watchers believed the verdict should have been for murder. Meanwhile, Casey has never backed away from her version."

"That someone drugged her with pills that just happened to be tucked away in her purse."

"She claims that anyone at the gala could have slipped something into her drink that night. Once they were in the house with her soundly asleep, that same person easily could have put some pills in her purse to make her look guilty, even if police tested her blood for the drug."

"Or else she's lying."

"Is that what you think, personally?" Laurie asked. "That Casey killed your brother?"

"Not at first I didn't. I liked Casey. Heck, if I'd met her before Hunter, I might have made a play for her myself. She was more fun than Hunter's usual type."

"He had a type?"

Andrew shrugged. "Beautiful but boring. Good for a date or two, a photograph on a red carpet, but all interchangeable. Not Casey, though. That girl was a firecracker."

"I'm not sure what you mean by that."

"Oh, nothing racy or anything. She was a challenge. When they'd been dating about two months, Hunter went down to Kiawah Island for a week without telling her. Didn't call her once, even though she knew darn well he had a cell phone with him at all times. She found out where he was when she saw a photograph of him at some hometown political fundraiser for a South Carolina senator. When Hunter came home, she wouldn't take his calls. When he showed up at her door, she slammed it in his face. No woman had ever drawn a line in the sand for him." Andrew was laughing at the memory. "She sure got his attention. Hunter was a changed man after that. Smitten to no end. He loved that woman."

"So why would she kill him?"

"To answer that, how much do you know about my father?"

"What I've read in his biography. And that he has an assistant who won't return my calls and might be a vampire," she added with a smile.

Andrew flashed her a thumbs-up of approval. "He's a good man, but he was a three-star general and the son of a senator. He's old school. In his world, men of a certain station owe the world a certain responsibility. They run foundations and serve the public."

Laurie could almost hear his internal voice completing the thought: . . . *They don't devote their lives to fishing and drinking.*

"And that kind of man requires a certain kind of woman at his side," he continued, "not the kind of woman who tries to wrap a man around her finger—at least as my father saw it. Not to mention the fights."

"Are you referring to the arguments that witnesses testified about during Casey's trial?" The prosecution had marched through a parade of Hunter's acquaintances to recount impassioned arguments Casey and Hunter had had in public.

"Those two would debate any and everything. Politics, of course. Casey was an outspoken liberal. She'd get so irritated when Hunter would call her a Woodstock hippie. But you'd barely have started the appetizer course before they'd be on opposite sides of any issue. She liked Michael Moore's movies. He thought Jackson Pollock's work looked like a child's finger paintings. The two of them would grill each other as if it were a Congressional hearing. It was off-putting to many of Hunter's friends, as they made clear at trial. But what the friends and my father didn't realize was that they both enjoyed their arguments. For them, it was like playing tennis."

"Arguments about movies and art certainly don't amount to a motive for murder."

"I think you're missing the bigger picture, Laurie. Casey wasn't fitting in. My point is that my father thought she wasn't sufficiently reserved."

"Pardon me for saying this, but I don't think most people expect women to stand silently at their husband's side anymore."

"Well, my father's not most people. A political wife—like my mother, like my grandmother—wouldn't have dreamt of contradicting her husband. Besides that, Hunter had previously been very serious with a socialite. My father loved her family background, and Casey couldn't compete with that."

"You've made it clear that your father didn't approve of Casey."

"*Didn't approve* is an understatement. First, he insisted on an ironclad prenup, thinking it would chase Casey away. I wasn't the least bit surprised when Casey said, *Tell me where to sign. I'm not marrying Hunter for his background or what comes with it*, she said. But that wasn't enough for our father. He was actively trying to dissuade Hunter from going through with the marriage."

"Are you telling me that Hunter was planning to break off the engagement with Casey?" That had always been the prosecution's theory.

"I don't know that for sure, but let's just say that I was the one willing to disappoint my father. Hunter never did."

At the risk of getting ahead of herself, Laurie was already picturing Andrew and his big, southern-accented personality on the television screen, and she liked what she saw. This was the kind of show she would love to watch.

"You mentioned that Casey slammed the door on your brother after he failed to call her during a trip. Was that the only time you saw her get jealous or possessive?"

"Absolutely not. She was aware of Hunter's reputation, as well as the fact that his previous girlfriends had all been her polar opposite. I think she was always wondering when the other shoe was going to drop. As a result, she could be intensely jealous and wanted everyone to know she wasn't just another flirtation. She had no qualms about making cutting comments to him in public, such as *Which one of us are you with?* One of her favorites was *Are you going to wait until we're married to stop acting like an eligible bachelor?*"

Andrew was describing a side to Casey that Laurie had not seen.

"Maybe you're right and Casey is guilty." Laurie was speaking to herself now as much as to Andrew. "Our show makes a point of being evenhanded. We ask tough questions of every person involved. And it's important to me that your family be represented in that process. I give you my word that our show always treats the victim's memory with respect. We want the audience to realize it's not just evidence in a case folder. We want them to remember the value of the life that was lost."

Andrew looked away and coughed. When he spoke again, his southern accent was nearly gone. "My brother was an exceptional human being, Laurie, one of the finest men I ever had the honor to know. He was incredibly bright. I barely got into U of Texas, but Hunter was Princeton and the Wharton business school. With his real estate prowess, he made my family's previous fortune seem like chump change. But he was entering a new phase of life. He was using his God-given talents for the public good, consulting with the mayor about using free-market principles to expand affordable housing. Our mom died of breast cancer when she was only fifty-two years old. I flew down to the Caribbean and stayed drunk for a year, but Hunter shifted the foundation's mission in her honor."

Once again, Laurie was tempted to start asking the tougher questions. Andrew was full of praise for his brother, but had living in the shadow of such an admired sibling led him to bitterness, as Casey alleged? And what did Andrew know about the possibility of financial irregularities at the foundation? She didn't want to scare off the only member of the Raleigh family who had bothered to return her call.

"Was Hunter thinking of running for office himself?"

"Oh sure, he was talking very seriously about it—perhaps mayor of New York once the current mayor left because of term limits. He would have been the rare politician who woke up every day asking how he could make life better for ordinary people. Hunter was, quite simply, beloved and deservedly so. And if I'd be allowed to tell your audience all that, then I'm happy to participate. Just tell me when and where."

"We hope to shoot soon. We want to do a scene with the six people who will be on the show sitting at the table where they were that last night. Cipriani has already agreed to make the ballroom available, schedule permitting. And it's my understanding that you inherited your brother's country home. I don't know how you'd feel about making it available—"

"Consider it done. In fact, as far as the banquet hall goes, our foundation still uses Cipriani for many of our events. We're having a function there next Sunday for our most important donors. Nothing as lavish as the annual gala, mind you, but if you wanted to get some footage that night, I'm sure we could arrange that."

"Really? That would be incredibly helpful." As of this morning, Cipriani had told Jerry they'd have to film before ten in the morning or wait at least two months to hold the ballroom for a day. She jotted down the date Andrew had given her, wondering if they could possibly be ready to start shooting by then. If it were up to Brett, she'd be filming right now. "I don't suppose you have any inkling of what your father might decide."

He craned his neck to look beyond the library's exit, and then answered in a whisper. "If I had to guess, Mary Jane didn't even tell him you called. I'll have a chat with him. As long as it's not going to be a hit piece on Hunter—"

"Of course not."

"I can probably even get him to sit down for your cameras. He's slaving away these days trying to finish his memoirs, but he can probably spare a few minutes."

"And what about Mark Templeton? My understanding is that he was one of your brother's close friends and was also at the gala that night." She still did not mention Casey's suspicions about the former financial officer of the family's foundation.

"I haven't spoken to Mark for years, but I'll see what we can do."

"And not to push my luck, but maybe you can work your magic on Mary Jane Finder? My understanding is that she was at your family's table at the gala. We like to cast a wide net on potential witnesses, and she might have observed Casey's demeanor that evening."

He feigned a frightened chill running down his spine. "Your cameras may not catch her reflection, but I'll try."

"Thank you, Andrew. Your help is invaluable."

The black security gate had just slammed behind her when Laurie made a call to Brett.

"I see you're calling me from your cell," he said once Dana connected her to his line. "Out of the office again?" he asked. His tone was sarcastic.

"This time, I know you'll approve. I just left the Raleigh family's townhouse. The brother's definitely in, and thinks the father will be, too."

"Excellent. As long as we have one of them, we should be okay. Start getting releases signed and nailing down the production schedule. I mean it about moving quickly."

She was tucking her phone back into her purse when it vibrated. According to the screen, it was Charlotte.

"Hey there," she answered. "What's up?"

"I'm about to meet Angela for a cocktail. You want to join us?"

"I actually saw Angela a couple of hours ago in my office. She was with her cousin. Is Casey going, too?" Laurie had just promised Andrew Raleigh that she would keep an open mind about the facts of his brother's murder. It would be inappropriate to be seen socializing with the woman who was convicted of killing him, not to mention the chance that she might actually be a killer.

"Definitely not," Charlotte said. "She walked Angela back to

Ladyform after they met with you, so I did get a chance to talk to her. Angela felt so bad about Casey having to go to the mall for clothes that we let her raid the sample closet. She's got enough sportswear to last for the next fifteen years. I got the impression she's had enough of the public eye over the last few days. Angela got her a car service so she wouldn't have to brave the train back up to Connecticut. Meet us at Bar Boulud, right across from Lincoln Center?"

Laurie liked the idea of having time with Angela away from her cousin. Maybe if she earned her trust, Angela could help get her aunt's approval, as well. "Sure, what time?"

"Now!"

Laurie glanced at her watch. It was 4:15. As Andrew Raleigh had said, it's five o'clock somewhere, Laurie thought. She deserved to celebrate. She finally had her next show.

22

Andrew Raleigh was pouring himself a scotch from the bar cart in what his father, and his father's father before him, insisted on calling the Kennedy Library. Laurie Moran may not have wanted a drink, but just the smell of this house was enough to drive him to the bottle.

He was fifty years old and still marveled at the daily pretentiousness that defined his family. The Kennedy Library? *It's not some monument at the national mall*, he wanted to yell. *It's a useless room at the top of the stairs filled with books that are more decorative than read*. Perhaps the room is not *completely* useless, he thought, as he felt the comforting burn of alcohol in his throat.

The sight of his father stepping from the library's anteroom had him pouring a second round. "How'd I do, Pops?"

As instructed, Andrew had scheduled his meeting with Laurie here so that his father could monitor the conversation from the next room. "You're drunk already," the General snapped, his tone icy.

"Not yet, but getting there."

Andrew resumed his spot in the wing chair, and then immediately regretted it. Even though Andrew was two inches taller and thirty pounds heavier than his eighty-year-old father had ever been, he suddenly felt small with his father standing over him. General James Raleigh was in his most casual attire, which meant a navy sports coat, gray flannel pants, and a heavily starched white shirt. To go without a tie was the equivalent of wearing pajamas in public for the General. Andrew was immediately conscious of his own attire, more fitting for one of the casino resorts he enjoyed so much.

Looking at his father, Andrew thought, Hunter was always your favorite, and you never stopped telling me about it.

He remembered when he was ten years old, his mother found him in his room, studying a photograph of him, Hunter, and their father. When she asked why he was staring at it, he began to cry. He fibbed and said that he was crying because he missed Daddy, who was in Europe on army business. The truth was that he'd been crying because he'd had a dream the night before that he wasn't really related to his family. Like his father, Hunter was lean and fit with a strong jaw and hair suitable for a news anchor. Andrew had always been softer and rounder.

You always treated me like your fat little baby, he thought, compared to my brother, the glorious charmer.

Now his father's face was formed in a disapproving scowl, as it was so often in Andrew's presence. "Why did you make it sound like I was the one pressuring Hunter to call off the engagement? Why didn't you tell her that you knew to a certainty that Hunter planned to drop that woman like a stone the moment they got home from the gala?"

"Because I know no such thing, *Father*." He could hear the derision in his own voice. "And you *were* pressuring Hunter to break it off, even though he loved Casey. I agreed to go along with this scheme of yours, but I won't risk getting caught in a lie on national television."

Despite what Andrew had told Laurie, he had no interest in helping her with the show. If it had been up to him, he would have turned on his usual charm, heard out her pitch, and then politely declined. It was, in Andrew's view, what any normal family would do. No point in rehashing bad memories. Protection of privacy. All that jazz. An easy out.

But the Raleighs were never normal, and James Raleigh never took the easy route. Andrew tried to persuade his father once again. "I really don't think we should get involved in this show, Dad."

"When you've done something to earn your last name, you can have an opinion."

Andrew felt himself shrink farther into the chair. "Well, I still don't understand why you didn't meet with her yourself," he muttered, taking another sip of scotch.

He couldn't believe it when his father snatched the glass from his hand. "Because a television executive would expect someone of my stature to spurn her invitation. I don't want to seem too eager to help or she might be suspicious of what I have to say. You on the other hand? Finally, your aw-shucks, go-along-to-get-along persona comes in handy."

Would his father ever understand that his personality wasn't a persona, like a coat that he could take on and off at will? His mind flashed back to a visit from his father at Phillips Exeter, before Andrew was "asked to leave" for a "less demanding" boarding school. His father had spent the entire evening fawning about Hunter's "exquisite command of the stage" during the student body's auction to raise money for scholarships for low-income students. What everyone neglected to mention was Andrew's role in rounding up so many student volunteers to support the event. Hunter may have been the Raleigh student that everyone admired, but Andrew was the one they enjoyed spending time with.

"So basically what you're saying is that I seem dumb enough to agree to do this show. But meanwhile, you're the one who wants us on it. What does that say about you?"

"Andrew, don't try higher-level thinking. We both know it's not your forte. When are you going to learn that you can only wield power from the inside? If we had no role in the show, we'd be giving away any hope of control. Imagine the lies Casey could tell about your brother. About me. About *you*, for God's sake. If we signed away all interest in participating, these immoral television people would rush to air without giving us any chance of rebuttal. We absolutely must be involved. Why do you think she asked about Mark Templeton?"

"Because he was at the gala that night. That show interviews anyone who may have noticed the smallest detail. She even wanted to speak to Mary Jane for whatever reason."

"We don't all have time to watch television," James snapped. "Mary Jane will say whatever I tell her. She's always been a loyal soldier. But you're naive to think that Laurie Moran's questions about Templeton were a coincidence. When I have Mary Jane send in my conditions, she'll make it clear that I'm begrudgingly going along with your suggestion. My role will be limited to speaking kindly of your brother."

"And mine?"

"More of the same. If I spilled the beans about that nasty piece of trash on some reality TV program, it would be unseemly. But when you told those stories about Casey's petulance, you seemed perfectly natural. By the time that show goes to air, Casey Carter will wish she had stayed inside that prison. Good job, son. Good job."

Andrew could count on one hand the number of times his father had praised him for anything.

23

Laurie couldn't remember the last time she'd been able to walk into a bar in the city without having to turn sideways to navigate her way through a crowd. Bar Boulud, a high-demand hotspot, was gloriously empty this late afternoon. Laurie could hear the sound of her own heels echo up to the vault-shaped ceiling as she made her way to the back of the bar, where she spotted Charlotte and Angela at the farthest table. They had already ordered three glasses of wine and a beautiful charcuterie board filled with prosciutto, salami, pâté, and a couple of things Laurie was afraid to eat.

Angela reached over and gave Laurie's free hand a quick squeeze. "You are such a doll for seeing Casey and me without an appointment today. Casey called me last night going absolutely nuts about those online comments." She quickly pressed her hand to her mouth. "Oh dear, bad word choice. I meant that she was very concerned."

"Who wouldn't be?" Laurie said. "It does seem odd that fifteen years later, someone would immediately resume talking about her on the Internet using the same nickname. It suggests a person who's not only obsessed with the case, but who wants Casey to know about it. Why use the same name unless you want to send a message that someone out there hates you?"

"Hello?" Charlotte said with a little wave. "No idea what you two are talking about. I'm the one who introduced you, remember? Fill me in, please."

"Sorry," Angela said, "I didn't want to mention it while Casey was at the office with me. She's so upset." It didn't take long for Angela to fill Charlotte in on the comments from RIP_Hunter.

"It could be one person who's obsessed with Casey," Charlotte observed. "Or it could be a bunch of different people all using the same online name."

"I don't understand," Laurie said. "Why would a group come together to post negative comments about Casey as if they're one person?"

"No, not anything like a conspiracy. I remember back in college, when I'd go on message boards to talk about the latest celebrity breakup—don't judge me—people would sign their comments along the lines of Team Jennifer or Team Angie. It's a way of taking sides in an Internet feud. Same thing with political candidates. These days, it would be on Twitter. A million people typing hashtag-whoever are signaling who they're supporting, but it's not written by one person. For all we know, RIP_Hunter could have been a label that caught on among people who were all on Hunter's 'side' so to speak, meaning they thought Casey was guilty."

"How could we find out what it really was?" Laurie asked.

"You'd have to check to see whether it was the kind of site where users had to create a verified account with a unique username, or whether anyone could just type RIP_Hunter as a signature."

Laurie made a mental note to follow up on the technological aspect of these posts. She had her fingers crossed that the defense lawyer had done the same back then, which would save her from wading into a morass of computer information she sometimes struggled to understand.

"I don't know about all that," Angela said, "but I've been wracking my brain trying to think of people who might have wanted to hurt Hunter. I realize that Casey may not have mentioned a couple of possibilities. One was her ex-boyfriend, Jason Gardner. He was terribly jealous. It always seemed like he was still in love with Casey and trying to get her back, even though she was engaged to Hunter. But after she was convicted, he really threw her under the bus. He even published a trashy tell-all book. And you should also look into Gabrielle Lawson. She's this pathetic aging socialite who was determined to snag a man like Hunter. Both of them were at the gala that night. Both of them stopped by our table. My worry is that if Casey goes through with this, it will kill her mother just the way her going to trial killed her father."

Angela was speaking with such an intensity that she didn't seem to notice that Charlotte and Laurie were sharing an anxious look. "Angela," Charlotte said gently, "maybe we should let Laurie enjoy her happy hour. How would you feel if she grilled us about the fall fashion show that has us so exhausted?"

Laurie hadn't known Charlotte long, but it wasn't the first time she'd seemed to know what Laurie was thinking. The truth was, Laurie loved talking about work, no matter what the hour, but it felt inappropriate to discuss the current investigation with Casey's family member in such an off-the-record way. Always the consummate professional, Charlotte had found a polite way to shift the subject matter.

"Oh my gosh, of course," Angela said sheepishly. "We're all officially off the clock. No work talk."

Laurie was grateful for Charlotte's save. "No problem at all," she said. "If it makes you feel any better, we already have both Jason and Gabrielle on our list of people to contact based on our review of the case."

"So," Angela said, searching for a new topic, "are you married, Laurie, or are you part of the single ladies club with us? I don't see a ring."

Charlotte wrapped a friendly arm around her friend's shoulder. "I should have warned you that my buddy Angela can be very blunt."

Laurie could tell that Charlotte was embarrassed, but, if anything, Laurie found comfort in the fact that Charlotte hadn't told Angela her background already. Sometimes Laurie thought that Greg's murder was the first fact anyone learned about her. "I'm not married either," she said. That seemed a sufficient explanation for the moment.

"Charlotte says I shouldn't care so much about finding a man. Be happy on my own, et cetera. But I admit, it gets lonely not to have found the right guy yet."

Charlotte rolled her eyes. "You make forty sound like ninety. Besides, you're more gorgeous now than most women could hope to be at any age."

"Oh sure, I go out a lot, but it doesn't amount to a hill of beans." She laughed. "I was engaged twice, but as we got near the wedding date, I asked myself if I'd want to see this guy's face every morning."

"Isn't this uplifting?" Charlotte said. "Besides, Laurie has more going on in that arena than she can handle."

Angela took the bait. "What's this? Sounds juicy."

"He's someone I worked with. It's complicated."

"You really don't think he'll change his mind about coming back to the show?" Charlotte asked. "It won't be the same without that perfect voice." She did her best, deep-voiced Alex impersonation. "*Good evening. This is Alex Buckley.*"

"No," Angela said, her mouth agape. "Alex Buckley? Really? The lawyer?"

Now Laurie wished they were talking about the case instead. She nodded. "The host of our show. Or at least, he was."

"Okay, now I have to admit I haven't seen the show yet."

Charlotte pretended to give her friend a little smack. "Laurie's taking your cousin's case and you didn't even watch her show?"

"I was planning on streaming it this weekend. Of course I was dying to watch it last month when your sister's case was featured, but you told me you didn't want everyone at work to watch, because it was so personal about your family."

"Well, obviously I didn't mean that about you," Charlotte said. "You're one of my best friends."

"Really," Laurie said, "you don't need to explain."

When the table fell into a silence, Angela shook her head. "Man, Alex Buckley. Now, that is a small world."

"You know him?" Laurie asked.

"Not anymore. But I went out with him once a million years ago."

Charlotte shook her head. "Why in the world would you tell her that?"

"Because it's a funny coincidence. And it was more than fifteen years ago. Ancient history." She waved off the thought.

Charlotte was still giving her friend a disapproving look.

"What? Laurie's not upset, are you? Trust me, this is a non-issue, just like with Hunter."

"Wait: You dated him, too?" Charlotte mused. "Who *haven't* you gone out with?"

"It's not like that, Charlotte," Angela said. "You didn't know me then. I went out every night of the week. I met baseball players, actors, a *New York Times* reporter. And don't go thinking what you're thinking. It was all very innocent. We were so young, thrown into these high-profile social situations where you're expected to have a plus-one. It's like Casey said earlier, Laurie: she felt like she knew everyone in New York City. I was the same way in my twenties. One moment, you'd be on a red carpet. Then when it was just a group of us alone, we'd giggle and act like kids. It was as if there were an unofficial club of a hundred popular New Yorkers, all keeping each other company. Nothing heavy."

She smiled at the memory. "But, my goodness, what a small

world indeed. Come to think of it, I met Alex when I tagged along to a picnic in Westchester with Casey and the Raleighs. I was unattached at the time. Alex was smart and so nice looking. Someone told me he was a lawyer at the host's law firm. We talked through most of the party so I took a chance and called him at the office to invite him out to lunch. When we met, I realized he wasn't even a lawyer yet. He was a summer associate, still in law school. I was several years older—not a big deal these days, but at the time, I felt like Mrs. Robinson. Of course, what a mistake in retrospect. Look how he turned out!"

Something about Laurie's expression caused Angela to pause. "Maybe I should keep my younger days to myself, but I promise, it was just one lunch. I'm very sorry if I've upset you, Laurie."

"Not at all. As you said, it's a small world. So if you met Alex at a picnic the Raleighs took you to, does that mean Alex met the Raleighs, too?"

She shrugged. "I can't say for sure."

Charlotte was signaling to the waiter for another round, but Laurie said, "That's all for me. I might actually have time to cook dinner for my son tonight."

"You sure? You're going to miss out on my grilling Angela about that long list of boyfriends from the nineties."

Laurie was indeed intrigued about something Angela had said, but there was only one person's past she was curious about.

She texted Alex. *Do you have a second?*

24

The tip of General James Raleigh's Montblanc pen hovered above his legal pad, but he hadn't been able to write a word this afternoon. He was working on his memoirs, already sold to a major publisher. His handwriting was as neat and orderly as the other attributes of his life, so Mary Jane had no difficulty reading his pages and typing them into manuscript format. Usually, the sentences flowed easily. He had been blessed with an exciting, challenging, and rewarding life. He had watched the world change and was filled with stories. He knew that others regarded him as an old man now, but he didn't feel like one.

He knew why he was having an uncharacteristic bout of writer's block. He was trying to write the chapter about losing his firstborn son, Hunter. He had experienced so much loss in his lifetime. His older brother, also his hero and best friend, had been killed in combat at such a young age. He watched the love of his life and the mother of his children waste away to cancer. And then three years later, Hunter—his brother's namesake—was stolen from him. That death had been the worst of all. Wars and disease are horrific, but expected parts of life. To lose a child, to have a child murdered—sometimes James was surprised he had not dropped dead himself from grief.

He placed his pen on his desk, knowing there was no point in trying to work in this state.

His thoughts suddenly shifted to the memory of Andrew sulking in the library today. James knew he'd been hard on his son, but the boy was such a disappointment. Fifty years old, he thought, and I still think of him as a boy. That speaks volumes.

James could only imagine what the Senator, as he and his brother had called their father, would have done to them if they'd ever behaved in such an entitled manner. Andrew had no sense of civic responsibility. He saw money in the basest, most hedonistic terms, something to be thrown about on a whim, solely for enjoyment. The partying. The practical jokes. The jumps from boarding school to boarding school. The gambling. *I am hard on you, Andrew, because I care about you. I won't always be here to guide you. Before long, you will be the only Raleigh left.*

So far James's efforts to drag Andrew into maturity had failed, along with every job he'd helped him land. He'd worked at the foundation but almost never showed up. James finally told him not to bother. He had pushed Hunter to become involved in the foundation when Hunter began talking about a shift into politics. That did not end well, so now the foundation was run primarily by paid staff instead of his own family.

It wasn't supposed to be like this. Hunter, if he had lived, eventually would have chosen a suitable spouse and would have carried on the family name. He might have proposed to Casey and put a ring on her finger, but he was never going to make it down the aisle with her. Of that much, James was certain.

As careless as Andrew was about his choices of companions, at least he had never brought them around in ways that embarrassed the family. He could not say the same for Hunter. Casey had been Hunter's Achilles' heel. James felt his blood pressure rise as he remembered the night that she began offering her strident political views at the dinner table, in front of a deputy attorney general and a newly elected congresswoman—as if she had done anything in her young, carefree life to have an informed opinion. He finally had to suggest that Hunter escort her home. The woman did not know how to behave, plain and simple.

He realized that his pen was back in hand. He looked at his notepad. He had written, *I am responsible.*

It wasn't the first time those words had come out when he least expected them. I was the one who told him that he could not let that woman into our family, he thought. I even went so far as to tell him that if he had children with her, he was forbidden to name them Hunter.

I saw forty-four years of military service. I have seen evil and confronted danger in many forms. But I never saw it sitting at my own dining table. I never thought I was putting my son in danger by expecting him to break things off with a woman who didn't deserve him.

I am responsible.

Now that murderous girl was planning to cry in front of the cameras to gain sympathy. He would not let that happen. If he had to fight until his last breath, the world would come to see her for what she was—a cold-blooded killer.

He had told Andrew that his role would be limited to putting on a stern face for the show, but he had learned the five p's in the military: *prior planning prevents poor performance.* Andrew would do his job of exposing Casey for the volatile sociopath that she was, but James's efforts would remain behind the scenes.

At the very least, Mark Templeton would not be saying a word to anyone about Hunter or the foundation. James had made sure of that earlier today when he'd spoken to Templeton for the first time in nearly a decade.

25

Laurie was stepping out of a taxi in front of Alex's office when her cell phone rang. According to the screen, it was Jerry. She wasn't surprised that he was still working. She picked up immediately.

"I've got bad news," he said. "Mark Templeton, the former CFO of the Raleigh Foundation, finally called you back. He wanted to know what this was about, so Grace connected him to me. I told him about the show. I hope you don't mind."

The fact that Jerry had said he had bad news indicated that Templeton wouldn't be participating. "Of course not, Jerry. I trust your judgment. I take it he's a no?"

"Unfortunately."

"That's a little fishy," Laurie said. "He was one of Hunter's closest friends." Maybe Casey was right about Hunter's death being connected to his audit of the foundation.

"I didn't want to raise the issue of the foundation's finances without running it past you. I said we wanted to talk to him about that night at the gala. His rationale for declining had a certain logic. He says he loved his dear friend and eventually concluded from the evidence that Casey was guilty. As the head of a reputable nonprofit, he feels a responsibility not to get involved in whatever it is Casey has — quote — *up her sleeve*."

"Okay, you made the right call by not pushing too hard." She'd made the same decision by not asking Hunter's brother about the foundation's finances. Ryan could ask about it once they were in production. She was hopeful that by then, they'd know more about the reasons Templeton resigned his position.

In the meantime, they had other suspects to research. "I was just talking to Casey's cousin Angela. She confirmed Casey's claim that Jason Gardner tried getting Casey back after they broke up, even after she was engaged to Hunter."

"Really? If even half of those nasty things he wrote about her in his book were true, you'd think he'd have run as quickly as he could in the opposite direction."

"I was thinking the same thing." The prosecution had tried to offer Jason as a witness at Casey's trial, to testify that she was a jealous and volatile person. The judge ruled that the testimony was inadmissible "character evidence." That didn't stop Jason from writing a tell-all book that made Casey look like Lizzie Borden. "Let's see what else we can find out about him."

"Got it," Jerry said. "Are you out for the rest of the day?"

"Yes. I'll see you tomorrow."

She needed to speak to Alex.

26

Alex greeted Laurie in his reception area with a lingering kiss. She realized how good it felt to have her body close to his. "Funny. I'm used to going to *your* office, not the other way around."

"Sorry to pop in on short notice." She let Alex lead the way down the hall.

Although technically Alex was a sole practitioner, he shared space with five other attorneys. They had separate assistants, but jointly funded a pool of eight paralegals and six investigators. The result felt like a small firm, though the decor wasn't what Laurie typically pictured for a law firm. Instead of dark wood, overstuffed leather chairs, and rows of dusty books, Alex had opted for a modern, open, airy feel, filled with sunlight, glass, and colorful art. When they entered his office, he stepped to the floor-to-ceiling windows with views of the Hudson River. "This is the perfect time of day, watching the sun move to the horizon. The sky's beautiful tonight, filled with pink and gold."

Laurie always admired the way Alex took the time to appreciate the joys that others took for granted. She was wondering now if she had made a mistake coming here. Maybe she was overreacting. She found herself thinking about Grace's breezy attitude toward dating. It was a world she did not understand. She had always thought Greg was a once-in-a-lifetime soul mate because nothing between them had ever been complicated. But maybe I have a way of making things harder than they need to be, she thought.

"So to what do I owe this pleasure?" Alex asked.

Now that she was here, she couldn't lie to him. She just needed to come out with it. "The other night, it seemed like you were trying to avoid talking to me about Casey Carter's wrongful conviction claim."

"Did it?" Alex looked astonished. "As I said, I just wasn't sure how much I should stick my nose in now that I'm no longer working on the show. Once you told me you wanted my opinion, I did my best to give you my assessment based on the coverage I remembered from the trial."

Something about his explanation sounded defensive, almost lawyerly. "And then you told me not to let Brett pressure me into a rushed decision. And you pointed out that Casey didn't really have anything to lose, unlike our previous specials."

"What are you getting at, Laurie?"

"It seemed as though you were giving me reasons to stay away from the case. Why is that?"

Alex was looking out the window again. "I don't know where all this is coming from, Laurie. I thought the other night at my apartment went really well. It felt good to be with you and your family without work overshadowing everything. You seemed happy when you left. Was I wrong about that?"

"No. But that was before I found out you dated Casey's cousin."

"I what?"

"Well, maybe *dated* is too strong a word. But you went out with Casey's cousin, Angela Hart, when you were in law school. Is that why you didn't want me to take the case?"

Alex seemed to be searching his memory.

"Are there really so many women that you can't remember this one? She was a model, for goodness' sakes. I think most men would remember that."

It was a low blow and she knew it. Early on, Alex had assured her that he was no "man about town," even though he was in his late thirties and had never been married and always seemed to have a beautiful woman on his arm in the social pages. Now she was holding those facts over him.

"A model? Do you mean Angie? Sure, I vaguely remember her. You mean to tell me she's Casey Carter's cousin?"

"Yes. She's the friend of Charlotte I mentioned. And she told me that you met at some law partner's party in the Hamptons. She was with the Raleigh family."

She could see the memory coming back to Alex. It really did seem as if he had not made the connection before.

"That's right. General Raleigh was at that picnic. All of the law students were starstruck. It was a big deal when he took the time to shake our hands."

"And the sons, Hunter and Andrew?"

"If I met them, I honestly don't remember. Laurie, I don't understand what any of this is about."

"Were you trying to hide the fact that you knew Angela Hart from me?"

"No." He held up his right hand in a pledge.

"Were you trying to hide the fact that you knew Hunter Raleigh?"

No again, with the pledge. "I don't even recall meeting him," he reminded her.

"Is there some other reason you don't want me working on this case?"

"Laurie, I'm starting to think your cross-examination skills are better than mine. Look, I know how much you care about *Under Suspicion*. It is your baby, from top to bottom, beginning to end. You and you alone should decide what case you think merits your show's attention. Okay? I have total faith that you'll have yet another hit on your hands, no matter what you decide, because your instincts are always spot-on."

He wrapped her in his arms and kissed the top of her head. "Any more questions?"

She shook her head.

"You know you're prettier than any model out there, right?"

"It's a good thing you're not under oath, Counselor. I'm heading home to make dinner for Timmy. Care to join us?"

"I'd love to, but I'm speaking at NYU tonight. A friend of mine is being inducted as a chaired professor at the law school."

He kissed her once more before walking her to the elevator. By the time she stepped out in the lobby, a sinking feeling had returned to Laurie's stomach. She pictured Alex with his right hand up in a pledge to tell the truth. No, he hadn't meant to conceal a connection to Angela. No, he didn't remember meeting Hunter. But was there some reason he didn't want Laurie looking into Casey's conviction? He never responded to the question, but Laurie's instincts, the ones that were always spot-on, were yelling the answer: there was something he wasn't telling her.

27

Three days later, Laurie, Grace, and Jerry were gathered in her office to discuss where they stood in securing agreements from everyone they wanted to participate in the next special.

Grace flipped through a file of signed releases. "Of the people who were at the gala that night, we've got Hunter's brother and father, both of whom have made it very clear they believe Casey is guilty. The assistant, Mary Jane, signed. Casey, of course, is participating, as is her cousin Angela. We have the housekeeper who will back up Casey's claim that Hunter's photograph with the President was on his nightstand. And we have Casey's mother."

Jerry let out a groan. "I'm not even sure we should go there. Paula seems like a nice woman, but she has called at least three times a day, asking questions about every last thing. *Are we sure Casey can't be sent back to prison? Does Casey need a lawyer? Can you blur our faces?* She doesn't have much to offer about the actual evidence, and I'm afraid if we put her on camera, she'll be a deer in the headlights."

"I'll think about that," Laurie said. "You may be right."

Viewers would tune in just to hear Casey, because she never testified at trial. But they needed something new other than the missing picture frame.

"I'm torn about whether to push harder to get Mark Templeton on board," Laurie said.

Grace flipped through her notes, trying to remember all the names. "That's the money guy, right?"

Laurie nodded. "Chief financial officer of the Raleigh Foundation, to be exact. He told Jerry he wanted to avoid associating his name with Casey because of his current role as director of a nonprofit, but he could have ulterior motives for lying low. The fact that the Raleigh Foundation had financial problems when he departed does raise questions—especially combined with Hunter's concerns about the books and the fact that it took Mark nearly a year to start a new job after he left the foundation."

Jerry tapped his pen against his notebook. "Do we have any evidence other than Casey's word that Hunter was worried about the foundation?"

Laurie raised her hand in the shape of a zero. "If we did, we'd have leverage to press Mark on the issue. Without it, we look like we're grasping at straws." Laurie was already missing the conversations she used to have with Alex. They would pore over the evidence together, looking at each piece from all sides.

"More like Casey's grasping at straws," Grace emphasized. "If Hunter had really been sniffing around about the finances and was suddenly murdered, wouldn't someone have come forward to tell the police? One of those forensic accountants he was hiring?"

"Unless he never got around to calling," Laurie said. "According to Casey, he said he noticed something unusual and that he was going to hire someone to inspect the books. But, again, that's according to Casey. I'm tempted to press Mark Templeton about the issue, but I'm worried he'll call the Raleighs and scare them off. I'm sure they don't want a whiff of scandal about the foundation. Until I have concrete evidence to connect Mark, I think it's a dead end."

"The good news," Jerry reported cheerily, "is that we have our two principal locations locked down. Hunter's Connecticut house was left to his brother, Andrew. My impression is that the man nearly forgot he owns it. His exact words when I called him to confirm were *mi casa es su casa*. And even though the Cipriani ballroom is booked for months, the Raleigh Foundation will let us piggyback onto their upcoming donor event, but it's next Sunday. That's in ten days, which I think we can pull off. We'd film before their event—in exchange for a nice donation, of course. I already did a walk-through, and it will be a beautiful setting."

"I have an idea about a location also," Grace said. "Tiro A Segno in Greenwich Village. It's both a private gun club and a restaurant. Where else can you get veal parmigiana and a target range? It was Hunter's favorite place to shoot. You might be able to find people who remember him and Casey."

"Congratulations, Grace. Good idea," Laurie said. "If only location scouting was always this easy." The trial had simplified matters, too. Her past specials had all involved cases that never led to an arrest, let alone court proceedings. She had to piece together the evidence from public records, newspaper articles, and the biased recollections of myriad witnesses. Not this time. She had spent the last few days poring over the transcripts from Casey's trial and had created a detailed overview of every aspect of the evidence. "Is it possible we might actually be able to meet Brett's absurd time line?"

She heard a knock at the door and yelled for the person to come in. It was Ryan Nichols. "Sorry I'm late."

He didn't sound as though he meant it.

28

What had been a fast-moving, natural conversation became clunky and awkward with Ryan in the room. "I didn't realize you were joining us," Laurie said.

"You sent me an email with the time. Why would you think I wouldn't come?"

Laurie hadn't thought of her message as an invitation to attend, let alone a directive. In the spirit of playing nice with the new kid in the sandbox, she had notified him that she'd be meeting with Jerry and Grace this afternoon with an eye toward setting a production schedule. "Alex usually didn't get involved until we had a full list of witnesses lined up and ready to go on camera," she told him. "Then of course we'd all work together to plan the lines of questioning."

Ryan said abruptly, "Laurie, I think I'd be more comfortable plugged in from the get-go. That's what I've talked about with Brett."

Jerry and Grace were sharing an apprehensive glance, like siblings who were watching their parents fight. They knew that Ryan had Brett wrapped around his finger, and Laurie was in no position to complain about Ryan's involvement. They also were certainly aware that she had gotten into the habit of treating Alex like a trusted sounding board.

Seeing no way out, Laurie gestured to Ryan to have a seat. "We were just going over the releases we've received from the people we'd like you to interview." She filled him in on the list they'd compiled so far.

"That's not much to work with," he said dismissively. "It would be nice to get some of their friends, just to give a sense of what Casey and Hunter were like together."

"We already thought of that," Laurie said, "but Casey's friends all dropped her when she was arrested, and Hunter's friends are obviously going to have a biased opinion of her."

"Who's to say it's biased?" he questioned. "Maybe she's just as awful as they say."

Jerry cleared his throat to cut the tension. "What about that guy Angela was dating?"

"Sean Murray," Laurie reminded him. "He called yesterday and doesn't want to get involved. He's married now with three kids. He said no wife wants to be reminded her husband was with someone else, especially not someone who looks like Angela. He asked me if she was still beautiful."

"Painfully so," Grace observed. "It's sort of hard not to hate her."

"Sean said he had nothing to offer in any event. He was out of town the night of the foundation gala and hadn't seen Hunter and Casey for at least a couple of weeks before that. All he could say was that they seemed very much in love. He wrote off their arguments as debates they both enjoyed. But after she was arrested, he would read the news coverage and wonder if there was a darker side to their relationship that he hadn't seen."

Ryan raised an eyebrow. "He sounds like a smart man. Where are we on alternative suspects?"

Jerry was ready with an answer.

"I've been looking into the names you gave me, *Laurie*," he said. He emphasized her name in an attempt to return control of the meeting to her. "I got renowned socialite Gabrielle Lawson on the phone, and I made an appointment for you to see her at three o'clock today."

Grace interrupted. "I'm sorry, but what the heck is a socialite? I mean, I'm a secretary, Laurie's a producer, Jerry's an assistant producer, and Ryan here's a kick-butt lawyer. What makes someone a socialite?"

Laurie smiled. "In Gabrielle Lawson's case I would say it's generally someone from a prominent family who likes to walk on the red carpets and see her name in gossip columns."

Once Grace was satisfied with that response, Jerry continued. "The day before Hunter was killed, a gossip column called 'The Chatter' ran a photograph of Gabrielle looking cozy with Hunter at a fundraiser for the Boys and Girls Clubs." He handed Laurie a printout of the picture in question. Gabrielle was staring at Hunter adoringly. "Perhaps not coincidentally, the reporter was Mindy Sampson, the blogger who has been posting constantly about Casey since her release. When Mindy was a newspaper columnist, she was practically tailing Hunter, claiming that he was back to his playboy ways and was on the verge of breaking off his engagement to Casey because of an infatuation with Gabrielle, who made no secret of her interest in Hunter."

Fifteen years later, Mindy Sampson's constant blog posts about Casey were the reason Brett was rushing them into production.

"I also found this 'Whispers' piece that ran the previous week," Jerry added.

"I used to love that column," Grace exclaimed. "It ran so-called blind items: whispers about hot gossip, without naming names."

Laurie read aloud the item Jerry had highlighted: " 'Which of the city's most sought after men might be heading back to the bachelor scene instead of heading down the aisle?' And we think this was Hunter?" she asked.

"The press certainly did after Casey was arrested," Jerry said. "That, plus the picture of Hunter with Gabrielle, suggested that all wasn't right in paradise."

As far as Gabrielle Lawson was concerned, Laurie had some inkling of what she'd say if interviewed for their show. "Gabrielle testified at Casey's trial. According to her, Hunter flirted with her at that fundraiser. Her exact words were that he was 'not behaving like a man who was spoken for.' At the gala she had approached their table, put her arms around him, and kissed him. The prosecution used that as further evidence to suggest that Hunter was about to break things off with Casey."

Laurie could tell from Jerry's eager expression that there was more to the story.

"But we know there's more today than Casey's defense lawyer knew fifteen years ago. Gabrielle Lawson has been married and divorced three times, with high-profile romances in between, which she always plays up in the press, whether real or imagined. Many of her advances on wealthy, powerful men have been rebuffed. One of her crushes, the director Hans Lindholm, even obtained a restraining order."

Laurie, Grace, and Ryan all murmured vague recollections of the momentary scandal, but Jerry was prepared with the details. "According to Lindholm's petition, he met Gabrielle in passing at the Tribeca Film Festival, and then she began showing up unexpectedly at other public events he attended. He claimed that she even called a gossip columnist and swore that the two of them were shopping for an apartment together."

"Who was the gossip columnist?" Laurie asked, her eyebrow arching.

"The one and only Mindy Sampson. Of course, there's no way to confirm that Gabrielle was Mindy's source, but the court did issue the restraining order."

Grace frowned. "She sounds like a literal Fatal Attraction. Maybe she decided that if she couldn't have Hunter, then no one could. She killed Hunter, and framed Casey for the deed."

"Notice that even Grace is starting to see another side to the story," Laurie said. "As you know, I'll be seeing Gabrielle this afternoon. I've also been doing some digging of my own into Jason Gardner."

"That's Casey's ex-boyfriend," Laurie told Ryan. "He was a junior banker and just happened to be sitting at his employer's table at the Raleigh Foundation gala."

"Seems like another possible stalker to me," Grace added.

"Ryan," Jerry explained, "Grace is our in-house conclusion-jumper."

"Put another way," Grace said defiantly, "I'm the one with good instincts about people. And I started out absolutely certain that Casey was guilty as sin."

"Join the team," Ryan snapped.

"Now I've opened my eyes," Grace declared. "And Jason's my number one suspect. Think about it. Your ex is newly engaged to Mr. Muckety-Muck. Your enormous company buys an obligatory table at the gala, where Hunter Raleigh is bound to be the center of attention. Any normal person would want to be anywhere in New York City other than in that room. Instead Jason shows up. I'm telling you: that guy was jealous."

"You may be onto something," Laurie agreed. "Both Casey and Angela claim that Jason tried getting Casey back, even after her engagement was announced. And like Gabrielle, Jason has accumulated some skeletons in his closet since Casey was first charged with murder. He raised eyebrows by writing a tell-all book immediately after she was convicted. But since then, he's been divorced twice. Both wives complained to the police that he would drive by the house after he moved out. He even confronted his second wife's new boyfriend in a restaurant. She alleged he had a substance abuse problem."

Ryan held up a hand to interrupt. "I don't know how you can possibly get either of these people to talk to me on camera."

Laurie thought she saw Jerry and Grace both cringe at the use of his word *me*. She was relieved when Jerry spoke up. "Laurie can be very persuasive. The ones who are innocent help because they trust us. And the ones who aren't so innocent pretend to trust us because they're afraid of looking guilty."

Laurie couldn't have put it any better herself. "If we can get Gabrielle and Jason on board, we should have enough to start production. If we get new leads, we can always do a second round of interviews."

"Sounds like a plan," Ryan said.

Our plan, she thought, not yours.

Jerry tucked his pen inside the spiral of his notebook. "It's too bad we don't know more about this financial issue with the foundation."

"Why?" Ryan asked.

"Because Casey told us she was suspicious of Mark Templeton. He left the foundation under a cloud. She said she thought Hunter was planning to order an audit of the foundation's books."

"According to media reports at the time," Laurie explained, "the foundation's assets had significantly dipped."

"That's very interesting." Ryan's voice was thoughtful, but he did not explain himself. "Very interesting." He didn't share whatever inferences he might have drawn from that information. The man was utterly useless.

"I need to run," Laurie announced. "My meeting with Gabrielle is in half an hour, and her apartment is near Gramercy Park."

She was surprised to find Ryan waiting for her a few minutes later outside the elevators. "I told Brett I'd be with you on the interviews for the show. Do you have a car coming or should I call my driver?"

29

For a man who had successfully tried multiple, complex jury trials, Ryan looked a little nervous. His eyes were darting between the doorman, front entrance, and the elevator as the doorman called upstairs to announce their arrival.

"This can't be the first time you've spoken to a potential witness," Laurie whispered.

"Of course not, but usually the person's under arrest or with their lawyer."

The doorman announced that Ms. Lawson would see them. "Penthouse floor," he told them.

Gabrielle Lawson was one of those women who could pass for any age between forty and sixty, but Laurie happened to know that she was fifty-two years old, the same age Hunter Raleigh would have been, had he lived. She was dressed in an elegant white suit with tasteful gold jewelry, and her red hair was swept into a perfect, high bun. She didn't look much different than she had fifteen years ago, when "The Chatter" published a photograph of her looking lovingly at Hunter Raleigh.

Fifteen minutes into their conversation, Laurie had managed to make eye contact with Gabrielle only twice. Gabrielle was absolutely riveted by Ryan, twenty years her junior. Based on everything she'd read about her, Laurie knew that she was singularly focused on attracting the attention of successful, preferably handsome men. Ryan checked both boxes.

Gabrielle ignored Laurie's question about her greeting Hunter at the Raleigh Foundation gala and instead launched her own inquiry for Ryan: "How did you go from being a television commentator to a producer?" she asked.

"Actually, I'm not a—"

"Mere producer," Laurie said, interrupting Ryan's correction. "He's also the new star of the show. He'll be the one working start to finish with all our participants. He's the heart of *Under Suspicion*, really."

She guessed that being the heart of a news-based television show wasn't quite the draw of the award-winning film director Gabrielle had stalked, but it was probably good enough to have her fawning over Ryan.

She hoped Ryan would take the hint and use the obvious dynamic to their favor, but instead he asked Gabrielle to confirm that she'd been thrice married and divorced.

"I see no reason to dwell on that," she said softly.

"I think what Ryan would really like to know is whether you went over to greet Hunter the night of the foundation's gala." It was the very question she had already posed, but Gabrielle seemed to hear it for the first time now that it had been attributed to Ryan.

"Let's see . . . did I talk to Hunter that night? Well, of course I did. At some length."

Laurie pointed out that Casey's defense lawyer had asked every prosecution witness whether they'd seen Hunter and Gabrielle together. No one had, other than a brief moment when Gabrielle walked up to Hunter near his family's table and flung her arms around him enthusiastically. It was a subtle point, intended to undercut the prosecution's claim that Casey killed Hunter because he was planning to break off their engagement to be with Gabrielle.

Casey's lawyer never argued that Gabrielle could have used the moment to slip a drug into Casey's glass.

"We were keeping things discreet," Gabrielle said demurely. "Hunter hadn't broken the news to Casey yet. He was dignified. He would never embarrass any of us. He would break things off quietly, and then we would have gone public after a respectable time period."

"Sounds reasonable," Laurie said, even though she did not believe a word of it. "Given that you were keeping things private, how did Mindy Sampson manage to get a photograph of the two of you together at a fundraiser for the Boys and Girls Clubs?"

Gabrielle smiled coyly, as if they were two girlfriends gossiping. "Well, you know how it is. Sometimes these matters need a little push. It didn't dawn on me that the picture would get Hunter killed or I never would have done it."

"So you admit you gave that picture to Mindy," Ryan said, as if nailing down a witness on cross-examination.

Laurie managed to suppress a wince. His statement was too bald and assertive. Alex never would have made that mistake. Sure enough, Gabrielle immediately denied the accusation.

"Heavens, no. I saw a photographer approaching and leaned in for the picture. But that's all."

Laurie immediately tried to regain some rapport with Gabrielle. "What about Casey? I've heard that she was quite a mess at the gala."

"Sloppy doesn't *begin* to describe it," Gabrielle dished. "She was visibly intoxicated, slurring her words and nearly falling down. It was embarrassing. Hunter was distraught, I could tell."

"As distraught as Hans Lindholm when he applied for a restraining order against you?" Ryan asked mockingly.

Gabrielle glared at Ryan. "You're as pretty as a Georgia peach, but your mother should have taught you some manners, Mr. Nichols."

Laurie offered a profuse apology and her warmest smile. "Ryan's a lawyer by training," she explained. "Law schools don't spend a lot of time teaching etiquette."

Gabrielle laughed. "I can see that."

"Millions of people watch our show. Would you be willing to share your observations with our viewers?" Laurie asked.

Gabrielle hesitated, eying Ryan skeptically.

"It would be essential to countering Casey's claims of innocence," Laurie pressed. "On the program we want to make sure we hear from *both* of the women in Hunter's life."

Gabrielle's face glowed at the description. "Absolutely," she said. "I owe it to him. That's why my other marriages never lasted. I could never replace my Hunter."

Gabrielle was still smiling as she signed on the dotted line.

As Laurie walked to the elevator, she found herself wishing Alex were here. As much as she resented Ryan's presence, she had often asked Alex to play a role in these preliminary interviews. If he had been the one who had accompanied her, they'd have been sharing their opinions immediately. But she had no interest in hearing Ryan's thoughts, so she replayed her own.

She believed Gabrielle's account of Casey's impaired condition, but that was consistent with having been drugged involuntarily. However, she did not believe that Gabrielle had had a close relationship with Hunter. She was certain that Gabrielle had been in cahoots with Mindy Sampson to plant that photograph of Hunter and her in the paper. But was she obsessed enough to kill Hunter? Laurie had no idea.

The elevator doors had barely closed when Ryan laid into her. "Don't ever apologize for me to another person again or make a joke at my expense. I'm good at my job."

"You should have been the one apologizing, including to me.

You may be a good lawyer in the courtroom, but you've now chosen a job that you seem to have little interest in learning about. You nearly blew that interview," Laurie shot back.

"You call that an interview? More like a cakewalk."

"Gabrielle agreed to go on camera, which you said an hour ago would be impossible. We're not federal prosecutors. We don't have subpoena powers. We get witnesses by being warm and fuzzy, not sarcastic and alienating. The tough questions come later, while we're filming."

"Please. The woman doesn't even know anything relevant. Hunter Raleigh was murdered by Casey Carter. Full stop."

Laurie walked three steps ahead of him through the building lobby and into the backseat of the awaiting car. "You have a lot to learn, and you don't even know it. If you mess this case up, I won't care how many of your family members know Brett—I won't work with you again. And now I'm taking *your* car to *my* next interview."

She pulled the backdoor closed, leaving Ryan standing alone on the sidewalk. Her face still felt flushed when she gave his driver the only address she had for Jason Gardner.

30

Fifteen years ago, Jason Gardner attended the Raleigh Foundation's gala at Cipriani as an up-and-coming analyst for one of the largest investment banks in the world. In light of that background, Laurie had expected to find Casey's ex-boyfriend working today as a billionaire hedge fund manager. Instead, when she appeared at the address listed on his LinkedIn profile, she found a tiny office in a dusty building overlooking the entrance to the Holland Tunnel. The name of the firm was GARDNER EQUITY, but based on the cheap furniture, she suspected Gardner had very little in the way of actual equity.

The receptionist at the front desk was reading a gossip magazine and chewing gum. When Laurie told her that she was looking for Mr. Gardner, the woman tilted her head in the direction of the only other person in the office. "Jason, Ms. Moran's here."

Jason's résumé was not the only thing that had taken a hit in the last fifteen years. The man who rose from the desk in the back corner was only forty-two but had deep lines in his face and bloodshot eyes. He looked nothing like the young, handsome man whose photograph was on the back of his tell-all book, *My Days with Crazy Casey*. Laurie suspected that the drugs and alcohol his ex-wives had mentioned to police were still taking their toll.

"Can I help you with something?" he asked.

"I have some questions about Casey Carter."

His face suddenly aged another decade.

"I saw the news that she's out. Hard to believe how fast fifteen years flew by." Jason's gaze was somewhere far away, as if he were watching the years pass.

"I don't think they were quick for Casey," Laurie said.

"No, I suppose not."

Laurie had not had a chance to read Jason's book in its entirety, but she'd skimmed enough to know that Jason had thrown his ex-girlfriend under the proverbial bus. The book described an ambitious, power-hungry young woman who cast aside her on-again, off-again boyfriend when she set her sights on Hunter Raleigh.

Laurie pulled her copy of the book from her briefcase. "Some people might have been surprised by your decision to write this. From what I've heard, you were quite in love with Casey."

"I did love her," he said sadly, "that's true. She was outspoken, energetic, fun. I have no idea what she's like now, but back then? Being around Casey made me feel more alive. But sometimes a personality like that comes with a price. There's a fine line between spontaneity and chaos. In some ways, Casey was a one-woman wrecking ball."

"How so?"

He shrugged. "It's hard to describe. It's like she felt everything a little too much. Her interest in art? She couldn't just appreciate a painting; it would move her to tears. If she got a negative comment at work, she'd be worried about it the rest of the night, wondering what she had done wrong. And so it went with me. When we first met in college, it seemed like we were soul mates. When she moved to New York, I hoped it was to be with me, but she clearly cared more about her job at Sotheby's. Then she enrolled in classes toward her master's degree and started talking about plans for her own gallery. Meanwhile, she was questioning why I wasn't working harder. Why someone got promoted over me. Like I wasn't good enough for her. When she broke it off with me, she said she wanted a 'time-out.' I figured it was another one of our off periods. But two weeks later, I see a picture of her in the society pages with Hunter Raleigh. She broke my heart. I got distracted. The troubles I was having at work snowballed. As you can see, I didn't exactly wind up in the Taj Mahal."

He sounded like a man who blamed Casey for his downfall. It wasn't a stretch to think he blamed Hunter as well.

"Yet I'm told you tried to get her back, even after the engagement was announced."

"You've got good sources. It was only once, and a large amount of whiskey was to blame. I told her that a snob like Hunter would squeeze every ounce of life from her. Little did I know that the situation would be the other way around."

"You think she killed him?" From what Laurie could tell, Jason's book never gave a direct opinion as to Casey's guilt.

"I'll admit that calling her Crazy Casey in the book title was a little unfair. Frankly, Arden Publishing insisted. But Casey was stubborn as a mule, with the temper to back it up. When we were going around, she would get all riled up if I spoke to another woman. I can only wonder what she would have done if Hunter tried to dump her the way she did me."

After Laurie left, Jason waited until he heard the elevator in the hallway depart before asking Jennifer—the latest in a long string of incompetent assistants willing to work for what he could pay—to take a short break. Once she was gone, he pulled up a number he had not dialed for years. His agent answered, then placed him on a brief hold. The man who eventually picked up again did not sound happy to hear from him.

"A television producer came to see me, asking about Casey," Jason explained. "It's for a show called *Under Suspicion*. They want to interview me. What do you think?"

"Sign the papers. Do the show. You might sell more books."

"She won't make me look good."

"What else is new? Just sign the papers."

Jason felt nauseous as he hung up the phone. He had told the truth to Laurie Moran. He really did love Casey. But then the woman he loved had been arrested for murder, and there was nothing he could do to help her. He could only help himself, and so he had. And now he hated himself for it. He opened the top drawer of his desk, popped one of the dwindling number of painkillers he had stored there, and tried not to think about Casey.

31

Tiro A Segno looked nothing like any gun club Laurie had ever seen. Tucked within a series of three nondescript brownstones on MacDougal Street in Greenwich Village, the club seemed more like a private home, noteworthy only for the Italian flag flying proudly at the entrance. Even when she stepped inside, Laurie was greeted by leather furniture, mahogany wood, and a pool table—not a gun in sight. The smells were of garlic and oregano, not gunpowder.

"Not what you pictured, is it?" her host asked. "I never get tired of seeing the look of surprise on the face of a new guest."

"Thank you so much for letting me pop in like this, Mr. Caruso." She'd called the club after she left Jason Gardner's office, just a few blocks away. "As I mentioned, my production team learned that your club was one of Hunter Raleigh's favorite places to target practice."

"Please, call me Antonio. And I was happy to help. You tell me, 'TV show'—my response is 'aaah, we don't like cameras so much.' But then you say you want to know about Hunter Raleigh. He was a good man, a real gentleman. Then to top it off, you are the daughter of Leo Farley. Of course, you are welcome here. Your father is an honorary member for life."

With the exception of perhaps the perpetrators he arrested throughout his career, everyone who'd met her father considered him a friend.

She'd come here with questions about Hunter and Casey, but now that she was here, she understood why Grace had suggested it as an ideal location for footage. "I can see why your club is so beloved, Antonio."

"It's transformed over the years, to be sure. We didn't used to be quite so elegant. Some of the old-timers still complain about losing the bocce court. These days, it's more about the food and wine and socializing, but of course we still have the range downstairs. We're strictly target shooting, as you may know. And no handguns, just rifles."

"Did Hunter ever bring his fiancée, Casey Carter, here?" Laurie asked.

A momentary darkness fell over Antonio's face. "Yes, of course. What a terrible ending. Of course, he brought many women here before he was engaged," he added.

"But being with Casey changed his bachelor ways?"

"So it seemed. The second time I saw them together, I said to Hunter, *You should have the wedding here*, and he just smiled. Do you know the saying, *Chi ama me, ama il mio cane*? It translates to 'Whoever loves me, loves my dog.' But what it really means is 'Whoever loves me, loves me as I am, warts and all.' That's how Hunter felt about Casey."

"Forgive me if I'm reading too much into this, Antonio, but it sounds like you're saying Casey had warts."

He shrugged. "Like I said, it was a terrible ending."

Laurie could already tell that it was going to be impossible to get an unbiased depiction of Casey as a young woman out of anyone. Everyone's recollections had been permanently transformed by the fact that she'd been convicted of killing Hunter.

"I heard that Casey was quite skilled at target shooting in her own right," Laurie said.

"You heard correctly. Hunter joked that the only reason she tried was because she was the most competitive person he knew. She was an athlete at some point, as I recall."

"Tennis," Laurie clarified. "In college."

"That's right. Hunter said she cleaned the court with him. And not to be bested, she certainly was catching up to him at his own sport. She was a very good shot."

"The police found bullet holes in the walls of Hunter's living room and bedroom, where he was actually killed. Does it strike you as odd that Casey would have missed twice?"

"That's hard to say. We only use still targets here. I never saw her shoot skeet or at another moving target. It's much harder than people realize. That's why in self-defense classes, they say you're better off running from a gunman, especially if you run in an unpredictable pattern. Plus, adrenaline and, as I understood it, intoxication, may have affected her skills. So the fact that she missed is not a smoking gun one way or the other," he added with a smile.

Laurie thanked Antonio again for his time and promised she'd tell Leo he said hello. As far as her show was concerned, some photographs of this Greenwich Village treasure might be worth a few seconds of local color, but she was no closer to knowing who killed Hunter Raleigh.

32

While she was waiting for Gabrielle, Mindy Sampson sat at a table in the back corner of the Rose Bar in the Gramercy Park Hotel. There was a time not many years ago when every person here, from the hostess at the front to the A-list actress at the booth to her right, would have recognized her face. For more than two decades, her photograph had graced the top of "The Chatter," one of the most read gossip columns in New York City. She'd take a new head shot like clockwork each year, but always wore pale makeup and dark red lipstick and kept her hair naturally jet-black. The look was iconic. Before the Kardashians and the Kanyes and the Gwyneths, Mindy Sampson had understood the value of branding oneself.

And Mindy's brand was associated with taste making. Who wore it better? Which celebrity couples were to be cheered for, and which scorned? Was the billionaire playboy guilty, or the victim of a reckless accusation? Mindy always had the answers.

Those were the days when papers still left ink on your fingers.

Then came the day when her managing editor told her to "hold off" on her annual tradition of getting a new photograph for her column. They might be making "changes," he warned.

Mindy was famous by then for gossip, but she still had a journalist's instincts. She'd seen what was happening in the newsroom. Advertising dollars were down. The paper got thinner each month. So did the workforce. The long-timers, seen in the past as the backbone of the paper, were too expensive to keep on the payroll. College interns were willing to work for free, and recent graduates didn't cost much more.

A month later, she was told "the news." They were turning her column, the one she had built and nurtured and branded, to "staff." No byline. No iconic photograph. She knew "staff" was shorthand for tidbits pulled from the wires.

She did not go easily. She threatened to sue for gender discrimination. For ageism. She even threw in a potential disability claim for chronic pain syndrome. The paper thought they were looking at years of litigation and a public scandal. But then she told her lawyer that she only wanted two things: six months' severance pay and the name. They could call their watered-down column whatever they pleased, but she would be taking the "Chatter" brand with her.

They may have written her off as an over-the-hill old-timer, but it wasn't the first time Mindy had been underestimated. She knew before they did that the new media was online. She used her severance pay to launch a website, and she became the one to hire unpaid interns. Now, instead of a salary, she earned money for ads that were sold, readers who clicked on those ads, and product placements. And instead of sifting her words through layers of editors, she could publish to the world with the click of a button.

She hit send on her phone. A new story was filed, just like that, all while she was waiting for Gabrielle Lawson. Of all the personalities Mindy had known over the years, Gabrielle was among the most dramatic. She carried herself like an old-fashioned Hollywood dame. She lived like one, too, thanks to a trust fund from a wealthy uncle who'd never had children of his own, not to mention her settlements from three divorces. She was lucid and functional, but seemed to live in a parallel reality in which her inflated sense of self played a starring role.

For example, when she had something to tell Mindy, she couldn't just say it over the phone or by email. She liked to meet in the back corners of a bar. In her alternative universe, Mindy was Bob Woodward to Gabrielle's Deep Throat. What news would she have today?

When Gabrielle arrived, they spent the first few minutes sipping champagne and engaging in small talk. As always, Mindy assured Gabrielle she would run a flattering photograph of her. It was an easy promise to make. Gabrielle had been a good source for her over the years, so she wanted to keep her happy.

On this particular occasion, however, the clandestine meeting was a waste of time. Gabrielle didn't tell her anything she didn't already know. When it came to Casey Carter, Mindy had never been lacking information.

33

That night at dinner, the smell of butter, thyme, and a perfectly roasted chicken filled Laurie's apartment. "This was such a treat, Dad."

Leo was supposed to have had a mini-reunion with some of his police pals at Gallagher's Steakhouse. To Laurie's surprise, he had dinner warming in the oven when she came home. The men's night had been canceled when two of Leo's friends, still on the job, had been called to Times Square on reports of an unattended van containing a suspicious package. Two hours later, the NYPD confirmed that the panic was a false alarm. The van's driver had inadvertently left the engine running while he ran upstairs to his sister's apartment to give a toy to his niece, and then stayed to visit with his family. The city was safe, and Laurie had enjoyed a delicious home-cooked meal.

Timmy was breathlessly replaying the reports that had come to Leo's phone earlier in the evening. "Mom, they evacuated three blocks—in the middle of Times Square! They had swat trucks and bomb-sniffing dogs. And Grandpa knew it all, before the news even reported it."

Leo reached over and patted Timmy on the shoulder, but looked melancholy.

After Timmy asked to be excused, Laurie asked her father, "Do you miss it? The job? Being in the middle of the action?"

She had probably asked him that same question a hundred times in the last six years. His answer was always some variation of saying that the best job he ever had was helping to raise his grandson. But tonight, he was absolutely honest. "Sometimes, yes. I remember that awful day in 2001. We all knew the world was changing in unimaginable ways, but I felt like I was helping. Tonight, I made a chicken. It's a quieter life."

She didn't know what to say, so she remained silent, kissing him on the cheek before clearing the dishes.

She was not surprised when Leo followed her into the kitchen and asked how the show was coming along. She had a hard time explaining her mixed feelings. On the one hand, she'd been lucky to get so many pieces connected quickly.

In theory, Gabrielle and Jason were both credible alternative suspects. She knew from the original police reports that both of them had said they went home alone after the gala, meaning either one of them could have gone up to Connecticut and killed Hunter. But she still lacked strong evidence pointing to a killer other than Casey.

"I don't know, Dad, maybe you were right. I may not have more to add to the original investigation after all."

He leaned against the kitchen counter and crossed his arms. In her eyes, she remembered him at the head of a squad room before roll call on Take Your Daughter to Work Day. She couldn't believe that since then a quarter of a century had passed.

"Look," he said, "I happen to think the system works 99.9 percent of the time, which means—yeah—I think the odds are slim this woman is innocent. But I'm also your father, so in the end, I'm on your side. With every production, you find yourself overwhelmed by the number of stories floating around. You manage to turn it into a riveting show, and you've delivered an impressive amount of justice in the meantime. Just remember that your main goal is to put out a fair and fine piece of television. Let the viewers decide what they think about Casey."

It was good advice, but her own desire for the truth always had a way of taking over. "Maybe I should have been a cop instead."

"Too rebellious," he said with a wink. "Besides, Timmy's going to be the next family member with a badge. Just you watch. Have you run any of these characters past Alex? He's always a good sounding board for you."

"He has been in the *past*," she said, involuntarily emphasizing the last word. "Now that he's not working for the studio, I'm not sure how much to burden him with work talk."

Leo shook his head. "When are you going to accept that nothing you ask of him is a burden? Alex cares about you. If you let him in, I'm sure he'd be more than happy to lend you an ear."

Alex cares about you, she thought. *If you let him in* . . . The words were echoing in her head and then, out of nowhere, she was crying.

Her father immediately grabbed her shoulders. "Laurie, sweetie, what is wrong?"

"I've been trying, Dad. You have no idea how much I've been trying to let him in." Her father was cradling her, telling her that everything would be okay, but a wave of emotion overcame her. The night Alex told her he was leaving the show. The moment Brett said he was hiring his best friend's nephew. The exhaustion of the last several days, working morning until night. And, finally, that unavoidable feeling in her stomach that Alex had lied to her.

"When I tried to talk to Alex at his apartment about the case, he seemed uncomfortable. I thought my complaints about Ryan were making him feel guilty. But then it turns out that he knew Casey's cousin, Angela." The words were spilling out of her. "And he met

Hunter and his family at a law firm picnic. Then when I asked him about it on Monday, he was . . . evasive. I could tell he was hiding something from me."

"Do you want me to call him? Talk to him man-to-man?"

She laughed and wiped the tears from her face. "How many times do I have to tell you that grown women can't have their fathers handle all their problems?"

"But this shouldn't be a problem, Laurie. We know Alex. He's a good, honest man."

"I know. But you're the one who has taught me always to trust my instincts. And I'm telling you, there's a reason Alex doesn't want me talking to him about this case. He's hiding something."

Her father was about to launch another defense of Alex when Timmy came running into the room. His iPad was outstretched in hands that were still small enough that both were required to hold his tablet. "Hey, Mom, I have something for you."

The last time he handed her his iPad, he'd gotten her hooked on a game in which plants battled against zombies. She couldn't afford that kind of distraction right now.

"I don't think I've earned enough free time for a new game, Timmy."

"It's not a game," he insisted. "I set up a Google alert on your name, and there's a new hit. Some blogger named Mindy Sampson wrote all about your next show."

34

Is Crazy Casey Playing with Fire?

Hello, fellow Chatterers. Have you been following the antics of Katherine "Casey" Carter since she flew the coop? Well, I have, and Casey has been awfully busy. It's not your everyday ex-con who goes directly from the prison exit to the closest fashion mall for a daylong shopping spree. Where was she planning to wear her new wardrobe? We all wondered.

But instead of making a comeback on the social scene, Casey seems to be on yet another shopping spree. This time, she's shopping for someone who might believe the same flimsy claims of innocence she's been spinning since the night she was found with Hunter Raleigh's blood on her hands.

At first, it appeared she might have found a sucker in Laurie Moran, the producer of Under Suspicion. *The series, which reinvestigates cold cases, has been on a roll, solving cases that had long been written off as unsolvable. The Chatter is able to report that Casey has met with Moran three times in person since her release from prison, once at her home and twice in Moran's offices at Rockefeller Center. For Casey to land under such a respected brand would have been a coup indeed.*

But, wait, not so fast! Moran might be making nice to Casey's face, but she appears to have other tricks up her sleeve.

Laurie could feel her father's eyes reading over her shoulder. "The mixed metaphors alone should be criminal," she muttered.

"Sshh," Leo urged. "Keep reading."

Casey may have thought that the television producer plans to present her side of the story, but she might want to think again. Turns out, her new pal Moran has been meeting with the likes of renowned anti-Casey types like Gabrielle Lawson and Jason Gardner. Savvy chatterers will recall that these insiders provided damning statements during Casey's trial.

Lawson was the luxurious lady who was ready to take Casey's place next to Hunter at the altar. Jaded Jason was Casey's ex-boyfriend who spilled the beans about her anger management problem.

With friends like these, who needs enemies? Twelve jurors unanimously agreed that Casey killed Hunter in a rage after he called off their engagement. Without a defense attorney at Casey's side, a successful journalist like Laurie Moran might convince the rest of the country that Casey is a cold-blooded murderer who got off easy.

Casey, if you're reading, you might think a television show can help you turn over a new leaf, but you better think twice. Do you really think Gabrielle and Jason will change their stories? You could be playing with fire.

The Chatter *suggests you stay home, and stay silent.*

Laurie clicked the button at the bottom of the tablet to blacken the screen, then handed the device back to her son.

"Mom, how does that website know so much about your show? Is all of that information true?"

Every word of it, Laurie thought. She already knew—or at least, strongly suspected—that Gabrielle had a habit of feeding information to Mindy Sampson, but this column contained more information than Gabrielle could provide on her own. Gabrielle knew that Laurie was planning to cover Casey's case for their next special. And she could probably make an educated guess that any responsible television producer would speak to the ex-boyfriend who wrote a tell-all hatchet job. But to know how many times Laurie had met with Casey, and where? Anyone who could guess that accurately should be playing the ponies.

She was replaying the entire column in her mind, thinking she had no idea who could have given Mindy Sampson the inside track on her production. And then suddenly, she thought of a moment that had passed a few hours earlier. *You may be a good lawyer in the courtroom, but you've now chosen a job that you seem to have little interest in learning about.*

Ryan Nichols. Was he trying to teach her a lesson? She immediately tried to shake the possibility, telling herself she was being paranoid. But Grace, Jerry, and Ryan were the only people who could have leaked all this information. She trusted Grace and Jerry with her life, but knew nothing about her new host, other than that he was so hungry for time in front of a camera that he'd been willing to leave behind a promising legal career to pursue television full-time. Was he leaking inside information to create gossip that was certain to generate plenty of interest in the show? Was this his first step in trying to undercut me and push me out of the picture? His uncle's best pal, Brett, rewarded those whose ideas resulted in better ratings.

As they say, just because you're paranoid doesn't mean someone's not out to get you.

• • •

She was still wondering whether she should trust Ryan when her cell phone rang on the counter. It was Alex. For the first time since she'd known him, she hesitated before accepting the call.

Finally, after three and a half rings, she answered with a *hey there*.

"Hey there, yourself."

"How did your talk at NYU go?" She hadn't spoken to him since she'd shown up at his office asking questions about his prior dealings with the Raleigh family.

"Fine. My friend was beaming ear to ear over his induction as an endowed chair. Sounds like nothing but a title to me, but it was good to see him honored. You would have been more impressed with the food, I think. They had those Baked by Melissa tiny cupcakes you love so much."

"They're both delicious and adorable. What's not to love?" She could hear him smiling over the phone. Before she knew it, twenty minutes passed as they fell into a comfortable rhythm talking about a local political story in today's *Post*, a new client who'd retained Alex the previous day, and nothing in particular.

Just when she was beginning to feel silly for being so paranoid— about Ryan, about Alex—he suddenly asked about Casey. "So you made a final decision to cover her case."

It sounded like an observation, not a question. To her knowledge, only *The Chatter* blog had reported the news. She couldn't imagine that Alex was a regular follower of Mindy Sampson's posts. She knew Timmy had set up a Google alert of her name, but had Alex? Or had Alex made a special effort to stay up-to-date with any news about Casey? Or was all of this in her head?

There was only one way to find out. "I take it you saw the story?"

He paused. Or at least, she thought he did. "What story?"

"On a website called *The Chatter*," she said. Only after she spoke did she realize that his response hadn't been a direct answer to her question, just as when she'd asked him the other night whether there was a reason he didn't want her working on the case. "I don't know how Mindy found out about the show," Laurie explained. "And she also knew about two of my witnesses."

The other end of the line was silent.

"Are you there, Alex?"

"Sorry, just thinking."

"I guess with a case that high-profile, it's not surprising that word got out that I was asking around," she said, wondering out loud. "And the witnesses she mentioned by name would be obvious guesses."

"Or someone inside the production is feeding her information," Alex said. His tone was serious.

"It did cross my mind that Ryan Nichols could have ulterior motives."

"Or someone wants to make sure you have a hard time flipping the public's opinion about Casey. Is your decision absolutely final, Laurie? Maybe I can help you find another case that would satisfy Brett."

She could not ignore this feeling that he was holding something back, something vitally important. "Alex, please, if you have information—"

"I don't."

"You don't, or you can't?"

He was silent again.

"Alex, what aren't you telling me?"

"You're smart, Laurie. You know you're dealing with some very powerful people."

"Alex—"

"Just promise me you'll be careful."

He hung up before she could ask why.

• • •

Six hours later, Laurie woke up in the middle of the night, her thoughts racing. She reached for the cell phone on her nightstand and opened her email. There was a new message from Jason Gardner, saying he had decided to tell his story to *Under Suspicion*. "The more truth, the better," according to him, but Laurie had a feeling that his first phone call had been to his publisher. She pictured a reprint of his book in the imminent future.

But Casey's ex-boyfriend was not the reason she had logged onto her account. She drafted an email to the head of information technology at Fisher Blake Studios. *Remember those old online messages I asked about re the Hunter Raleigh case? Posted by RIP_Hunter? Please send me what you have ASAP.*

The RIP_Hunter posts. Mindy Sampson's insider knowledge. Alex's guardedness. Somewhere in her dreams, they felt connected. Tomorrow, she thought. Tomorrow, it might make sense.

35

Casey's mother was pacing in circles around the living room. Sometimes Casey wondered if her mother arranged her furniture with walking routes in mind.

"I knew it," Paula huffed under her breath. "Casey, you kicked the hornet's nest, talking to this television lady. You haven't even been out of prison two weeks, and already you're all over the news."

Casey was sitting cross-legged in a chair across from her cousin Angela and Angela's friend Charlotte. Angela had been with Charlotte in the city when Casey called her in a panic about Mindy Sampson's latest post. Charlotte had insisted on driving Angela to Connecticut. Now that she was here, Charlotte looked as though she wanted to shrink into an invisible speck on the sofa, away from Paula's judgmental glare.

It's a good thing my mother doesn't gamble, Casey thought. She wouldn't have a roof over her head, that's how readable her expressions are. Her mother didn't trust Laurie Moran, which meant she didn't trust her friend Charlotte.

"How do you know you can trust that producer, Casey?" her mother protested. "She doesn't care about you. All she wants are ratings. It's a conflict of interest. She's probably feeding these little teasers to the tabloids to generate buzz."

"We don't know that, Mom."

Paula's pacing halted abruptly. "Shut UP, Casey!" Casey could not remember her mother ever using that phrase with her. "What is WRONG with you? It's like you're addicted to drama. You invite this kind of chaos into your life, and you don't listen to another soul. That's what got you into this mess in the first place!"

The room fell silent as Casey glared at her mother. "Go ahead and say it, Mom. You think I did it. You always thought I did it."

Her mother shook her head, but did not deny the allegation.

Angela reached for her aunt's hand. "This is all too much," she said gently. "It's late, and you're both upset. Why don't you both sleep on it and talk again tomorrow?"

"Why bother?" Paula threw up her hands futilely. "She's going to do whatever she wants."

Casey didn't stop Paula from going to her room. Once the door closed and her mother was out of earshot, she felt a weight lift from her body and allowed herself to sprawl in her chair. "I don't know how much longer I can take it. One of us is going to end up dead."

"Don't even kid about that," Charlotte said.

Casey wanted to tell Angela's friend to mind her own business, but then she stopped herself. Other than Laurie Moran, Charlotte was the only new person in her life who had been kind to her since she was released. And here I am, resenting her very presence, she thought. Was I always this mean? Or did prison make me like this?

"You don't know what it's like," she complained, reserving her bitterness for her mother. "My parents stuck by me, but they never believed that I was framed. Did you know that she even prays for me at church? She's always telling me that I've paid my debt to society, as if I ever owed one. I swear, sometimes I wish I was back in that cell."

Angela sounded sheepish when she spoke again. "Don't get mad at me for saying this, Casey, but she might have a point. About kicking the hornet's nest, so to speak. RIP_Hunter is posting ugly comments about you. And somehow the *Chatter* website got the inside track on your plans for the show—"

"It wasn't Laurie," Charlotte said, unprompted.

"Whether it was Laurie or not doesn't matter," Angela said. "My only point is that you wanted to do this show to clear your name, and now it might be backfiring. I thought Jason or Gabrielle might be alternative suspects, but without new evidence, they'll repeat all the horrible things they said about you at trial. Do you really want every negative thing about your past thrown in front of cameras again?"

"What are you saying?" Casey asked.

"That maybe you should rethink this, Casey. Your mother might be right—"

"That I'm *guilty*?" Casey could hear the anger in her own voice. She could feel Charlotte's eyes boring into her.

"No," Angela said gently. "About lying low for a while. Give yourself time to get settled into a new life."

"Absolutely not," Casey snapped. "I know you're looking out for me, but you don't understand. I'm not doing this to clear my name. This is for Hunter. I owe him."

"You can't blame yourself—"

"But I do. Don't you get it? Someone drugged me and killed him. But if I hadn't been drinking that night, we would have known earlier that something was desperately wrong. We would have left the gala and gone to the emergency room. I wouldn't have passed out. He wouldn't have been home. But instead I thought maybe I'd had a little too much wine. He'd still be alive if it weren't for me."

Angela held Casey when she broke out into sobs. After Casey recovered her ability to speak, she looked directly at Charlotte Pierce. "You tell me, Charlotte: Can I trust Laurie Moran?"

Charlotte answered immediately. "Unequivocally."

"Then it's settled. I don't want to hear another word about backing out of the show. I'm done being silent."

• • •

That night in bed, Casey listened for sounds of her mother roaming around the house, but heard nothing. She thought about going to her room to apologize for the dustup, but didn't want to start another round. They could clear the air in the morning.

She picked up her iPad and re-read Mindy Sampson's blog post. *Do you really think Gabrielle and Jason will change their stories? You could be playing with fire.*

As Casey stared at the airbrushed, Photoshopped image of Gabrielle Lawson's face, she felt her blood pressure rise. She might be willing to spend another fifteen years in prison to see that horrible woman meet a deserving fate.

Mindy Sampson's reporting wasn't always accurate, but she sure was right about Casey's feelings toward Gabrielle Lawson. Rage didn't begin to describe how she'd felt when she saw the *Chatter* column about Hunter and that horrible woman. Didn't he realize how it would look? *The women at work would all be talking about me like I'm a fool!*

What people often described as her temper was simply passion for ideas and arguments. But that day? She'd been truly angry.

As she fell asleep, she spoke the words aloud, hoping that the intended listener could somehow hear her. "I'm sorry, Hunter. I'm so very, very sorry."

36

A week later, every surface of Laurie's usually tidy office was blanketed with paper. Three whiteboards, covered with colored ink, framed her conference table.

Jerry was raking his fingers through his hair so intensely that Laurie was worried about premature baldness. When they first started on this special, it had felt like everything was falling into place. Hunter's family agreed to participate. Location scouting was a cinch: the principal sites were Cipriani and the country home that Hunter's brother now owned. The trial transcripts had given Laurie a tremendous head start on the facts. But now, they were flooded in paper—three days from production—and Laurie was regretting ceding to Brett's ridiculous demand for speed.

Most of the disorder in her office was attributable to Laurie's obsession with identifying the Internet user who called himself RIP_Hunter.

"Privacy, schmivacy," Jerry cried, every syllable marking his frustration. "There has to be some way to know who posted all of these messages."

Monica from Information Technology tried for the sixteenth time to lower expectations. She was twenty-nine years old with a slight frame and barely five feet tall. Other members of the IT Department had more years of experience under their belts, but Laurie trusted Monica as to computer matters implicitly. She was hard-working, thorough, and most importantly, able to explain technical details in a straightforward way.

"You're forgetting," Monica explained, "that fifteen years ago the Internet was treated by most people as a computerized bulletin board. To use it at all was fairly cutting edge, but for the most part, the information flowed in one direction. You'd pull up a page and read it. The idea of responding, let alone engaging in a conversation, was groundbreaking. News providers posted content online, but there was no way to respond."

"Oh, how I miss those days," Laurie sighed. As far as she could tell, only the most extreme viewpoints were expressed on the Web. Her own show's social media pages were filled with praise from viewers, but Laurie always felt the sting of the harshest comments.

Monica was tapping away at the keyboard excitedly. "The desire to engage was out there," she explained, "but the mainstream media pages weren't creating a forum. The early adopters found their own cohorts through message boards. Fortunately, I've found shadow sites where the content is archived. It took days to print out all the buried conversations about Hunter's murder and Casey's trial. If the sites were still operational, I could try to find a company willing to share IP addresses with us. But these sites are no longer active."

"Can you break that down to regular English?" Grace asked.

"What we're looking at," Monica explained, "are just words, as if tapped on a keyboard; the underlying data can't be accessed. In short, I'd have to be psychic to tell you who actually wrote this stuff."

Hunter's murder had made national news. In the public eye, Casey quickly went from grieving girlfriend to "presumed guilty." With Monica's help, they had also sifted through thousands of on-line comments written by followers of the trial, who found one another on message boards and debated the case intensely.

The first step had been to identify all comments authored under the name "RIP_Hunter." When they were able to read all of these posts together, they noticed two trends. The author tended to speak with authority, as if he or she had inside information about both Casey and Hunter. *All of Casey's friends know*, for example, or *Casey has always had a raging temper*, was a *phony*, and *and also had the easy route handed to her*. Throughout the entire case, it seemed as if someone with inside information was "trolling" Casey and feeding gossip to Mindy Sampson.

It was Jerry who noticed another, more subtle characteristic. The author had a tendency to introduce additional points with the phrase "and also." *Anyone who knows Casey will tell you that she has to have the last word*, and also *has to be the center of attention*.

On the chance that whoever authored the RIP_Hunter notes had posted other comments, Monica had found another fifty-seven comments that appeared to suggest firsthand knowledge of the case, and another twenty using the phrase "and also," with some overlap between the two groups.

"Bravo for our organizational skills," Laurie said, "but what in the world are we supposed to do with all of this now?" She collapsed onto her office sofa, her head beginning to hurt from reading so many printouts.

She grabbed a notepad and made a list of all of her unanswered questions. Who is RIP_Hunter? Who tipped off Mindy Sampson about her show? Why did Alex warn her to be careful, and did it have something to do with the fact that Alex had met General James Raleigh as a law student? Did Hunter audit the foundation's books, and was that related to Mark Templeton's departure from the foundation four years later?

Laurie thought about the principle of Occam's Razor: the simplest explanation is usually correct. Was there any one thing that could tie together all of these loose threads?

She barely noticed the sound of her phone ringing and Grace

picking it up, until Grace told her that General Raleigh's assistant, Mary Jane, was on hold. "She wants to know how much time she should allot for the General's interview as well as hers. I offered to juggle the schedule if they had somewhere else to be, but she said his time is tight every day of the year. She said Arden's pushing him for pages, whatever that means."

"He's working on his memoirs," Laurie said. Something about Grace's question was bothering her, but she couldn't quite put her finger on it. Most likely, it was that she had no idea how long Ryan would take to conduct his interviews. Was she ever going to get used to working with Ryan instead of Alex? "See if he can give us an hour. I assume she'll be more flexible."

Of the suspects Casey had identified, Mary Jane seemed the least likely. Hunter may have worried about the assistant's motives, but fifteen years later, she appeared to still be working as a dutiful servant. And General Raleigh did not seem like a man who would be taken advantage of easily.

While Grace returned to the phone, Laurie went back to her list of questions, but Mary Jane's phone call was still nagging at her. *Arden.* Where had she heard that name recently? Who else had been talking about a book publisher? And then she remembered her conversation with Casey's ex-boyfriend Jason. *I'll admit that calling her Crazy Casey in the book title was a little unfair. Frankly, Arden Publishing insisted.* Could it possibly be a coincidence that General Raleigh's and Jason's books shared a publisher?

"Jerry, when you talked to Mark Templeton, did you ask him about the gap between his employment at the Raleigh Foundation and his new job at Holly's Kids?"

"No. As I said, I wanted it to seem like we only wanted to talk to him about seeing Casey and Hunter at the gala. I thought you should be the one to decide whether to push him on the rumors about the foundation's assets."

Laurie walked to her computer, typed *Holly's Kids* into the search engine, and pulled up the website for the nonprofit that currently employed Mark Templeton as its director. She clicked on the list of the board of directors. Her eye immediately moved to one name in particular: Holly Bloom, as in Holly's Kids, listed as both board member and founder. She clicked through to Holly's bio and then tilted the computer screen toward Jerry. "The Holly of Holly's Kids is the president of Arden Publishing, also known as the publisher of Jason Gardner's book and General Raleigh's forthcoming memoir."

Jerry was staring at the screen. "Whoa. I think I just felt the room tilt."

Laurie still didn't know who killed Hunter Raleigh, or even whether Casey Carter was innocent. But she was putting certain pieces of the puzzle together. If she was right, then Casey never had a fair shot at trial.

She picked up the phone and called her father. "Dad, I have a favor to ask. Do you know anyone with the Connecticut State Police?"

"Of course. I may be off the job, but my old Rolodex still comes in handy."

"Can you see if anyone who worked on the Hunter Raleigh murder case would be willing to talk to me off the record?" She remembered his wistfulness last week when he seemed to miss being in the middle of an investigation. "Maybe you can come with me."

37

The next morning, Leo waited at the curb outside her building behind the wheel of a rental car, blinkers flashing.

"Thanks for this, Dad," Laurie said as she hopped in the passenger seat.

"And for this," he added, handing her one of two Starbucks cups from the car's console.

"Best dad *and* driver ever."

Yesterday, Leo had called his friend, the former commissioner of the Connecticut State Police, to ask for a meeting with Detective Joseph McIntosh, the lead investigator on the Hunter Raleigh case.

"So who's taking my job for the day?" he asked.

"Kara."

"That's great. Timmy likes her."

As hard as Timmy tried to convince Laurie that he was no longer in need of a babysitter to walk him to and from school when his grandfather was unavailable, all protests ceased when it came to Kara, who loved sports, made chocolate chip pancakes from scratch, and shared Timmy's growing love for jazz.

"When it comes to your role in Timmy's life, you've got tenure, Dad. You know where we're headed?"

"Already got it in the GPS. Detective McIntosh, here we come."

• • •

Detective Joseph McIntosh was still with the Connecticut State Police, but his current title was lieutenant. He did not look happy to meet Laurie, but was considerably warmer to her father. "Commissioner Miller had a world of good to say about you, Deputy Commissioner Farley."

Once they began talking about the evidence, it was clear that McIntosh had no doubts as to Casey's guilt. "You've got to understand that the defense lawyer even suggested I was responsible for Rohypnol being found in Casey's purse. Until we found those pills, we were on her side. She seemed genuinely distraught when we arrived. We only tested her hands for gunshot residue as part of the protocol. In our eyes, she was one of the victims. She'd lost her fiancé to horrible violence. From all appearances, her sickness that night probably saved her life. And when her cousin arrived, she suggested we test Casey Carter's blood to see if she had been drugged. Ms. Carter consented and we asked the medic on the scene to take a blood sample. Later it was confirmed that she had Rohypnol in her system. At that point, we still believed it was possible the killer had drugged her."

"How would you describe Hunter's father, James, when you broke the news of his son's death?" Laurie asked. "Did he consider Casey a suspect?"

McIntosh gave her a half smile. "I see where you're going with this. Powerful family, eager for answers. You're wondering who was pulling the strings."

Laurie was still trying to make sense of everything she knew, but yes, that is what she was wondering. It was no secret that James had been pressuring Hunter not to go through with his marriage to a woman he viewed as trouble. When Hunter was killed shortly after

Mindy Sampson photographed him with Gabrielle Lawson, he would have naturally suspected Casey—whose jealousy was well known in the family—as the murderer.

So was it possible General Raleigh tried to tip the scales of justice against her? Whoever was behind the RIP_Hunter posts clearly admired Hunter. Had the General written them? At the time of the murder he would have been in his mid-sixties, pretty old to be an early user of the Internet, but could Mary Jane have helped him? Had he gone further and bribed the police to frame Casey? If so, and Mark Templeton knew about it, it would explain why the General publicly praised the resigning CFO even as the Raleigh Foundation floundered. It couldn't be a coincidence that the same woman who was publishing the General's memoir had also hired Templeton at her nonprofit, in addition to publishing Jason Gardner's very negative book about Casey. Laurie found herself wondering again why Alex had warned her about taking this case.

She wasn't about to share all her suspicions with Lieutenant McIntosh. "Did General Raleigh immediately suspect Casey," she asked, "or did he come around to that conclusion gradually?"

"Well, his initial response was utter shock and grief. Then he asked if Casey was okay. When I said she was, he replied, and I quote, *Hear this in no uncertain terms: she's the one who killed him.* So, yes, I think it's fair to say he suspected her," he chuckled. "But I don't take orders from anyone, not even General James Raleigh. We did a thorough investigation, and, sure enough, all evidence pointed to Casey."

"Did you ever figure out where she obtained the Rohypnol?"

He shook his head. "That would've been nice, but the drug was easy enough to buy on the street, even back then. I hear your show is going to reinvestigate the case. I can't imagine what you think you're going to prove. We had means, motive, and opportunity."

Laurie listened patiently as McIntosh laid out the case. Means:

As Hunter's future wife, Casey had taken up his hobby of shooting and knew where he kept his guns. She began firing at Hunter in the living room. When she missed, Hunter ran to the bedroom, perhaps to lock himself in the master bathroom or to grab another gun in self-defense. Once he was cornered in the bedroom, Casey fired the two fatal shots.

Motive: Casey's engagement to a member of the Raleigh family raised her social station considerably. She could also be extremely jealous where Hunter was concerned. Hunter's father was pushing him to break up with Casey, and just days before his murder, Hunter was photographed with socialite Gabrielle Lawson at his side. After the fact, even some of Casey's former friends were willing to entertain the possibility that she might have "lost it" if Hunter broke off their engagement.

Opportunity: Casey faked her illness to create a partial alibi, claiming to be asleep during the murder. Then after she shot Hunter, she took Rohypnol so it would appear as if someone had drugged her.

"You should have seen her face when her own defense lawyer shifted gears during closing argument," McIntosh said. "The lawyer went from *she didn't do it* to *well, maybe she did, but if so, she was out of her mind*. Casey looked like she wanted to send her lawyer to the grave, too. *That's* how strong our case was: even the defense attorney could see the writing on the wall. If you ask me, that jury just didn't have the stomach to put an attractive young woman in prison for life. Manslaughter? How can you believe it was a spur-of-the-moment killing without explaining why she had those drugs in her purse? She had those pills for a reason."

It was Leo who interrupted the lieutenant's narration. "And that's why the defense lawyer accused you of planting them or tampering with evidence."

"She certainly raised the possibility. She said maybe the real killer put the pills there, but she also went so far as to suggest that the pills I took from Casey were not the ones that were sent to be tested. They somehow got switched. But again, Casey wasn't even a suspect at that point. We let her cousin take her back to her apartment in the city while we finished processing the scene. In a homicide case, we are thorough. Trust me, the last thing I suspected to find in or next to her purse were so-called roofies."

"Did you need permission to search her purse?" Laurie asked.

"No, it was left at the crime scene, on the couch, behind a pillow. And it was overturned and the pills were clearly visible."

"You knew right away what they were?" Laurie asked.

He nodded. "They're stamped with the pharmaceutical company's name, and we were starting to see more and more of them in use by bad guys, unfortunately."

Laurie was glad he mentioned the thoroughness of his searches. "Did you happen to see a framed photograph of Hunter with the President when you searched the house? It was in a crystal frame."

He shook his head. "I certainly don't remember that. Not sure I would, though, and I've got a darn good memory. Why?"

She told him about the photograph that had been on Hunter's nightstand prior to the murder, but appeared nowhere in pictures of the crime scene.

"Maybe the housekeeper's mistaken about the timing," he said. "Hunter had an apartment and an office in the city. He could've moved it. Or maybe it broke. There could be a million explanations. Regardless, not sure I'd call a missing picture reasonable doubt."

Laurie could tell by the way Leo avoided her eye contact that he agreed.

"What do you remember about Mark Templeton?" she asked, shifting gears.

"Name sounds familiar—"

"He was the chief financial officer at the Raleigh Foundation and one of Hunter's closest friends."

"Oh, sure. Good guy. He was terribly broken up."

"Did you check whether he had an alibi for the time of the murder?"

McIntosh laughed at the suggestion. "You really are casting a wide net, aren't you? Well, I wouldn't describe it in those terms, but we got a time line from every person we talked to about that night. Hunter's father took a few VIP donors to his private club for a nightcap after the gala. His driver took him home from there, and he has a live-in assistant. So in case you also suspect General Raleigh"—his sarcasm was apparent—"his alibi's locked down. But everyone else at Hunter's table that night went home alone from the gala."

Laurie knew the table seating by heart: Hunter, Casey, Hunter's father and brother, Mary Jane Finder, Casey's cousin Angela, and Mark Templeton. Neither Mark nor Angela had a date. Angela's boyfriend at the time, Sean Murray, was out of town, and Mark's wife stayed at home with their children. After confirming each name with the lieutenant, Laurie asked what he recalled about Hunter's phone call on the way to the gala, asking a friend for a referral to a private investigator.

"We knew about it because the friend contacted us after the murder. Hunter wanted a background check on someone, but didn't have a chance to identify the person. Personally, I thought it might be Casey. Maybe he was beginning to share his father's concerns and wanted to know more about the woman he was planning to marry."

"Which is what the prosecution argued," Laurie said, "but it was complete speculation. It seems equally possible that he was looking into his concerns about his father's assistant, Mary Jane. He was determined to have her fired. Mary Jane was at the gala that night, but did she accompany the General when he brought donors to his club afterward?"

The lieutenant squinted, trying to access the information from memory. "No, she didn't. But she told us the next day that she heard him come home after she turned in, and then she was the one who answered the telephone when we called to tell him there had been a shooting."

"So you have no idea exactly what time she returned from the gala. She could have gone up to Connecticut and back before you phoned the house. In fact, for all you know, she came home after the General and was lying about hearing him return."

"I suppose that's possible." Then he added with a wry smile, "But not likely."

Laurie began to slip her notes into her bag. "Thank you again for your time, Lieutenant. I admit I didn't expect you to be so forthcoming."

He held up both hands. "The way I see it, if I do my job right, you can go over it with a magnifying glass, and I've got nothing to worry about. You don't seriously think Hunter's best friend or his father's assistant killed him?" He still seemed amused.

"Did you know that in addition to inquiring about a private investigator, Hunter was also looking into financial irregularities at the foundation?"

McIntosh's smile fell from his face. "Now, *that* I would remember. No one ever mentioned such a thing."

"It's just a possibility at this point." She saw no reason to tell him that Casey was the only source on this issue. "But Mark Templeton did resign suddenly four years later, with the foundation's assets significantly reduced, and did not get a new job for almost a year."

The lieutenant was squinting, as if a memory was tugging at him.

"Does that ring a bell?" she asked.

"Maybe. Remember I said we do a thorough search of the home? There was a note on Hunter's desk that had a couple of phone numbers jotted down. According to the phone records, he never actually called the numbers. But here's the thing: they were both major accounting firms that specialized in forensic accounting, and in the margin next to the numbers, Hunter had written: *Ask Mark*."

"I assume that's Mark Templeton. So did you ask him?"

"Sure did. He said he had no idea what the note meant. Maybe the Raleigh family needed a new firm and he was planning to get Mark's opinion. But like I said, take your magnifying glass and go for it, Nancy Drew. I know we convicted the right person."

38

Laurie's father had just buckled his seatbelt when he asked what she was thinking. "Do you really believe Hunter may have been killed because of problems at the foundation?"

"I'm not sure, but I definitely get the feeling that Hunter's father put his thumb on the scales of justice at some point." She explained the role of the General's editor, Holly Bloom, in assisting both Mark Templeton and Jason Gardner.

"But you can't believe the General was actually involved."

"Of course not." The possibility was unimaginable. James Raleigh was a national hero and by all accounts adored his older son. Even if she doubted him, his whereabouts were accounted for up until the moment he was notified of Hunter's death.

"Why would he cover up for his own son's murderer?"

"If he thought his other son was responsible. According to Casey, Andrew Raleigh could be very resentful of his older brother, especially when he was intoxicated. Even when I met with Andrew, he made it very clear that Hunter was the favored son. Or General Raleigh may have genuinely believed that Casey was guilty. But what if he was wrong?"

"Or maybe he was right, Laurie. Even if he did get Jason Gardner that book deal, even if he had something to do with the RIP_Hunter posts, even if he was trying to stack the deck against Casey—she could still be guilty."

Maybe, Laurie thought.

They were only two days from filming, and she was finding more questions than answers. She now knew that police had found the numbers of forensic accountants on Hunter's desk, along with a note to *Ask Mark*. That likely corroborated Casey's claim that Hunter was looking into irregularities at the foundation. She was going to have to take another run at Templeton.

In the meantime, she had one more stop to make before they could return to the city. The rental car's GPS instructed her father that their destination was on the left.

"You coming in?" she asked.

"No thanks. Never met a defense lawyer I liked until Alex. I think I'll quit while I'm ahead."

The lawyer Laurie was going to see was Casey's trial lawyer, Janice Marwood.

39

Laurie rang the bell of Janice Marwood's office. When no one answered, she opened the door and stepped in. This is an *office*, she thought. At a glance she could see that the space had probably served as a family home in the early twentieth century. On her left, what used to be the living room was now a reception area with several chairs and a table with magazines.

What was missing was any sign of life—not a person in sight.

"Hello?" Laurie called out, as she stepped into the reception area. She heard footsteps coming down the hall.

A woman emerged from the back of the house, a jar of peanut butter in one hand, a spoon in the other. "I'm here—Oh."

Oh, Laurie thought. She introduced herself even though she strongly suspected from the woman's reaction that she already knew who she was. "I've called a few times on behalf of Casey Carter."

Marwood finished swallowing the lump of peanut butter in her mouth and freed her hands for a quick shake. "Sorry, I'm juggling a ton of cases right now. I swear I was going to call you today, come hell or high water."

Laurie didn't believe it for a second. "Did you get the waiver we faxed over? I'm eager to talk to you. We start production in two days." *Faxed over* in this context meant faxed, emailed, and sent certified mail. *Called a few times* translated to daily phone messages.

And yet Laurie had not heard one word from Casey's trial lawyer. "The courthouse doesn't allow cameras inside, but we have permits to film out front. Or we'd be happy to do it here if that's more convenient. Most of all, I'd love to pick your thoughts. It's been fifteen years, and Casey has never wavered once about her innocence."

Janice worked her jaw as if she were still eating. "Yeah, about that. It's Casey's right to forgo attorney-client privilege, but I've looked into the issue of whether I'm obliged to participate in a television show against my own desires. The answer is no."

Laurie had imagined multiple scenes that might have played out when she arrived at Janice's office, but this hadn't been one of them. "You owe a duty of loyalty to your client. She spent a good part of her life in prison and is now desperate to clear her name. You're supposed to be her advocate. I'm sorry, but I don't understand the conflict here."

"My job is—was—to fight for her at trial. And on appeal. But the litigation is over. I'm not some reality TV star. It's not my job to appear on camera."

"Casey signed the papers."

"That's fine, but she can't order me to talk to you any more than she can tell me where to go to dinner tonight. I did pull her case files from storage. She has every right to those materials. And she's welcome to call me for any type of consult she'd like. But as far as your show goes, I won't be participating."

Once again, Laurie found herself wishing that she had Alex by her side. She had assumed that Casey's lawyer would at least feign an interest in taking up the gauntlet on her former client's behalf, but now that Marwood was resisting, Laurie had no authority to contradict her. Before she even realized what was happening, the attorney was walking her across the foyer into a room with a conference table, where two banker boxes marked "C Carter" were waiting on the table.

"What would have happened to these if I hadn't driven up from the city today?" Laurie asked.

"Like I said, I was about to call you. FedEx would have picked them up in the morning."

Once again, Laurie didn't believe a word she was saying. "During the trial, someone was trolling Casey with negative comments online. Did you ever look into that?"

"Everything I have is in the files."

"One of the jurors was even told by his daughter about a comment claiming that Casey confessed. He reported it to the judge. Why didn't you ask for a mistrial?"

She pushed one of the boxes in Laurie's direction. "With all due respect, ma'am, I don't owe you any explanations about trial strategy. Now do you need help taking these boxes with you? Because that's all I have to offer."

Alex had graded Janice Marwood as a C-minus lawyer, but Laurie wanted to give her a giant F.

When she walked outside, file boxes in tow, she could see her father in the rental car, fingertips tapping against the steering wheel. She suspected he was listening to the sixties channel, his favorite station on satellite radio.

He popped the trunk when he spotted her and hopped out to help. "Looks like that went well," he said, grabbing one of the boxes.

"Not at all," she said. She had no proof, but found herself wondering whether Hunter's father could have gotten to Casey's own lawyer.

40

It was five-thirty by the time Leo and Laurie got back to the city. Leo tried to get Laurie to go straight home, but she wanted to type up her notes from the trip to Connecticut and always worked better at the office.

She was used to finding Jerry late at his desk, but was surprised to see Grace still at work, too. She was even more surprised to see Ryan wave as he passed her in the hallway, a coffee from Bouchon Bakery in his hand.

"Why is Ryan here?" she asked Grace.

"He's been waiting around for his office to be ready. It was supposed to be done hours ago, but you know how slow the maintenance staff can be. They didn't even start painting until this morning. Anyway, he used the time to get to know Jerry and me a little better. I think he's eager to no longer be the new kid at school."

Laurie noticed a Bouchon pastry bag on Grace's desk that matched Ryan's cup. She had a strong feeling why Grace had stayed late.

Laurie stopped by Jerry's office and knocked on the open door.

"Please tell me Ryan didn't start dating my assistant while I was out of town for the day."

Jerry laughed. "You know Grace. She's a born flirt, but that's all it is. Besides, Ryan Nichols is much too high-maintenance for her.

The only reason his office isn't ready is because he's been telling the building staff where to place every item and hang each picture of himself, down to the centimeter." Laurie took a small amount of satisfaction in the eye roll that followed.

She couldn't believe that Brett had given Ryan an office. The idea of providing one for Alex had never even been raised.

"I was actually about to call you," Jerry said, sounding more urgent. "I think I found something important."

Once they were seated in her office, he explained his excitement. "I was thinking about the 'Whispers' piece we found—the one that was probably about Hunter."

Shortly before Mindy Sampson published the photograph of Hunter with Gabrielle Lawson, her paper's "Whispers" column had published a "blind item" reporting that one of the city's most sought after men was about to become un-engaged. Laurie said she remembered it.

"It made me think we might have missed something when we were researching Mark Templeton. The write-ups about his departure from the Raleigh Foundation only hinted at improprieties, at worst." The reports simply noted that he'd left, that assets were down, and that he hadn't announced a new position. Perhaps there was wrongdoing at the foundation, and perhaps Templeton was involved, but there wasn't enough evidence for the reporters to raise the possibility directly.

Laurie could see where Jerry's thought was going. "That's when gossip columns resort to blind items," she said. "The paper can't get sued if they don't name names." When she had researched Templeton, she had conducted a media search for any mentions of either his name or the Raleigh Foundation. But a blind item that intentionally omitted the specifics would never turn up in such a targeted search. "You found something?" she asked.

"I think so." He handed her a printout from an archived "Whispers" column, dated several months after Templeton resigned as CFO of the foundation: *What unnamed former fiduciary of what unnamed political-royalty non-profit was seen walking into the federal courthouse with a criminal defense lawyer two days ago? Are charges forthcoming? Stay tuned.*

"This is good work, Jerry. I suppose it's possible they were talking about someone else, but a 'political-royalty non-profit'? This sounds like it has to be Templeton. Can we feel out the reporter who published it? They might confirm off the record."

"Unfortunately, I tried that already. 'Whispers' never gave bylines to its contributors. I took a stab in the dark and contacted the guy who was the paper's main financial reporter at the time, but he said it didn't ring a bell. He said it's possible their crime beat reporter came up with it, but he passed away several years ago."

If they couldn't nail down the specifics of the story through the reporter, they'd have to find another way. Templeton had made it clear he had no plans to talk about his work for the Raleigh Foundation. That left only one other option.

She asked Grace which office the studio had given Ryan, then found him there, adjusting the throw cushions on his new sofa. "Do you still have contacts at the U.S. Attorney's Office?"

Ryan had only worked at the federal prosecutor's office for three years after his Supreme Court clerkship, but he'd racked up an impressive trial record prosecuting white-collar criminals. "Sure," he said. "Not everyone can be rich and famous."

The wink that followed made her want to point out that, so far, he was neither. His uncle's friend may have given him a job and an office, but Laurie knew what he was being paid. Brett's frugality bent for no one.

Laurie handed him a copy of the blind item that Jerry had found. "It's possible that whatever happened between Mark Templeton and the Raleigh Foundation was serious enough that he hired a criminal defense lawyer. What would it mean if he went to the courthouse with his lawyer, but there's no record of any actual charges?"

Ryan took a quick glance at the printout and then exchanged it for a baseball from the top of his desk. He tossed it from hand to hand. "It's possible he was testifying, maybe in front of a grand jury. More likely, he could have been meeting with prosecutors, possibly as an informant."

"Any chance you can look into that?"

"Sure. But even if something fishy was going on at the foundation, it might have nothing to do with Hunter's murder."

"If Templeton knew Hunter was onto him, that would be a powerful motive to silence him."

"I just don't see it." He continued passing the ball from side to side. "White-collar types don't like to get their hands dirty."

She resisted the temptation to list all of the stories she'd worked on that challenged his assumption. "Can you ask around or not?"

"Like I said, no problem."

She had thanked him and was almost out of his office when she heard his voice behind her. "Laurie, think fast."

He looked surprised when she effortlessly caught the ball headed her way. "Thanks," she said, slipping it into her jacket pocket. She smiled as she returned to her office. Maybe she'd even give it back to him at some point.

She was about to leave work when she got a text from Charlotte. *Short notice but time for a drink?*

Laurie barely remembered the days when she could do whatever she wanted after work. *My kid may stop recognizing me if I don't go home. Want to swing by my place?*

She felt silly the second she hit send. She couldn't imagine that Charlotte would want to spend a Friday night in her apartment with her son and father.

Only if your cute dad will be there, too. I'll bring the wine.

Laurie smiled. Now that was a good friend.

41

"Should I open another?" Leo was holding up a bottle of Laurie's favorite Cabernet.

Charlotte held up her empty glass. "Well, let's see. The three of us just finished an entire bottle of wine."

"So that's a no?" Leo asked.

"Of course not. Pop the cork, Lieutenant Farley."

"Actually," Laurie corrected, "Dad retired as first deputy police commissioner."

"My apologies for the demotion, Leo." As Timmy cleared the last dinner plate, Charlotte looked impressed. "That's some young man you've got there."

Laurie could feel herself beaming.

"If you guys are having more wine, does that mean I can have ice cream?" Timmy asked from the kitchen.

"I suppose that's fair," Laurie responded.

Timmy was back with one scoop of chocolate and one scoop of vanilla by the time Leo was finished pouring the wine.

"So tell us more about the fashion show you're planning, Charlotte," Laurie said.

"Are you sure? I can't imagine the men want to hear about that."

"Of course we do," Leo said, even though Laurie knew her father was definitely not interested in the logistics of a women's fashion show.

"It's not the typical runway show. Because we do sportswear for real women, we're using famous athletes and actresses instead of typical models. We'll even feature some of Ladyform's employees and their friends. Just normal people."

Timmy's teeth were stained with chocolate when he smiled. "You should use my mom. She's a normal person, depending on your definition of normal."

"Nice," Laurie said.

"JK." It was Timmy's new version of *just kidding*. "Where's it gonna be, Miss Pierce?"

Charlotte smiled again at Timmy's good manners. "In Brooklyn. Does anybody know where DUMBO is?"

Leo jumped in. "That's Down Under the Manhattan Bridge Overpass." Then he explained the nickname to Timmy.

The area was between the Brooklyn and Manhattan bridges. It used to be a wasteland known mainly for its ferry landing. Then a savvy developer bought it and turned it into a hotspot for galleries and tech start-ups, and gave it the trendy name. Now DUMBO was a haven for hipsters.

"We found the perfect spot," Charlotte said excitedly. "It's one of the last real, open warehouses. It's been cleared out for a condo conversion, but the developer hasn't found financing yet. So for now, it's three stories of concrete floors and exposed bricks and beams. Very industrial. We're going to have a different theme on each floor, and people will walk through the whole building, instead of watching models on a catwalk. I feel like we're putting on a Broadway production."

When Timmy finished his ice cream, Laurie announced, "All right kiddo, it's time to hit the hay. It might be Friday night, but you've got soccer practice in the morning."

"And I'm going to be there cheering from the sidelines," Leo said, "so I'm heading home. It was nice to see you again, Charlotte."

Charlotte insisted on helping Laurie wash the wineglasses before leaving. "Thanks for a very lovely night, Laurie. You may have ruined my life, though. I think I need to have a kid."

"Really?"

"No," she said with a laugh. "Or 'JK' as he would say. But seriously, he's a keeper. I guess I should go. I'm dreading tomorrow. I have to call a guy from Accounting at home on a Saturday and tell him he'll be attending sensitivity training first thing Monday morning. I'm sure that'll go over well."

"What did he do?"

"Looked at some extremely inappropriate websites on his company computer. Our Information Technology Department runs a monthly list of Internet usage."

"Wow. Is that typical?"

"These days, it's practically required. Your studio probably does, too. I'm sure the policy is buried in the small print of an employee handbook somewhere. Anyway, I've got to nip that sort of thing in the bud, and I insist on doing it myself. We're still a family-run business. I'm responsible for maintaining the culture of the office. Hey, before I leave, I wanted to ask how things are going with Alex." Laurie had mentioned to Charlotte that things had been awkward between her and Alex lately, but hadn't given details. "Any updates there?"

She shook her head. "That's a long conversation that we shouldn't start now. I'm sure everything will be fine."

Once she closed the apartment door behind Charlotte, Laurie checked the screen of her phone. No new calls.

She was not at all sure that everything with Alex would be fine.

42

Two days later, Laurie stood in the Cipriani ballroom. She remembered coming here with Greg when they were choosing a venue for their wedding. Despite the astronomical prices, her parents had insisted that they look at it. "Are they crazy, Greg?" she had asked, as she marveled at the size and beauty of the space. "We could invite every person we know and still fill only half the room. This place is fit for royalty, with a price tag to match."

Despite Leo's protests of *you're my only daughter* and *this is the only wedding I'll ever pay for*, they had insisted on using a more reasonably priced place. And everything had been perfect.

She remembered Greg smiling at her as Leo walked her down the aisle.

A voice pulled her back into the present. "It's very festive, isn't it?"

"Beautiful," Laurie echoed. In fact, the only thing in the room that was *not* festive was the person standing next to her, General Raleigh's assistant, Mary Jane. The woman looked as though her face might crack if she tried to smile.

"At the General's instruction, I had the tables decorated early so you could film prior to our event tonight. As you requested, we even used decor similar to the gala that took place the night before Hunter was killed." Mary Jane's deepening frown conveyed her disapproval.

Laurie did not remind her that her studio had agreed to make a generous donation to the foundation, which more than covered the expense. "The family was seated at the head table," Mary Jane said, gesturing toward the round table closest to the dais.

"And by the family, you mean . . . ?" Laurie already knew who was seated there, but she wanted to hear what Mary Jane had to say.

She seemed put out by the question, but began listing the family members: "Andrew and Hunter, Casey and her cousin, the General and I."

Laurie noticed the way Mary Jane listed herself with the General, as if they were a pair. "Only six?" Laurie asked. "These look like eight-tops."

"Of course, the foundation's chief financial officer was the other person. His wife did not attend because at the last minute their babysitter canceled."

"Right," Laurie said, as if her memory was being triggered. "What was his name again?"

Mary Jane's expression was flat, and she said nothing in response. "You'll probably want to get started soon. You absolutely must have these cameras out of here in three hours. Guests will begin arriving shortly thereafter."

"On that note, Mary Jane, you scheduled General Raleigh's interview with us tomorrow in Connecticut." Their plan was to question both James and Andrew Raleigh at the country house where Hunter had been shot. "But, as I hope my assistant made clear, we'd like to tape your segment today."

"Let's see how the day goes. Right now, the fundraiser is my priority."

"But you've already agreed to participate. We need to keep to a schedule."

"And you will. Now, your three hours are fading fast. If worse comes to worst, you'll have me at your disposal tomorrow. I'll be accompanying the General to New Canaan."

Of course you will, Laurie thought. The man had served his country on every part of the globe, but if you believed Mary Jane, he could do nothing without her at his side.

Other people might ooh and aah over the setting's soaring ceilings, marble columns, and perfectly placed centerpieces, but Laurie was energized by this room for reasons that had nothing to do with the party that would start here in a few hours. Laurie was excited because she loved being on set. She loved the feeling that came with knowing that she was about to tell a story—not just with words, but with images, dramatic pauses, and sound effects. No matter what happened, she knew she would make a high-quality program. And with a little bit of luck, they might also obtain some justice.

She found Ryan pacing in the hallway, next to the pay phones. "Are you ready for your *Under Suspicion* debut?"

He held up a finger until he finished mouthing words to himself from a note card. "I'm good."

He did not look good. He looked nervous and was still wearing the towel that the makeup technician had tucked into his front collar. Laurie had been afraid this was going to happen. Alex had been the rare attorney who was comfortable doing his job in front of a television camera. In contrast, some of the most gifted courtroom lawyers turned to stone once cameras were rolling, while the "talking head" types might be good on camera, but only with a teleprompter or canned sound bites. She had no idea whether Ryan could combine the two talents.

"Are you starting a new fashion trend?" she asked, pointing to her own neck.

He looked down, seemingly confused. "Right," he said, pulling off the towel.

"Have you found out anything more about Mark Templeton hiring a defense lawyer?"

"I'm working on it." He was still paying more attention to his notes than to her.

"When you called the U.S. Attorney's Office, what did they say?"

"Like I said, Laurie, I'm working on it. Give me a little more time."

For all she knew, *I'm working on it* was code for *I forgot all about it*. But now was not the time to lecture him about workplace communication. They were about to start shooting and needed to focus.

Their first witness, Jason Gardner, had arrived.

43

As Ryan questioned Jason Gardner, Laurie's gaze bounced between the live conversation and the screen feed beside the cameraman, hoping that the televised version would somehow be better than reality. When she caught the cameraman's worried expression, she knew there'd be no such luck.

Jerry leaned down to whisper in her ear. "It's like the two of them are having a contest to see who can talk faster. I can't tell who's more nervous. And what's up with those note cards? Even if we zoom in to crop Ryan's hands in post-production, his eyes will be downcast the whole time."

"Cut," Laurie called out. "Hey, I'm sorry, guys. This is going great, but we've got a lighting issue. Too much glare off the chandeliers. It'll just be a few minutes to adjust, okay?" She signaled for Ryan to follow her out to the hallway. Once they were alone, she held out a palm. "Give them to me. The note cards, all of them."

"Laurie—"

"I'm serious. You don't need them. We've gone over everything backwards and forwards." She was no fan of Ryan, but his résumé was undeniable. He was never going to be Alex, but he could certainly be better than what she'd just seen in front of the camera. "This isn't a Supreme Court brief. There's no judge here. The judge is the audience. They need to trust you, and that won't happen if you make them uncomfortable."

"But I've got all my questions here—"

"No," she said, snatching the cards from his hand. "You have them in that Harvard-trained mind of yours. Tell me five things we want to know about Jason Gardner."

He looked at her, clearly frustrated. "Pretend I'm Professor Bigshot and just called on you in a packed lecture hall. Quick: five things."

He rattled off five points as quickly as if he were reciting the alphabet. She was impressed.

"There, you're ready."

Five minutes into the next session, Ryan was walking Jason through his time line the night of the gala. His body language was comfortable and his confidence seemed to grow by the second. Laurie could feel her fists begin to unclench.

According to Jason, he spoke to Casey only briefly after he first arrived at the gala at about eight-thirty. At that point, she seemed as if she might have enjoyed a glass of wine or two, but did not appear impaired and did not complain of any kind of illness. Jason noticed Casey leave with Hunter, but stayed with his co-workers until the end of the party, then went home alone. By the time Ryan wrapped up the time line, he had already met one of his five goals for Jason's session: he had established that Jason had no alibi for the time of Hunter's murder.

"Now, you said your employer had bought a table at the gala, correct?"

"That's right. Taking a table is one way for a firm to support a charitable cause."

"And your firm had only one table?"

"Yes, as far as I recall."

"That's eight seats. But your firm had more than a hundred financial analysts, not to mention support staff and other personnel. So how does the firm determine who attends any given event? Do they force you to go?"

"Oh no. It was a volunteer type situation."

"So you knew in advance that you were attending a gala to benefit the Raleigh Foundation?" Ryan asked.

"Of course."

"Then you certainly would have anticipated bumping into your ex-girlfriend and her fiancé, Hunter Raleigh."

Jason finally seemed to realize where the questions were heading, but it was too late to avoid the obvious implication. "Yes, I suppose that's right."

"Here's what confuses me, Jason. Your book, *My Days with Crazy Casey*, describes a woman and a relationship that—well, I think the title says it all. If you believed Casey was volatile to the point of insanity, why would you purposefully show up at a gala that her fiancé's family was hosting?"

"Well, I thought it would be a nice gesture."

"So you were still on good terms with her?"

He shrugged.

"Even though, as you wrote in your book, you bolted yourself in your apartment bathroom one time because you were afraid that she was going to attack you physically?"

"I'm not sure *afraid* is the right word."

"Should we get a copy of your book? I believe your exact words were that you feared for your life and wished you'd hidden the kitchen knives."

"That might have been an exaggeration. Obviously, the publisher wants to sell books."

Ryan was finding a rhythm. He had just nailed down a second

point: Jason's book was not the same thing as testimony under oath.

"Speaking of your book, it was published by Arden Publishing. I believe your editor was a woman named Holly Bloom. Can I ask how you came to be published by Arden?"

"What do you mean? I had an agent and he helped me."

"Right. But did the agent send the book around to all the New York houses, or did he go straight to Ms. Bloom?"

"I'm not really sure. You'd have to ask him. His name's Nathan Kramer."

Laurie recognized the name as the same agent who had negotiated the deal for James Raleigh's upcoming memoir, also to be published by Holly Bloom with Arden. Ryan confronted Jason with those coincidences. "Jason, isn't it true that General Raleigh helped you obtain the publishing deal for the extremely negative book you wrote about Casey?"

Jason's eyes darted around the ballroom, searching for guidance. Ryan leaned forward, and Laurie braced herself for whatever sarcastic, alienating comment was going to come out of his mouth.

Instead, Ryan placed a comforting hand on Jason's shoulder. "Hey, it makes perfect sense. The General's son had been murdered. You were Casey's ex. Once he realized you had a story to tell, why wouldn't he help you? It was a win-win."

"That's right," Jason said nervously. "We both wanted the truth out there."

A third point was on the board: Jason's book had General Raleigh's fingerprints all over it.

"But then some things got exaggerated along the way," Ryan added.

"Right."

"Jason, I want to thank you for being so forthcoming today. I just want to ask one more question that could really help us make sense of something Casey and her family have told us. We won't have a he-said, they-said scenario. I think we all know that love can be complicated. Relationships are on and off. One day, we're head over heels, the next we're full of resentment. Am I right?"

Ryan actually had his arm around Jason now, like old buddies telling war stories from the dating world.

"You're telling me," Jason said. By now, he was agreeing with everything Ryan said.

"Okay, so I just want you to come clean about one last thing. You still loved Casey, didn't you? In fact, that's why you went to the gala that night. She didn't think you should be in contact anymore now that she was engaged. So you went to the gala to ask her one last time to take you back."

Jason said nothing. Ryan pushed. "Casey already told us. Her cousin, Angela, did, too."

"Yes, okay. It's like you said: it was complicated. We were toxic for each other, until we weren't, and then it felt like magic. Our relationship was crazy. We were crazy." Ryan had just nailed down his fourth point, and the word choice couldn't have been better. "I thought I'd try one last time — a grand gesture to declare my love, and if she chose Hunter, I'd let her go."

"So you surprised her by going to the gala and poured your heart out to her. But she didn't take you back, did she?"

He shook his head. "She said she finally understood how love should feel. That it didn't have to be difficult. I'll never forget: she said Hunter 'felt like home.' "

"And how did that make you feel? That you made her crazy, and he felt like home?"

Jason suddenly jerked away from his new friend. "Wait. You don't think — "

"I'm just asking questions, Jason."

"Look, I told you everything. My career wasn't going as planned, and I was tight on money. I accepted the Raleigh family's offer to help me get a book deal. We were all tired of Casey playing Little Miss Innocent. But if you think I killed Hunter and framed her, then maybe *you're* the one who's crazy. I'm calling a lawyer. You can't air this," he stammered, pulling off the microphone from his lapel.

The second Jason left the ballroom Laurie raised both hands and gave Ryan a round of applause. "Not bad for the new kid."

He took a mock bow.

Four facts were now established: Jason had still loved Casey, Jason's book was an exaggeration, arranged by Hunter's father, and Jason had no alibi. But had Jason murdered Hunter Raleigh? They still didn't have an answer to Ryan's fifth question, but they were making progress.

And Ryan might not be Alex, but he had stepped up to the plate when it mattered.

"Laurie," he said while the crew took a break, "thank you for the pep talk. You were right. I just needed to be myself. I have the best instincts. Like they say, behind every great man is a woman."

She could feel her newfound goodwill toward him blow away, like air from a balloon. More like *behind every cocky man is a woman rolling her eyes*, she thought.

Grace and Jerry were walking quickly toward them, looking excited. "Gabrielle Lawson's here," Grace announced.

"And you will not *believe* what she is wearing," Jerry said. "It's a dream come true."

Laurie had instructed the show's participants that business attire would be appropriate for filming, but Gabrielle Lawson apparently played by her own wardrobe rules. It was only three-thirty in the afternoon, but she arrived in a sequined ivory gown, her hair and makeup ready for a nonexistent red carpet. Something about the gown was familiar.

As Laurie was thanking Gabrielle for coming, she realized where she'd seen the dress before. "Gabrielle, is that the same gown you wore to the gala fifteen years ago?"

"It sure is," she gushed. "I knew someday it would have historical importance. I was wearing it the last time I saw Hunter. I've preserved it in a bag for the day the Smithsonian calls. It still fits like a glove, too."

While Jerry got Gabrielle mic'ed up, Grace whispered in Laurie's ear. "I know I said Casey has crazy eyes, but this lady takes the cake. Let me know if you need me to call the men with the straightjackets and butterfly nets."

44

Laurie checked the screen to make sure that what she was seeing in front of her was being captured on film. Gabrielle Lawson was leaning forward in her chair—almost at a forty-five-degree angle—staring intensely into Ryan's eyes. Whatever damage Ryan had done with his abrasiveness at her apartment had been forgotten.

Jerry passed Laurie a note he had jotted on a pad: *Get a room!*

Ryan was handling the situation like a professional—businesslike for the cameras, but warm enough to keep Gabrielle talking. He began by walking Gabrielle through a shorter version of her trial testimony. According to her, Hunter realized that Casey was too "coarse" and "unsophisticated" for him to marry. He was interested in pursuing a relationship with Gabrielle "after an appropriate amount of time had passed."

Ryan then moved on to the same line of cross-examination Janice Marwood had pursued, establishing that no one had been able to corroborate Gabrielle's claims of a relationship with Hunter. Gabrielle had an explanation for everything. Hunter was "subtle." They weren't "crass" enough to be seen in public. They had a "special connection" and an "unspoken understanding" about their future commitment to each other.

Ryan continued to nod politely, but Laurie could tell he was about to move into unchartered territory. "Gabrielle, it's been fifteen years, and there's still no way to know for certain that Hunter was planning to leave Casey for you—which formed the basis of Casey's supposed motive to kill Hunter. What would you say to people who think that you're either lying about your relationship with Hunter, or perhaps even imagined it as a kind of wishful thinking or fantasy."

She let out a childlike giggle. "Well, that's just silly."

"But here's the thing. This wouldn't be the only time you've been accused of doing exactly that. Can we talk for a minute about Hans Lindholm?"

Not even the pound of makeup on Gabrielle's face could hide the fact that she suddenly went pale. "That was a misunderstanding."

"Our viewers probably recognize the award-winning director's name. They may also remember that he obtained a restraining order against a woman he met at a film festival. He suspected that the woman even planted a gossip report that the two of them were moving in together. What our viewers may not realize is that you were the woman named in that restraining order."

"That was a long time ago." Gabrielle looked away from Ryan for the first time since the cameras began rolling.

"And the gossip columnist who reported—falsely—that the two of you were moving in together was a woman named Mindy Sampson. That's the same columnist who ran the photograph of you with Hunter, speculating that he might not be getting married to Casey after all."

"What's the point of all this?" Gabrielle asked.

"It seems as if Mindy Sampson has a way of knowing—or at least *reporting*—about your supposed romantic relationships, whether they exist in reality or not. Isn't it true that *you* were the source of both reports?"

"You're twisting things around."

"That's not my intent, Gabrielle." His voice was gentle, like an ally's. "We spoke a couple of weeks ago off the record. Do you remember that?"

"You were very rude at the time," she remarked, apparently rethinking her latest opinion of Ryan.

"I'm very sorry we got off on the wrong foot. I want to make sure I understand your side of the story. You conceded then that you may have—quote—*leaned in* toward Hunter when you saw the photographer. That—quote—*Sometimes these matters need a little push*. Maybe it's possible you spread the word to Mindy about relationships that were . . . let's say, in the early stages, like planting a seed in the hope things would blossom. Is that what happened with Hans Lindholm?"

She nodded tentatively. "As I said, it was a misunderstanding. I was shocked when he accused me of stalking him. It was completely humiliating."

"And did you also *plant a seed* with Hunter? Did you call Mindy Sampson so she'd have a photographer at the Boys and Girls Clubs fundraiser, then lean in toward Hunter when the photographer came around?"

Now she was shaking her head in denial. "No. I admit I contacted her about Hans. I thought if he realized I was good publicity for him, it would spark his interest. But the only reason I thought to call her is that *she* had been the one to contact me about Hunter."

"What do you mean, she contacted you?"

"She said she'd heard rumors that Hunter was interested in me. She said he was going to the Boys and Girls Clubs fundraiser a few nights before his own gala. Mindy told me Casey had an auction at Sotheby's that night and couldn't attend. She was the one who suggested I go to the fundraiser. She told me she'd send a photographer. Hunter was so happy to see me. He was so sweet and asked me all kinds of questions about what I'd been doing since we last saw each other. I'm telling you, we had a connection. There was an understanding. He was going to leave her for me."

Jerry was writing another note next to Laurie: *he just didn't know it yet!!*

Ryan managed to maintain a neutral expression, even though Gabrielle was beginning to sound completely delusional.

"You said Mindy was the one who contacted you about rumors concerning you and Hunter. Was that news to you?"

Gabrielle mulled the question carefully before answering. When she finally spoke, the tone of her voice had changed. She came across as lucid and thoughtful.

"It was widely speculated that Hunter's father could not possibly approve of Casey. And there were rumors that Hunter might be caving to family pressure on that point. And yes, I suppose I wanted to believe that maybe he was remembering our dates fondly and thinking I might be a more appropriate choice."

"So how do you think Mindy Sampson knew that Hunter would be attending an event without Casey?"

"Honestly, I always assumed it was Hunter's father. As we were saying, sometimes things need a push. Maybe he thought his son needed a push toward a different kind of wife."

"Do you know for certain that General Raleigh was pressuring Hunter to break off his engagement?"

"Well, I can't be certain, but you should ask Hunter's brother, Andrew. The night of the gala, he was even drunker than Casey. I saw him fetching his umpteenth scotch at the bar. I said something like 'Aren't you supposed to be working the crowd?' He said no one cared whether he was there, and he was thinking of going outside because Hunter and his father sucked all the oxygen out of a room. He complained that his brother acted so rich and accomplished even though the family business had been handed to him. I made some joke because I thought the entire conversation was unseemly. And then he said, 'If I were engaged to someone like Casey Carter, my father would see her as too good for me. But God forbid that the chosen son should marry a normal person. Well, good going, General Raleigh.' Then he held up his glass, like he was giving a toast, and said, 'Keep going down this road, and this loser will be the only son you have left.' To tell you the truth, when I first heard about Hunter's murder, I thought about Andrew's dark mood that night. But once they arrested Casey—well, it goes without saying, she's the one who killed my Hunter."

45

As soon as Gabrielle Lawson was gone, Laurie checked her watch. They had about half an hour before they needed to pack up their equipment. She looked for the General's assistant, Mary Jane, but did not see her.

Spotting a young woman placing flower arrangements near the podium, Laurie asked where she could find Mary Jane. If they moved quickly, Ryan could interview her now, leaving tomorrow's session at the country house entirely for Andrew and James Raleigh.

The woman with the flowers said she'd seen Mary Jane getting into a car on 42nd Street less than ten minutes ago.

Laurie pulled up Mary Jane's number on her phone and hit enter. She recognized the stern voice on the other end of the line. "Yes," Mary Jane said coolly.

"It's Laurie Moran. We have some time left in the schedule if we could have a few minutes with you."

"Why don't we speak tomorrow when things won't be so rushed."

"It will be quick," Laurie promised. "And since you were so instrumental in planning the gala that night, it seems only fitting that you should speak to us at Cipriani rather than the country house."

"Well, I'm afraid that's impossible. You see, I'm on my way to pick up tonight's seating charts, which I managed to leave behind at the townhouse. With traffic, I won't be back for at least another forty-five minutes."

Laurie thought the woman was more likely to forget her own birthday than the seating arrangements for a Raleigh Foundation event. She was tired of Mary Jane stonewalling her.

"Is there a reason you don't want to be interviewed, Mary Jane?"

"Of course not. But you're not the only person who has a job to do."

"Speaking of jobs, were you aware that Hunter actively disliked you and was trying to get you fired from your job?"

There was a long pause before she spoke. "I'm afraid someone has misinformed you, Ms. Moran. Now, please, keep your word and have your camera crew off the premises by the time I return."

As the line went silent, Laurie was certain that Mary Jane was hiding something.

46

After they were finished at Cipriani, Jerry, Grace, and Ryan gathered in Laurie's office to recap the events of their first day of production. As usual, Jerry and Grace did not see eye to eye on the subject of Andrew Raleigh.

"He was pretty lit up and talking out of turn," Jerry insisted. "Please, if I got accused of murder every time I said some petulant thing about my brother, I'd be on death row by now."

"No, no way." Grace raised her index finger in the air, which was always a sign that she felt strongly about her point. "It's one thing to say your brother's a bore or a blowhard, but calling Hunter the *chosen son*? That shows serious resentment, against both brother *and* father. That's some call-your-therapist business."

"If we don't make better progress," Laurie said, "*I* might be the one calling a therapist."

After such a successful day in front of the cameras, Laurie had been prepared for Ryan to try to take over the meeting, but so far he had been silent, fiddling with his phone to catch up with missed messages.

Laurie was an only child, and so was her son, so she didn't have much experience with sibling rivalry. On the one hand, she'd seen Andrew in action and could see he was a heavy drinker. She could imagine him speaking irreverently, but harmlessly, at the bar. On the other hand, she sensed when she met him at the townhouse that he was the disfavored son in an extremely accomplished family. His comment about being *the only son* his father would have *left* was disturbing, coming only hours before his brother's murder.

"We know that General Raleigh entertained a circle of donors late after the gala," Laurie said, "but Andrew supposedly went straight home."

"See?" Grace exclaimed. "That explains why he'd do it. Hunter left early because Casey was sick. Andrew probably thought, This is my chance to step up and show my worth. And then Dad didn't even invite him to the after-party. I bet he snapped."

"That doesn't make any sense," Jerry retorted. "Why would he frame Casey? And how did he just happen to have Rohypnol for that very purpose? Besides, you're the one who said from the very beginning that Casey was guilty."

An idea was floating at the edges of Laurie's consciousness, but she couldn't quite vocalize it. She looked to Ryan to see if he had any input, but he continued to tap messages on his phone. She forced herself to concentrate. She played back Jerry's comments about the Rohypnol pills, and then thought again about Gabrielle's interview.

"The father," she muttered.

"He sounds like a nightmare," Jerry said. "Used to being in charge at work and at home. You know what I think? I think Hunter really did love Casey. He wasn't going to cave to his father's pressure. And *that's* why Andrew said he'd be the only Raleigh son left. Maybe Hunter was going to choose Casey over his family. But the General had other plans. He plotted with Mindy Sampson—or had his assistant, Mary Jane, do it to keep his hands clean—to get that picture of Gabrielle and Hunter together. He was sowing discord. And then after Hunter was killed, he kept greasing the wheels, controlling the media coverage and planting online comments to make sure Casey was convicted."

"That's it," Laurie said. "The Rohypnol. This whole time, it was the drugs that didn't quite make sense in any scenario. But what if it was Hunter's father?"

On this point, Jerry and Grace agreed. They were both shaking their heads. The General loved his son, plus he had an alibi.

"No," Laurie explained. "He didn't kill Hunter. But what if he was the one who slipped the drug in her drink so she'd be an embarrassment—so Hunter would finally see her as an unsuitable wife. He could have put a few pills in her evening bag with the intention of making her look even worse if she claimed to have been drugged involuntarily. Then after Hunter was killed, he could have been so certain of her guilt that he decided to help the case along with the prejudicial online comments and Jason's book deal. And given Mary Jane's constant presence at the General's side, she probably knew about it or even did the dirty work herself, which would explain why she's trying to avoid being interviewed."

The room was silent. Her theory made sense. If they had an explanation for the Rohypnol that wasn't directly related to the murder, then it opened all sorts of possibilities about Hunter's killer. Even his brother could be guilty.

Ryan was typing on his phone again.

"Ryan, do you have an opinion?" she asked.

"Sorry. I need to make a call."

"Seriously? We're going to question Andrew and James Raleigh tomorrow at the country house. We need to firm up a strategy. You need to get your head in the game."

Jerry and Grace were both staring at her. They'd never heard her yell at work before.

"I just need to make a call."

The three of them watched as he left Laurie's office without further explanation.

"Just to be clear," Grace said once he was gone, "I knew Brett never should have hired that man."

"Sure you did," Jerry said. "Sure you did."

"It's late," Laurie said. "You two get going."

Twenty minutes later, when Ryan returned, Laurie was alone in her office. Ryan knocked before entering.

"I thought you left," she said.

"No. Are Jerry and Grace gone?"

"Yep."

"Can I come in?"

"Do you need to?"

"That's why I asked."

"Are we finally going to talk about how to handle the Raleighs tomorrow?" Laurie had worked in journalism for fifteen years, the last ten as a television producer, but she felt as though she was swimming in the dark here. She knew what it was like to lose a family member to violence. She remembered what it was like to know—or at least suspect—that some people were whispering *the wife's always guilty* when Greg's murder went unsolved for five years. It was possible that Hunter's father drugged Casey. And it was possible that Andrew was somehow involved in Hunter's murder. But if not, they were victims. They were grieving. They went to sleep at night missing Hunter. She would take no pleasure in asking them the kinds of questions she was carrying in her head.

"Yes, we'll talk about the Raleighs eventually," Ryan said. "But first I have to tell you something else. I know I probably wasn't your first choice as your show's host—"

She held up one hand. "This isn't necessary, Ryan. All I want is a good show. And you were great today. But the work isn't all in front of the camera. You need to treat an interview like a cross-examination, the way you did today with Jason and Gabrielle. The whole plan is fluid and constantly changing. What we learned today informs tomorrow. And Gabrielle dropped a bomb on us with respect to Hunter's family. We need to regroup before their interviews in"—she looked at her watch—"about fifteen hours. And when I tried to bring you into the fold for the work, you were totally out to lunch."

"Except I wasn't. I told you I had to make a call, and you didn't believe me. Just like when I told you today that I was working on getting information about Mark Templeton, and I could tell you didn't believe me. You're treating me like I'm Brett's nepotism project—"

"You said it, not me."

"Wow. Okay, I actually feel bad about having to tell you what I need to tell you, but here goes. You seemed skeptical about whether I'd actually reached out to my contacts in the U.S. Attorney's Office about Templeton? Well, I made several calls, right after we talked about it. And the reason I was being quiet about it is that I really am serious about this crossover into journalism, so I wanted to verify my sources before repeating mere innuendo. Brett told me how devoted you are to maintaining journalistic integrity. That was the reason I agreed to do this show, Laurie. I've never been your enemy. I had other offers for media opportunities, and this is the one I wanted. My sources won't go on record, but I trust them. And I finally have two, which I understand to be the industry standard."

"Just tell me what you're trying to say, Ryan."

"You were right about something being fishy with Templeton's resignation from the foundation. He didn't find a job for quite a while because, despite what James Raleigh was saying publicly, he was refusing to give Templeton a reference."

"That would be fatal to his employment prospects. So what changed?"

"He cut some kind of deal. No criminal charges were ever filed, but the U.S. Attorney's Office was involved. Templeton signed some kind of nondisclosure agreement with the Raleighs right around the time he started his new job. Voilà. Problem solved."

"Okay. Thanks for digging, Ryan. I'm sorry I doubted your follow-through. Why did you feel bad about telling me this?"

"The defense attorney Mark Templeton was seen with at the federal courthouse? It was your beloved former host, Alex Buckley."

47

When Ramon opened the door at Alex's apartment, Laurie could tell from his expression that he knew something was wrong. He usually welcomed her with a wry joke and an offer of a cocktail, but tonight, he simply told her that Alex would be out soon, and left her by herself in the living room.

When Alex emerged from the hallway leading to his bedroom, his hair was damp, and he was still adjusting the collar of his shirt. "Laurie, I'm sorry you were waiting. When you called, I was at the gym. I rushed home, but obviously you were quicker. Can I get you something?"

She very much wanted a glass of Cabernet, but that would come later. "I'm here about the show. Based on Ramon's demeanor at the door, I assume you figured out this wasn't entirely a personal visit."

"I didn't know for certain."

Not for certain, perhaps, but he must have been expecting this moment to come in some form. After all, he was the one who was always telling Laurie that she was better than any investigator he'd ever worked with.

"The last time we spoke, you warned me to be careful with this case—that I was dealing with some very powerful people. You were referring to James Raleigh, weren't you?"

"You don't need me to tell you that a three-star general whose name was at one point frequently mentioned as a presidential candidate is a powerful person."

"No, but I needed you to tell me that you have some kind of involvement with him."

He reached for her, but she pulled away. "Laurie, what *I* need is for you to remember that I have a job that existed well before I knew you or your show. Please don't expect me to say any more than that."

"I'm tired of you speaking in code, Alex. You've been talking to me like a lawyer since the first time I mentioned Casey Carter's name."

"That's because I am a lawyer."

"And because of that, you have attorney-client privilege. But your client isn't James Raleigh. Your client is—or was—Mark Templeton. But you knew James Raleigh first. You met him at a picnic when you were in law school. And then you went on to become one of the city's best criminal defense attorneys. And somehow that connection to General Raleigh is what led you to represent Mark Templeton when questions arose about his handling of the Raleigh Foundation."

"That's not fair, Laurie. I can't confirm or deny knowing Mark Templeton—"

"Are you kidding me right now?"

"I don't have a choice here, Laurie, but you do. You can choose to believe me. You know me, and you know I care about you, including your work. And I swear to you: You can—and should—leave Mark Templeton out of your story. You are barking up the wrong tree here."

"So that's it? I'm supposed to take your word for it and move on?"

"Yes." He made it all sound so easy.

Laurie felt completely powerless. Ever since she began working on this case, she had been acutely aware of Alex's absence, and it wasn't just because Ryan Nichols was such an annoyance. Something about Alex put her at ease. When they spoke, ideas flowed like water. Following her instincts came easily, at least when it came to work. And now Alex was telling her to ignore the facts, based solely on his word, and her instincts were screaming in opposition.

He reached for her again, and this time she let him pull her into a gentle embrace. He stroked her hair. "I'm sorry I can't say more, but please trust me. Why won't you trust me?"

She stepped back so she could look him in the eye when she answered his question. "Because I think you've been lying to me."

"Laurie, I have never lied to you, and never will. If what you're asking me is whether Mark Templeton was involved in Hunter Raleigh's murder, I will personally vouch for his innocence."

"You're still working for your client, aren't you? Alex, I'm talking about *us*. I was here, in your apartment, with my family right after I first met Casey Carter. Even then, you seemed to be steering me away from the case. Why didn't you tell me then that you knew some of the key players? You've been forcing me to drag every snippet of information from you, like it's a cross-examination."

"I didn't lie. I just didn't tell you everything."

She shook her head. She could not believe that the man she knew she loved was standing in front of her, defending the difference between a lie and a failure to tell her the full truth.

"Please, Laurie, play back the conversation we had after you met Casey. You never once mentioned Mark Templeton, Hunter's father, or the foundation. It was a fifteen-year-old homicide case, not a case about whatever may have happened years later at the foundation. And his murder was always thought to be about Casey and Hunter's relationship, which I know absolutely nothing about. So even *if* I knew something about the foundation, why would I have brought that up, especially *if* I was forbidden to talk about it?"

"You sound like the worst kind of lawyer right now—"

"And you're treating me like a suspect on your show."

"Okay, I get it, you're never going to tell me the truth. But tell me this: Do you owe a duty of loyalty to your clients, even if they're guilty?"

He sat down on the sofa, resigning himself to entering a new phase of the argument. "Of course."

"And that duty is forever; I think you told me once that it extends beyond the grave." He didn't need to answer. They both knew where she was going. "So it follows that if one of your clients—someone like, hypothetically, Mark Templeton—were desperately afraid that a show like mine would reveal that he did something horrible—like, for example, kill his friend to cover up embezzlement—it would be part of your job to undermine that show."

"Yes. Yes, Ms. Moran, you've got me. You're a better cross-examiner than I am. You win. Are you happy now?"

No, she was not happy at all. "You said you don't have a choice, Alex. Well, neither do I. Just before he was murdered, Hunter was looking into hiring a forensic accountant to audit the foundation's books. That gives Templeton motive. And his wife and children were asleep by the time he got home from the gala, so he has no alibi. Call your client: he can either talk to us on camera, or deal with the repercussions of what we choose to say about him in his absence. We plan to wrap filming in two days."

48

Laurie nearly tripped over a soccer ball when she opened her front door. She started to pick it up but then saw all the other signs of Timmy's presence scattered along the hallway floor: his trumpet case, video game cartridges, and enough sports equipment to teach a PE Class. Until Manhattan high-rises came with attached garages, this was the necessary decor, and it suited her just fine.

"How are my guys?"

Leo and Timmy were next to each other on the sofa watching the family's favorite detective show, *Bosch*. An empty pizza box was sandwiched between two crumb-filled plates on the coffee table. This was Timmy's version of paradise.

"You started without me?" The three of them were supposed to be binge-watching together.

Timmy hit the pause button. "We tried waiting, but the pizza smelled so good."

"We just started," Leo said. "Go change clothes. I'll reheat some pizza while Timmy rewinds."

She was on her second slice, engrossed in the show, when her cell phone buzzed on the end table. She stole a glance at the screen, hoping it was Alex. It was Casey. She decided to let it go to voice mail. She could return the call tomorrow from the Raleigh country house, where they'd be interviewing James and Andrew Raleigh. Casey and her family would be filmed last.

Instead of a new message alert on the screen, her phone buzzed again, and then a third time. Casey was hitting redial.

"Turn that off," her father said. "It's way past office hours."

"I remember Mom trying to tell you the same thing for years," Laurie said as she carried her phone to the kitchen.

Casey sounded excited on the other end of the line, skipping any kind of greeting. "I was just talking to Angela and my mom about the show. We think it would be wise not to mention the picture frame that was missing from the house."

Laurie quietly sighed. The last thing she needed was editorial notes from the show's participants. "I'm a little confused, Casey. I thought you believed the missing picture of Hunter with the President was the most compelling proof that someone else was in the house that night."

"It is, and that's why you shouldn't describe the picture in any kind of detail. We were thinking you could say that something was missing—or maybe even that a picture was missing—without saying it was a photograph of Hunter and the President."

"Okay, and why would we do that?" She immediately regretted asking, but curiosity had gotten the best of her.

"It's like the way the police hold back one fact so they can test people who come forward with information. I assume your show will bring in potential tipsters. To separate the real ones from the crackpots, we could find out if they know anything about the picture. See what I mean?"

What Laurie could see was that Casey and her family had been watching too many cop shows. "Let me think it over. We'll probably ask you about it when we film, but just so you know, we always edit the interviews later. Hey, while I've got you on the phone, tell me more about Mark Templeton. How long had he known Hunter?"

"Since freshman year at Yale. They were in the same residential college. Hunter was sort of a big deal on campus because of his family name. Mark was a financial-aid student, a bit out of his element at an Ivy. Hunter took Mark under his wing. That's how he was."

"And was that always the dynamic of their friendship?"

"That's a fair statement. Hunter was a big personality. Mark was in his shadow to some extent. That's what made me think it was even remotely possible that Mark might have been stealing from the foundation. Maybe over the years, he became resentful and felt like he was deserving in some sense."

Laurie had been wondering the same thing. "When the President decided to honor the Raleigh Foundation, did Mark also get invited to the White House?"

"No. Hunter was only allowed to bring one other person."

Laurie asked who he had chosen as his guest, even though she was certain she already knew the answer.

"He took me." Casey paused as she realized the reason for Laurie's question. "Oh my gosh, is Mark the one? Did you find more proof?"

Laurie wasn't sure what to think at this point, but she was certain of one thing: she already missed talking about these issues with Alex.

49

Laurie was surprised to see a can of beer in Andrew Raleigh's hand as a makeup technician applied powder to his face. She knew the man enjoyed a drink, but it was only ten-thirty in the morning, and he was about to be interviewed on camera about the murder of his older brother.

Perhaps spotting Laurie's wary look, he held the can up in her direction. "Only the one, I promise. Sorry, but being in this house always gives me the willies. I mean, this isn't the same sofa, but it's still the place where my brother was killed. I'll be lying on the couch watching a game and suddenly picture him running down the hall to the bedroom where it all happened. It's almost like I can hear the shots."

"I'm sorry." It was the only thing she could think to say.

"Wow, I really know how to lighten the mood, huh?" In the mirror he made eye contact with the makeup woman and asked, "How do I look, sweetheart? A work of beauty?"

She took a final look at her handiwork and pulled the towel from his collar. "A regular Adonis," she declared.

Andrew winked. "I think that's what they call sarcasm."

"Is General Raleigh here?" Laurie asked. They'd been at the house for more than an hour, and Laurie still hadn't spotted him.

On the other hand, the house had to be at least seven thousand square feet.

"No. A driver's bringing him and Mary Jane from the city. PTA twelve-thirty P.M."

"PTA?"

"Precise time of arrival. Nothing about my father's schedule is estimated." Andrew shook his empty can. "I feel a second one calling my name unless we get started pretty soon. Is your guy ready to roll?"

She turned to see Ryan clipping on his microphone outside the kitchen. "All good."

As Ryan eased into a conversation about Andrew's memories of his brother Hunter, Laurie thought about the remarkable progress her new host had made in just two days in front of the camera. He seemed completely comfortable, like a friend having a discussion in any normal living room. She turned to Jerry at her side. "What do you think?"

"He's actually getting good," Jerry whispered. "Does this mean we don't hate him anymore?"

She smiled. "Baby steps."

Jerry pressed a finger to his lips. Ryan was about to get to the good part. He reminded viewers that the prosecution's theory of motive was that General Raleigh was pressuring Hunter to break off his engagement with Casey. "Just how strongly did your father disapprove of Casey?"

"Pretty strongly. But he wasn't pressuring Hunter to do anything against his will. My father has a certain demeanor that comes from a military background, but at heart, he's a dad who loves his sons, and he was worried Hunter was making a big mistake. He spoke up in the hope Hunter would see the light."

"See the light about Casey?"

"Yes. He had good reason to be concerned. She was very temperamental. Impetuous, if you will."

Impetuous did not sound like a word Andrew would choose. This entire narrative sounded rehearsed and was a marked change from his tune when Laurie interviewed him at his father's townhouse. Gone was any sign of resentment of his father's heavy hand over his sons' lives. And he no longer sounded vaguely amused by Casey's willingness to rock the family boat.

"She could be very grating, with an opinion about everything. And if Hunter even hinted that her behavior was inappropriate, she'd say things like *Sometimes you're just as stiff as your father*."

Laurie found herself hiding a smile. She could imagine herself saying something like that if the situation called for it.

"And she could be terribly jealous. She was all too aware that other women were attracted to Hunter, not to mention the fact that he'd previously been very serious with a socialite who was quite different from Casey."

Andrew continued a monologue devoted to every one of Casey's faults. He was on his fourth anecdote about Casey speaking out of turn in "proper company"—this time at the gala the night Hunter was killed. "We were all concerned that she might have had too much wine."

Ryan interrupted. "Let's be fair here, Andrew. It's not unusual for people to partake a bit at these sorts of functions, right? In fact, weren't you also hitting the bar pretty hard at the gala?"

Andrew laughed like he'd heard an inside joke. "Unfortunately, that's probably true."

"Do you recall encountering Gabrielle Lawson? She said you were in a somber mood that night, talking about your father's interference in Hunter's relationship. In fact, according to her, you said your father would have no problem with Casey if she were marrying you. She just wasn't good enough for Hunter. She quotes you as saying that if your father wasn't careful, you'd—quote—*be the only son he had left.*"

Andrew's face suddenly fell. "I was hungover when I found out my brother was dead, and that was the first memory I replayed in my mind. I'm ashamed every time I think of that night. It was a horrible choice of words. Obviously I had no idea we'd lose Hunter within hours."

"So what exactly did you mean?"

"I didn't mean anything. Like Gabrielle apparently told you, I was drunk."

"Really? Because in context, it sounds like you were saying that your father might lose his relationship with Hunter. It gives the impression that your father was pushing Hunter to decide between him and Casey, and you believed your brother was going to choose Casey."

"Maybe. I don't know; it was a long time ago."

Ryan looked quickly to Laurie, and she nodded. Viewers would see the point. Andrew believed that Hunter was going to disobey his father, which undermined the prosecution's theory about Casey's motive for murder. It was time for Ryan to move on.

"Let's return to the subject of your brother's work for the foundation. By all accounts, he poured himself into it. It has been fifteen years since that night. How has the foundation fared without Hunter?"

"Pretty well, I think. We just had an event for donors last night at Cipriani. Every time we're there, we always have a moment of silence for both my mother and brother."

"Did you step into Hunter's shoes at the foundation?"

Andrew chuckled. "No one could step into Hunter's shoes in any aspect of his life. I work with staff on the silent auction for the annual gala, meet with press on occasion, but no, I'm definitely not engaged at the same level as Hunter. But thanks to his groundwork, the foundation is largely able to run with staff."

"But that staff no longer includes Mark Templeton, your former chief financial officer, correct?"

Andrew's expression remained blank, but the change in his body language was unmistakable. He shifted uncomfortably on the sofa and folded his arms.

"Mark was your brother's close friend, correct? It seems like he would have been a natural successor in leading the foundation. But instead, he resigned just a few years after your brother was killed. Were there problems?"

"No."

Ryan paused, waiting for further explanation, but Andrew remained silent.

"Have you stayed in touch with him?" Ryan asked.

Andrew smiled politely, but his usual charisma was gone. "He was more Hunter's friend than mine."

"How about your father? Is he on good terms with Mark Templeton?"

"Why are you asking so much about Mark?" When he began to reach for the microphone clipped to his shirt collar, Ryan effortlessly shifted gears back to Andrew's favorite memories of his brother.

Good job, Laurie thought. We weren't going to get any more information out of him, and you kept him in his seat. Ryan was finding his sea legs.

Once the interview had wrapped, Ryan immediately asked Andrew if he could show Jerry and a camera team around the property. "We want viewers to see why your brother considered this his home."

When Andrew and Jerry walked out the back door, it was 12:17. General Raleigh's "PTA," as his son had called it, was in thirteen minutes. Just as they'd planned, Andrew's tour of the grounds should keep him from notifying his father that they'd been asking about Mark Templeton.

But then twelve-thirty became twelve-forty and then twelve-fifty. Laurie's phone rang shortly before one o'clock.

"This is Laurie."

"Ms. Moran, this is Mary Jane Finder calling for General Raleigh. I'm afraid the General won't be able to make it to Connecticut today."

"We thought you'd already left the city. We're already filming."

"I understand that. I'm afraid time got away from us. But Andrew is there. He should be able to get you whatever you need in terms of access to the house."

"We need more than access to the property. Both you and the General agreed to tell us whatever you know about the night Hunter was killed."

"Frankly, Ms. Moran, the evidence speaks for itself, doesn't it? Not that you asked my opinion, but I'd say Ms. Carter has cost the Raleigh family enough without wasting their time with this futile reality show." She said the words *reality show* as if they were dirty.

"I was under the impression that General Raleigh still believes strongly that Casey Carter is guilty. We thought he'd want an opportunity to express his beliefs. You found a reason not to sit down with us on camera yesterday. Did you persuade your employer to stand us up today?"

"You underestimate General Raleigh if you think anyone pulls his strings. Please, Ms. Moran, I'm sure your show craves drama, but there's no conspiracy here: he is on a very tight writing schedule right now for his memoirs, which, with all due respect, are a better venue for his thoughts than your program. You're free to do whatever you want with your production, but General Raleigh won't be able to participate in the coming days."

"And you? You're also a witness to the events of that night."

"I'll be busy helping General Raleigh with his book."

"Speaking of the General's book, that's for Holly Bloom at Arden Publishing, correct? We'll be reporting Holly's role in publishing Jason Gardner's tell-all book about Casey, not to mention her assistance in securing a job for the Raleigh Foundation's former chief financial officer, Mark Templeton. Does the General know that we'll be reporting these connections, Ms. Finder?"

"Have a good afternoon."

Mary Jane didn't need to acknowledge Laurie's question. The answer was already clear. Of course General Raleigh knew the information they were reporting. That's exactly why Laurie was looking at an empty chair in the living room.

50

Forty-five miles from New Canaan, in his Manhattan townhouse, General James Raleigh watched his assistant hang up the phone on his desk. He had only heard Mary Jane's side of the conversation.

"She thinks you're pulling my strings, does she?" he said with a wry smile.

"Pity the person who would try such a thing."

"How did she handle the news that I would not be coming up to Connecticut?"

"Not well. As you predicted, she tried fear tactics. And I'm afraid I need to apologize. I realize that when I first called her assistant, Grace, I mentioned the name of your publisher. She's connected it to Jason Gardner's book."

The General waved off the apology as unnecessary. "I'm actually surprised no one realized earlier that Jason's agent and editor were both friends of mine. I see nothing wrong with the fact that I encouraged a man who knew that woman's dark side to tell the truth about her."

"She also mentioned Mark Templeton."

The General steepled his fingers. "I knew when she first mentioned his name to Andrew in the library that she'd be going down that road."

The General and Mary Jane had been on their way to Connecticut when Andrew sent Mary Jane a text message, warning them that Ryan Nichols had been asking extensive questions about the foundation and Mark Templeton. The General had immediately ordered the driver to turn around.

"Do you think she knows the truth about the foundation?" Mary Jane asked.

He shook his head. He had spoken to Mark Templeton personally. He could not imagine that Mark would be stupid enough to cross him.

"She still wanted to interview me, too," Mary Jane said. "Apparently Casey told her that Hunter despised me and was determined to have me fired. Is that true? Did Hunter dislike me?"

The General smiled. One of the reasons he trusted Mary Jane was because, like him, she never let emotions get in her way. She, too, came across to others as cold as steel. But, also like him, she did have feelings. He had never told her how much Hunter distrusted her, because he knew she would be hurt.

"Of course not," he said briskly. "Hunter liked you."

He could tell she wasn't completely satisfied with his answer. "Did he know about my last job?" she asked.

"No," he assured her. "Regardless, I would never fire you, Mary Jane. What would I do without you?"

51

At six o'clock that evening, Laurie's office was so covered in boxes, notebooks, and loose paper that she longed for the relative cleanliness of her own apartment, Timmy's clutter and all. She had just balled up a page of scrap paper and scored another two points in her recycling bucket when she heard a knock on her office door.

"Come in."

She was surprised to see Jerry and Ryan. They had stayed in Connecticut with the camera crew to finish up footage outside the police station and courthouse, and were supposed to go home directly from there. "What are you guys doing here?"

"We could ask the same of you. Seemed like a team effort might be needed," Ryan said.

"Grace offered to come, too," Jerry said. "But tonight was her monthly dinner with her godmother. I told her you wouldn't want her to cancel."

"You read my mind, Jerry."

Ryan began picking up balls of paper from around her recycling bucket. "Not sure you're ready for the Knicks based on these." Once the floor was clean, he plopped down in one of the chairs across from her desk. Jerry did the same. "I'm sorry today didn't go better."

"Not your fault," she said.

"Not yours, either," Ryan said.

"For what it's worth," Jerry added, "I was watching Andrew like a hawk after his interview with Ryan, but he did go to the bathroom at one point. I suppose he could have contacted his father then."

Laurie held up a palm. "Trust me, Jerry, short of going into the bathroom with him, there's no way you could have stopped him from contacting the General. Andrew wasn't our problem. If I had to guess, the General was Jason Gardner's first phone call from Cipriani, and Gabrielle Lawson ran straight to Mindy Sampson, who also tipped him off. And I blew it by losing my patience with his keeper, Mary Jane, yesterday." She also found herself wondering what role Alex may have played in the General's decision to stand them up.

"So I'm not sure how this works," Ryan said, "but should we talk about where we go from here?"

She opened the top drawer of her desk and pulled out Ryan's baseball. "Think fast," she said. He caught it with one hand. He had done good work the last two days. He was never going to be Alex, but at least he had gone more than twenty-four hours without being a jerk. As she had said to Jerry, they were taking baby steps.

Laurie looked around at all the documents she'd been scouring for hours and felt less alone. "Let's make two lists: what we know, and what we suspect."

The "suspect" list was much longer than the "know." Laurie accepted the fact that her show might not always reach a definitive conclusion, but she had hoped they'd at least be able to show that Casey was deprived of a fair trial. Between her bad defense lawyer, the anonymous online trolling, Mindy Sampson's column, and General Raleigh's involvement in Jason Gardner's book, the deck had been stacked against her.

But now they were almost done with production, and Laurie felt as if they'd accomplished nothing.

"Let's take another tack," Ryan suggested. "If you had to bet your entire life savings, what's your gut?"

Jerry volunteered to go first. "My life savings is about two hundred and seventeen dollars, but I'd go with Mark Templeton. I think the General—or Mary Jane at his behest—drugged Casey so she'd make a fool of herself that night. And then Mark, knowing that Hunter was about to expose him for embezzlement, saw an opportunity. He left the gala, went straight to Connecticut, killed Hunter, and framed Casey."

"So why won't General Raleigh help our show at this point?" Ryan asked.

"You already made me bet my life savings. Now you're hauling out the Socratic method? Okay, my guess is that General Raleigh is still convinced that Casey's guilty. That's the only reason he would've tried to manipulate this entire process. In his mind, whatever happened at the foundation with Mark is separate, and in some way he is protecting Hunter's legacy by keeping it quiet."

It was a good theory, Laurie thought, the one she'd been working on herself. "How about you, Ryan? What's your bet?"

"You sure you want to hear it?" he asked. "We're finally getting along. I don't want to find myself back in your doghouse."

"Stop it. Consider yourself initiated. What's your theory?"

"Honestly? I think Casey's guilty. I thought it from the beginning, and I think it still. And before you say I'm just sticking to my guns, I've kept an open mind. But the simplest explanation is that Casey did it."

"Occam's Razor," she said.

"Exactly. The simplest explanation is that Casey is guilty. Okay, Laurie, your turn."

"I honestly don't know."

Jerry and Ryan both groaned. "No fair," Ryan said. "We both went out on a limb. Tell us what you think."

Jerry jumped to the rescue. "That's not how Laurie works. She jumps from theory to theory, pulling her hair out, vowing to remain neutral. And then—BAM!—she's like an oracle: out comes the truth!"

"Bam?! An oracle? This is what you think of my work process, Jerry?"

They were still laughing, and Ryan was opening the scotch, when there was a knock at the door.

"I wonder who else is working late," she said. "Come in!"

It was Alex. She recognized the man next to him as Mark Templeton. "Can we talk?"

As they sat astonished at the presence of the two visitors, Alex explained, "Laurie, I called your home and Leo said you were working late. I took a chance that you'd still be here."

Jerry hurried to pull two chairs up.

"The extra chairs won't be necessary, Jerry," Alex said. "The conversation we are about to have is for Laurie's ears only."

Ryan and Jerry looked at Laurie, who nodded toward the door. "We'll be in my office," Ryan said.

As the door closed behind them, Laurie studied Mark Templeton. She had never seen him in person, but she recognized an older version of the man she'd viewed in numerous photographs, almost always next to his close friend Hunter Raleigh. Tonight, he was attired in a suit nearly identical to Alex's: dark gray with a white shirt and conservative tie. She knew that it was the exact wardrobe that Alex recommended for both trial lawyers and their clients for court appearances. It was a uniform. Just like Coco Chanel believed it was about the woman, not the clothes, Alex believed that it was about the evidence, not the man.

"Mr. Templeton, you've made it clear a number of times that you have no interest in speaking with me," she said.

"No, I made it clear that I wouldn't be participating in your show.

And I won't be changing my mind about that, for reasons I hope you'll understand. But Alex told me that you're likely to present me as an alternative suspect in the murder of my friend Hunter Raleigh, and I can't let that stand."

"Then I can arrange for you to be interviewed on camera tomorrow morning," Laurie said.

Mark shook his head vigorously. "No, no, no. All I want is for you to hear me out."

Alex spoke for the first time since they sat down. "Please, Laurie. I understand you're determined not to do me any special favors, but I know how you work. You care about the truth. You should at least listen to what Mark has to say."

"No promises, but please, go ahead."

Mark looked to Alex for reassurance. Alex nodded.

"A little more than three years after Hunter was killed," Mark explained, "the board of directors suddenly realized that the foundation's assets were nowhere near the targets Hunter had set in his five-year plan for fundraising. Because he wasn't there to raise our profile and market the foundation, I didn't think it was a surprise to anyone. But there was enough of a shortfall that the board decided to hire a consultant to do a full-scale study of the foundation from top to bottom—strategic mission, publications, investments, the works."

It sounded sensible so far. She nodded for him to continue.

"When they looked at the books, they saw not only that our fundraising was down, but that I had approved a significant number of bad investments and questionable expenditures, including large withdrawals in cash. I walked into what I thought was a routine board meeting, and James Raleigh cornered me, demanding explanations for each individual expense."

"Wouldn't that be something the CFO would be expected to have?" she asked.

"Ordinarily, but nothing with the Raleighs is ordinary. I refused to answer."

Laurie felt her eyes widen involuntarily. "I'm surprised they didn't fire you on the spot."

"They basically did. My—quote—*resignation* was announced by the end of business."

"And then it took you nearly a year to find another job. And in the meantime, you felt the need to hire Alex."

"I didn't hire him," Mark said.

Alex reached over and placed a hand on Mark's forearm. "Mark, I want to remind you again—"

"You don't need to remind me. I need to say this, to hell with the consequences. James Raleigh was the one who brought in Alex. After the board let me go, General Raleigh called all of his powerful friends to persuade the U.S. Attorney's Office to investigate me for embezzlement. He was certain I had swindled the foundation for nearly two million dollars. When the FBI first came to my door, I took the Fifth, refusing to answer questions. Then they went to my wife, asking her how we paid for a trip to Grand Cayman and her new Audi station wagon. At that point, I was tired of covering for him. I was determined to tell the truth. But I decided to play General Raleigh's game and give him a choice in the matter."

"You're losing me, Mr. Templeton."

"The reason I didn't answer his questions at the board meeting is because the questionable transactions were all Andrew Raleigh's. His father began pressuring him to become more involved in the foundation when Hunter started exploring the possibility of running for office. Andrew ran up his foundation credit card very quickly. When I asked him about the charges, he said he was traveling to network with his prep school friends to raise money for the foundation. Andrew wasn't part of the same New York social circles as his brother. He was out of his element and thought he'd be a more effective fundraiser in other parts of the country. I believed him at the time, but Alex tells me you think Hunter had concerns even when he was alive. The problem got worse over the years."

"Are you saying Andrew was embezzling?" Laurie asked.

Mark shrugged. "That may be too strong of a word. I think his heart was in the right place, but Andrew's a gambler by nature. He spent far too much money entertaining potential contributors at places like casinos. He chose risky investments. And the more he lost, the more desperate he became to make up the losses, leading to even worse choices."

"You were willing to be fired to protect Andrew?"

"*I resigned,*" he emphasized with a sad smile. "Even if I'd told the truth, they probably still would have wanted my head. I was innocent of any criminal wrongdoing, but, in truth, I didn't keep as close of an eye on Andrew as I should have. And I felt protective of him. Hunter was my best friend, so Andrew was like my own kid brother in some ways. I made a decision under pressure to leave the board meeting in silence, unsure what to do. Then the General's assistant, Mary Jane, called to say they'd be announcing my resignation. I thought I'd simply move on, but I couldn't get a new position without the General's recommendation."

"I don't understand. Why did General Raleigh hire Alex to represent you before the U.S. Attorney's Office?" she asked.

"Kicking me out wasn't good enough for him. He brought in the FBI to conduct a criminal investigation. Once they began asking me questions, I had a choice to make. If I'd told the FBI the entire truth, Andrew's crimes would have been exposed and the foundation would have had no future. I didn't want that to happen to Hunter's legacy. So instead, I told the FBI that someone else close to the foundation, with the instincts of a gambler, was responsible. Of course I knew that whatever I said would work its way back to the General, who immediately realized that Andrew was the guilty party. Everything with James Raleigh is a game of chess. He's always thinking eight steps ahead. At that point, I had him at 'check.' "

"If he didn't help you out, you'd expose Andrew," she said.

"Exactly. The next thing I know, Alex here is calling me, offering to represent me. I worked out a deal where the foundation agreed not to press charges. Technically, I was guilty of failing to supervise Andrew's actions at the firm. It would not have looked good for me, and my future employment prospects, if that had come out. I paid back to the foundation a token amount for the losses I was supposedly responsible for, and it was agreed that I would get a glowing recommendation from General Raleigh once I signed on the dotted line."

"That's a conflict of interest." Laurie was looking at Alex now, not Mark. "You led the government to believe you committed a crime someone else committed so they wouldn't scratch beneath the surface."

Alex's eyes were flat as he explained the mechanics of the deal. "It's not a defendant's job to correct the government's mistakes. Mark was satisfied with the outcome of the transaction. He also signed a nondisclosure agreement that he just violated by bringing this information to you. Our hope is that you will refrain from dragging Mark's name into the show now that you know the truth."

"How can you possibly expect that? You may have cleared your own name, but now Andrew is a suspect."

Mark looked at Alex, his face suddenly pale. "Andrew? No. You can't possibly think—"

"You just told me that he stole from his own family's charity. His brother knew there was money missing, and I can't imagine the shame Andrew feared if his father discovered the truth." Andrew also didn't have an alibi for the time of the murder, she reminded herself.

"But that's insane. Andrew loved his brother. And when his father did find out about Andrew's wrongdoing, he *didn't* shame him.

Instead, he threatened me with disaster if I didn't cover for him. Look, I no longer have a reason to protect Andrew Raleigh. The guy's an overindulged loser. He ruined my life, or at least that's what I thought before I landed on my feet. But there's no way he would have hurt Hunter. To be honest, he'd probably have murdered his father before he'd have touched a hair on the head of his older brother."

Laurie suddenly pictured Andrew at the country house, reminiscing about his perfect big brother. He may have had moments of resentment, especially after too much scotch, but she believed he had loved Hunter.

"Okay, thanks for coming here tonight, Mark. Please call me if you change your mind about going on camera."

"That's not going to happen. Can you please leave me out of this show? I'm just a normal guy trying to live my life."

"I can't make any promises."

Alex asked Mark to wait in the lobby while he finished up with Laurie. "It shouldn't have come to this," he said quietly.

"You mean it shouldn't have come to you doing dirty work for General James Raleigh behind closed doors?"

"I helped a decent man, Laurie. And now he's going to bed tonight terrified that his world is going to explode all over again, because you wouldn't take my word for it. If one of us should be judged, it isn't me."

52

After Alex left with Mark Templeton, Laurie phoned Ryan's office and asked them to come back. When they came in, she said, "It's been a long day. Let's wrap it up."

"Not to step out of bounds," Ryan said, "but shouldn't we talk about why Mark Templeton was here?"

Of course they should. But she knew Alex had a point. At this point, there was no longer reason to suspect Mark Templeton of murdering his friend Hunter. It was only because she had threatened to cast him suspiciously that he'd felt the need to violate his nondisclosure agreement with the Raleigh family. Laurie had seen the kind of influence General Raleigh was willing to wield to protect his family's name. The fewer people who knew Templeton's secret, the better.

"I can't talk about it right now."

"What do you mean you can't talk about it?" Ryan pressed. "Our last day of filming is tomorrow. Once we're done with Casey and her family, we're supposed to wrap it up."

Jerry held up an impatient hand. "If Laurie says she can't talk about it, she can't talk about it. That's how we do things here. We trust each other."

His words felt like a punch in the stomach. Jerry was showing her the kind of faith that she hadn't had in Alex when he'd asked for it. "Go on home. We can see where things stand in the morning."

53

She may have told Ryan and Jerry to call it a night, but Laurie couldn't bring herself to leave. An hour later, she was reviewing every document in the boxes she had picked up from Casey's defense lawyer, Janice Marwood. At this point, she was reading the pages just to stay busy. She knew that once she was home, alone in her room, the full impact of the conversation with Alex would hit her.

All these months, she'd been trying to make room in her heart for him, hoping he'd still be there for her when she was ready. But now he might really be gone from her life. She might have blown any chance they had at a future together, all because of this case.

It can't be for nothing, she told herself, flipping more quickly through the defense lawyer's files. There has to be something here that will lead me to the truth.

As Laurie pulled more and more documents from the boxes, she realized that Janice Marwood's files contained far more than the records Casey had given her.

Casey hadn't been certain whether Marwood had looked into the negative comments posted online, but Marwood's files indicated she had. In fact, one file folder was clearly labeled "RIP_ Hunter." Laurie flipped it open and found printouts of many of the comments she'd been able to locate in her own search. There were also copies of letters Marwood had sent to various websites, unsuccessfully seeking information about the identity of the author of the posts.

Another notebook was labeled "Pre-trial Motions." It was clear from the contents that Marwood had challenged much of the evidence that the prosecution wanted to present against Casey, and sometimes succeeded. In addition to getting Jason Gardner's "character testimony" about Casey suppressed, Marwood had also kept a supposed friend of Casey from college from testifying that Casey once said the simplest way for a woman to have power was to marry well. She also barred the testimony of a co-worker at Sotheby's, who claimed that Casey had set her sights on Hunter the moment he walked into the art auction.

This wasn't the work of an attorney who threw the trial. More disturbingly, Laurie had to wonder why Casey hadn't given her more complete information about her own defense.

Laurie needed a second opinion. To her surprise, her first instinct was to pick up the phone and call Ryan. She was even more surprised when he answered.

"You're still here," she said.

"Where I come from, you never leave before the boss."

Laurie was impressed at the speed with which Ryan was digesting the trial transcripts. It was like watching the law version of a master chef in his kitchen.

He paused to look up after reviewing the notebook of pre-trial motions. "This does not look like the work of a lawyer trying to take a dive at trial," he said.

"I was told she did a C-minus job," Laurie said.

"I would have said the same thing three weeks ago. She didn't put Casey on the stand, even though she had no prior record and could have presented herself well to the jury. Then she shifted gears at closing—suddenly moving from 'she didn't do it' to a manslaugh-ter theory. But now that I see all the work she did behind the scenes, I'd give her a B-plus, maybe even an A-minus."

"Then why didn't she move for a mistrial when one of the ju-rors reported that he'd seen RIP_Hunter's comments about Casey online? Is it possible she was trying to help Casey initially, but then somehow General Raleigh got to her?"

"I don't know," Ryan said, picking up another stack of docu-ments from the files. "General Raleigh pulling strings to get Casey's ex-boyfriend a book deal is one thing. But bribing a defense lawyer? And it's hard to imagine any decent lawyer willing to risk her career. I suppose it's possible, but—"

He stopped mid-sentence and flipped back to the page he had just finished reading. "Hold on a second, I think we have a problem. One of the motions to suppress has an attachment. Take a look at this."

The page he handed her was from the police department's inven-tory of evidence logged after the search of Hunter's country home. It only took Laurie a quick skim to realize the significance of what she was looking at.

"This inventory log wasn't in any of the documents Casey gave me," she said. "Let me make two phone calls to confirm our suspicions."

Fifteen minutes later, they had a new understanding of why Jan-ice Marwood had refused to speak to Laurie. Just like Alex, she had a duty of loyalty to her client, fifteen years after Casey was convicted. She didn't want to answer questions about Casey, because she knew her client was guilty.

"That's why she didn't ask for the mistrial," Laurie said. "She re-alized Casey did it. If the state retried her with a new jury, there was a chance they'd find even more evidence against her in the interim.

She got so much of the character evidence suppressed that she figured it was better to go to verdict and argue manslaughter."

For the first time since she'd met him, Ryan looked excited about the case. "The good news is we now have a plan. I'll make a copy of this for tomorrow. Casey won't know what hit her."

54

The following morning, Casey was staring at a copy of that same document. Her grip was so tight at the corners of the page that Laurie could see her knuckles turning white.

They were filming from a set in the studio. Unsurprisingly, the Raleigh family had refused to let Casey enter the country house. Even Cipriani had been reluctant to open its doors to her. Sotheby's declined, as had Casey's graduate school. She was a woman without roots.

Today, that worked in Laurie's favor. Laurie didn't want Casey to be on her own turf. In fact, Laurie had canceled this morning's interviews with Angela and Paula, asking Casey to come to the studio alone since her mother and cousin weren't "fully supportive" of her decision to participate in the show.

Now that questioning was under way, Casey was trying to keep her cool, but the page was beginning to shake in her hands. She dropped it on the table as if it burned.

"It looks like some kind of police report," she said, finally answering Ryan's question.

"Have you seen it before? It wasn't among the many documents you provided to the studio when we agreed to investigate your case."

"I'm really not sure. I'm not a lawyer, Mr. Nichols."

"No, but you've had fifteen years to work on your own defense.

You set out to prove that you were wrongfully convicted, and essentially treated that as your full-time job from a prison cell."

"I gave you everything I had. Maybe my lawyer didn't give me all the records. Or I probably narrowed things down over the years so I could focus on the most important parts."

Laurie wasn't buying it. Last night, she and Ryan had compared the defense attorney's records to the files Casey had given them. It was clear that Casey had selectively edited the file to make it look as if Janice Marwood hadn't fought on her behalf. She had also pulled this sheet of paper from the police's evidence inventory.

Ryan picked up the page and handed it to Casey again. "Can you please read the second entry on that list?"

"It says 'outdoor trash can.'"

"And then there are several items listed beneath that heading, correct? Please read the sixth item on the list."

Casey opened her mouth to answer, and then caught herself. She pretended to count each item, as if she had no idea which entry was at issue. "You mean this one? It says 'plastic garbage bag, contents: shards of broken crystal.'"

Exactly what the missing picture frame would have been if shattered to pieces.

Laurie's first phone call the previous night had been to Hunter's housekeeper, Elaine Jenson. She asked Elaine whether she remembered picking up any broken glass when she'd cleaned that day at the country house. She did not. On the rare occasions when she broke something while cleaning, she always set aside the pieces in case the homeowner wanted to try to repair or replace the broken item. She was also vigilant about recycling glass. According to Elaine, any trash bag containing broken glass or crystal must have been carried out by either Hunter or Casey.

Her second call had been to Lieutenant McIntosh of the Connecticut State Police. He chuckled when she asked him about the garbage bag. "Figured that one out, did you?"

"You knew?" she asked.

"Not for sure, not until you asked me about that missing photograph. We wondered when we found that bag in the garbage if perhaps something had been thrown during a fight or broken during a struggle. But the prosecution said it was too speculative to argue at trial. Then you come to my office telling me that his favorite crystal picture frame was missing from the house. I'm willing to bet that's what we found in the garbage. Breaking his favorite memento in some kind of temper tantrum."

"Why didn't you mention this when I asked about the missing frame?"

"Because once your show aired, I was going to use that to let the air out of Casey's tires. Can't help you too much, after all. Like I said, we got the right person. For what it's worth, I hinted at it. Said it might've been broken. That was a professional courtesy to your dad. And now you've figured it out."

"Do you still have the bag's contents? Can we prove to a certainty that it was a picture frame?"

"Nah. We keep the big, bad stuff like DNA nowadays, but a bag of garbage we never used as evidence? That's long gone. We thought it was a vase or something, but we never tried to piece it all together. Didn't seem to matter at the time."

It mattered now. Laurie remembered Grace's reaction when she first heard about the missing photograph: *She probably threw it at him when they were fighting, cleaned up the shards, and buried the picture in the woods before calling 911.* Ryan had reached the same conclusion: *For all we know, the frame got broken during an argument and Casey managed to clean it up before calling the police.*

This had to be why Casey had called her two nights ago, trying to convince her not to mention the missing picture frame during the production. Casey was afraid that the police would connect the dots.

Laurie had looked in Casey's eyes and believed she was innocent. How could she have been so wrong?

Ryan had predicted that Casey would storm out of the studio the second he confronted her with the evidence log, but she didn't budge from her seat, even when Ryan continued to tear into her. "Isn't it true that that bag contained the remnants of the picture frame you broke during a violent fight with Hunter? The picture that meant so very much to him? Or did it break when you chased him into the bedroom, firing shots at him?"

"No. It wasn't the picture frame!"

"In fact, didn't you even call our producer at her home two nights ago, asking her not to mention that picture frame?"

"That was for a totally different reason. It was strategy. You're twisting everything around!"

Casey was nearly screaming by the end of her response, pounding a fist against the table for emphasis.

Laurie felt herself flinch, but Ryan remained completely calm. "Then make it simple, Casey. This was your last day with Hunter. You must have replayed it in your head a million times. Just tell us what was broken that day. What were those shards the police found in the trash can behind the house?"

"It was a vase."

"And how did it get broken?"

"Things break. It happens."

"Let me be honest, Casey. If you were my client and gave an answer like that, I wouldn't put you on the stand, because any jury would see that you're not being honest. You remember more than you're saying."

"Fine, I broke it. I saw that picture of him with Gabrielle Lawson in the *Chatter* column. I got so angry that I threw the paper on the counter, knocking over a vase. I was immediately ashamed. I cleaned it up and took the garbage outside, hoping Hunter wouldn't notice."

"Why were you ashamed?"

"Because as hard as I tried, I couldn't get my jealousy in check. I can't believe I ever doubted his devotion to me, even for a fleeting moment."

"That wasn't the only time you felt jealous, was it? We've heard from others that you often spoke up publicly if you thought Hunter was being too cozy with other women."

"It wasn't always easy to be with a man who was so beloved. He was a hero. His family was practically royalty. By comparison, I was the tacky little commoner who had wheedled my way into the fold. It didn't help matters that the one serious girlfriend he had before me was a demure socialite—my exact opposite. When I would see him posing next to those kind of women, it wasn't just jealousy. It really hurt my feelings. But Hunter saw all of it as an expected part of the social scene."

"And how did you see it?"

"As a matter of respect."

Laurie felt Jerry and Grace staring at her, urgently wanting to talk about what was happening in front of them. Until today, Casey had presented her relationship with Hunter as a perfect fairy tale. Now they were seeing a different side of the story.

Laurie shook her head subtly, signaling for them to keep their poker faces.

"Hunter didn't respect you?" Ryan asked sympathetically. His cocky, smart-alec demeanor was completely in check. His tone was perfect.

"He did, but—he didn't understand. He was born the most important person in the room. No one ever judged him. He didn't know what it was like to be me. To have all those women assessing me, wondering how I was so lucky to be chosen by him."

"It sounds like this is a topic that came up repeatedly. Is it fair to say that you argued about it?"

"Of course. But not in the way my trial depicted. These were arguments like any normal couple would have. He was learning to be less flirtatious. I was getting less jealous as I became more confident in our relationship. And that's why I was so disappointed in myself for overreacting to that photograph of Gabrielle and him."

"So why didn't you tell us this?" Ryan asked. "Why did you remove this page of the police inventory from the documents you gave us? And why did you make it sound like your defense lawyer had done nothing on your behalf?"

"I didn't want you to think I was guilty."

The silence that followed spoke volumes. Casey's eyes desperately searched Ryan's for a reaction, and then looked past the camera to Laurie. "*You* still believe me, don't you?"

Laurie's face must have answered her question, because Casey immediately broke down in tears. "I'm sorry," she sobbed. "I'm so sorry."

The elevator doors had barely closed when they all let out a collective sigh of relief. They couldn't have asked for much more.

"I knew she did it," Grace said, holding up a fist in triumph.

"That is going to be the best scene we have ever aired," Jerry declared. "It's just too bad she already served her sentence. It felt like police should swarm in and haul her away."

Ryan waited until Jerry and Grace headed back to their offices to deliver his verdict. He leaned in close and said dryly, "If I were a lesser man, I'd be tempted to say 'I told you so.' "

"Good thing you're modest," Laurie said. "And it's a good thing

I'm a confident enough woman to admit a mistake. You were right: Casey's guilty."

Once she was alone, Laurie called Alex. Listening to his outgoing message, she realized how much she missed hearing his voice.

"Alex, it's Laurie. Can we please talk? You can tell Mark Templeton we won't be bothering him anymore. I'm sorry things got so out of control yesterday." She tried to find the right words. "Let's talk. Please call when you have a chance."

For the rest of the afternoon, she watched her screen, waiting for the phone to ring.

55

Paula Carter was on her hotel bed, flipping channels on the remote control to pass the time. At the desk next to her, her niece, Angela, typed furiously on her laptop.

"It was unnecessary of you to get us a hotel room, Angela. But very thoughtful."

"It's nothing. I couldn't imagine Casey wanting to get right back on the train after filming. Besides, Ladyform has a corporate rate here."

"I was so relieved when Laurie called last night to say she didn't need the two of us after all. And I understand why Casey decided to go alone, but why hasn't she called us? She should be done by now. How can you even concentrate?"

"I don't have a choice," Angela said, continuing to type. "We have our fall show this weekend. I'm doing what I can remotely, but Charlotte and I need to go to the warehouse to check on the design work on the sets."

Paula turned off the television. "Angela, I don't think I've ever told you how proud I am of you. How proud Robin would have been—to see how much you've accomplished as a professional woman. To go from being just a model to having such a successful career."

"Just a model?" Angela said, glancing from her computer screen. "I worked harder as a model than I've *ever* worked at Ladyform."

"That's not what I meant, Angela. You were always so beautiful — and, of course, are still stunning. But that was never your only value. Looks fade. Talent doesn't. I'll be honest. When you girls were little, I'd find myself comparing the two of you. Robin was always talking about how pretty you were. And, I'm sorry to say this, I would think, *My Casey will come out ahead in the long run.* I know how horrible that sounds now, but sisters are competitive, even about the next generation. I never would have thought that you'd be the corporate executive, and Casey would be the one who was —"

She couldn't bring herself to finish the sentence.

Angela closed her laptop, sat next to Paula on the bed, and pulled her into a hug. "Thank you, Aunt Paula. It means a lot to know you're proud of me. I'm sure somehow Casey will find a future for herself." Angela's eyes began to water. She wiped away a tear and laughed to lighten the mood. "Okay, now I'm the one fretting. We should have heard from Casey by now."

Paula was reaching for her cell phone when they heard the beep of a hotel key card in the door. Casey's eyes were red, and her face was smeared with makeup.

"Oh no, what's wrong?" Angela asked.

"Everything," Casey yelled. "*Everything* is wrong! They ambushed me. Charlotte's friend Laurie pretended to believe me, but then she sicced her attack-dog lawyer on me. He skewed all the facts. If they had at least given me notice, I would have had better answers. I could have explained everything."

Paula immediately regretted not fighting Casey harder about her decision to pursue this show. "Maybe it's not that bad," she offered meekly.

"Mom, it was awful. I'll end up looking awful. The whole point was to clear my name, and instead I look even guiltier than I did before. I could tell they weren't going to believe me. Yes, Hunter and I argued, but that's normal for a couple. We always worked it out. I shouldn't have tried to cover anything up, but I wanted to make sure she took my case."

Paula looked to Angela for guidance, but she seemed just as confused as Paula. "Honey, I'm not sure we're following you."

"When I gave my file to Laurie, I left something out. I left a lot of things out. So stupid. I should have known they'd find out."

"What exactly did you omit?" Angela asked nervously.

"I made the defense lawyer look worse than she really was. But the main problem was a page from the police inventory, showing shards of broken glass in the garbage."

"How could that possibly matter?" Paula scoffed.

"Because they think it's the crystal picture frame that was missing from the nightstand. They think I was the one who broke it during an argument with Hunter, and that's why I left the page out of the files I gave them."

"Well, are they right?" The words left Paula's mouth before she could stop them.

Her daughter's eyes were filled with pain. "Of course not. It was just a broken vase. I took that sheet out because I didn't want Laurie to assume it was the picture frame."

"So they're just speculating," Angela said. "I honestly don't see the problem."

Paula couldn't help but notice that Angela sounded less patient than usual. She chalked it up to Angela needing to leave for work soon.

"The problem is that I'm the one who broke the vase. A few days before the gala when I saw that photograph of Hunter and Gabrielle I was so mad that I slammed the newspaper down. It knocked the vase off the table and it shattered to smithereens."

Paula felt a pit growing in her stomach. "And you told them this today, on camera? That was the prosecution's theory of your motive." She put her hands to her face. "Oh Casey—"

"I know, Mom. Please don't start. That missing frame was the one thing I had on my side to prove that someone else was in the house that night. And now my attempt to hide that broken glass from them backfired. Not to mention, they made it sound like I was trying to manipulate them by suggesting we hold back the one detail about the picture frame. I didn't even make that connection. And now I'm going to look horrible."

Paula wondered whether her daughter was ever going to be honest with her—or herself—about what she'd done on that horrible night. Regardless, Paula was going to do what she always did—love her daughter and do what she could to protect her. Casey always said Hunter loved her unconditionally, but she never seemed to notice that her parents always had as well.

And because Paula always did what she could to protect her daughter, she told Casey to go into the bathroom to wash the makeup from her face. Once Casey was gone, she began pulling on her jacket.

"Where are you going?" Angela asked.

"To talk to Laurie Moran, mother to mother. There has to be some way to stop this show and let Casey live her life in peace."

56

Laurie must have looked pleased when she emerged from Brett Young's office. "The boss is happy?" his secretary, Dana, asked as she passed.

"Is he ever? But, yes, compared to his usual state, he's downright sunny."

Their highest hope during production was to rattle loose new facts they might piece together to shed light on an unsolved case. The idea that someone would actually confess on camera was beyond their wildest dreams. Casey didn't directly admit to killing Hunter, but she did concede that she'd been jealous of Gabrielle Lawson and that she'd lied to the show so they'd believe her claims of innocence. Her final sobs of "I'm sorry" were filled with regret. Just a short video snippet of that single moment would convince viewers she was guilty. No wonder her defense lawyer had advised her not to take the stand.

Brett predictably was pushing Laurie for an airdate already. She told Brett that she wanted to track down one or two people who knew Casey from the past, but thought they'd be done with production soon.

She was thinking of potential subjects to interview when she heard the sound of a raised voice coming from the direction of her office. She turned the corner to see Grace standing in four-inch heels, trying to calm down a very strident Paula Carter. She heard Paula say, "If I need to spend every penny I have, I'll hire a team of lawyers to tie this studio up in court for years. You're destroying our lives!"

"Mrs. Carter, why don't we talk inside my office?" Laurie asked.

Laurie let Mrs. Carter vent uninterrupted for several minutes. When she finally paused for air, Laurie handed her a copy of the release her daughter had signed. "That's a photocopy in case you're thinking of ripping it up. The language is clear. Casey agreed to a no-holds-barred interview and gave us the absolute right to air it. She has no editing power or any other authority to stop us. And please remember that your daughter was the one who approached me to help her. I did not insert myself into your family."

Paula was looking at the release. Laurie could tell that all the fight was falling out of her.

"Are you a mother?" she asked quietly.

"I am," Laurie said more brightly. "I have a nine-year-old son."

"Pray God that he never breaks your heart. I can't think of anything more painful other than losing her entirely."

Finally, confirmation that even Casey's mother believed she was guilty. That's what she meant when she said Casey had broken her heart. She'd broken it by committing an unspeakable crime.

"How long have you known?" Laurie asked.

Paula shook her head, lips pursed.

"You're not on camera, Paula. I'm not going to repeat whatever you say to me here."

"We tried to believe. Frank and I even prayed not to lose faith in our daughter. But the evidence was impossible to ignore. Gunshot residue on her hands. The drugs in her bag. And we of all people knew how fiery she could be. When Hunter started teaching her to shoot, Frank even joked that Casey might not be the best person to trust with a weapon. She wanted nothing more than to be Mrs. Hunter Raleigh III. If she thought she was going to lose that . . ." She let the thought trail off. "That's why Frank wanted her to plead guilty. He thought prison might even help her. But fifteen years? He never got to see her outside the prison walls again. Laurie, my daughter is seriously troubled. Is there any way I can convince you—mother to mother—to move on to another story?"

Laurie shook her head. The least she could do was level with the woman.

"I knew it was a mistake to do this show," Paula said softly. "After you first came to the house, even Angela asked me if there was any way I could talk Casey out of it. She had a feeling that Casey would slip up and come out looking even worse than at trial."

"Are you saying that Angela thinks Casey's guilty? She gave me the opposite impression."

"She gives everyone the opposite impression. I try not to resent Angela for being the one Casey credits with undying loyalty, but the truth is that Angela has her doubts, too. She always says, 'If Casey says she didn't do it, then she didn't do it,' but that doesn't mean she really believes it. But I made my peace a long time ago. I worried Casey wouldn't be able to get through her prison sentence if she didn't believe she had at least one person truly on her side. I continue to let Angela play that role."

"Paula, it's none of my business, but what are you going to do when our show airs? Are you going to continue to stand by silently while Casey blames everyone for Hunter's death but herself? She's already served her sentence. Maybe the way for her to find peace is to admit the truth about what she did—at least to her own family."

"I said before that I hope your son never breaks your heart. Mine was truly broken once I realized my daughter would never trust me with the truth. And if you ever repeat what I told you today, I'll deny it, just like my daughter."

57

Laurie had just put Paula on an elevator when the doors to the next one opened. Charlotte stepped out, wearing blue jeans and a black Ladyform-logo hoodie. Laurie was used to seeing her in elegant pantsuits on workdays.

"This is a surprise," Laurie said. "Are we planning a heist?"

"That would be much more fun. I'm on my way to Brooklyn." She said it as if it were a foreign country. "We need to get the warehouse in shape for the fashion show. The set builders started yesterday, but there's a lot of work to do. Angela and I need to go over the final plans."

Laurie had been so wrapped up in the show that she'd completely forgotten that her friend was under her own pressures.

"Can I help somehow? Not that I know anything about fashion shows."

"Unfortunately, I'm here for a different kind of favor. It's about Angela's cousin. Can we talk?"

Charlotte was clearly surprised when Laurie told her that Casey's mother had already beaten her to the punch. "She just left. I explained that Casey's signed agreement is straightforward. She can't revoke her consent now."

"I told Angela I didn't think there was anything I could do. But she sounded desperate when she called, and she's my friend, so—"

"I get it. But if my show is successful, there's always going to be at least one family torn apart by the truth. Everyone has a family. It sounds cold," Laurie said, "but I can't concern myself with that."

"What if you had found out something terrible about my sister? Would you have run with the story, even after my mother put so much trust in you?"

It was the first time Laurie had ever contemplated the question, but she answered without hesitation. "Honestly, yes. But, Charlotte, your sister was a victim. Casey's not. I know she's your friend's cousin, but she's a killer. Think of what she has put her family through. If I feel sorry for anyone, it's the Raleigh family." James Raleigh lost his son, and Andrew lost his brother. If the show was going to explore every aspect of the re-investigation, Laurie was going to have to expose their wrongdoing, too.

"General Raleigh isn't a perfect man," she continued. "I don't approve of his tactics. He had Jason Gardner write the book that convinced everyone Casey was crazy. He, in concert with his sidekick Mary Jane, was probably the source of the RIP_Hunter posts."

At that she stopped. The General had silenced and even threatened Mark Templeton to cover up the fact that Andrew used the family foundation as his personal ATM. But his concern was always for his sons. He wanted to make sure that Hunter's killer was punished, and he was desperate to protect his sole surviving son.

"I'll talk to Angela directly if you want. You shouldn't be dragged into the middle."

"I wasn't dragged. She's my friend, so I said I'd talk to you. But you're my friend, too, so I understand you need to do your job. Down the road, Angela will understand, too. Right now, she's in shock about Casey. She was so certain of her innocence, and now she's beginning to wonder."

Laurie's face must have revealed her apprehension. Charlotte asked if something was wrong. Laurie wasn't going to repeat what

Casey's mother had told her, but she did want Charlotte to know that Angela might not be as shocked as she was letting on.

"I think Angela may have already had suspicions about her cousin's guilt. If she asked you to get involved, it might be because she feels guilty for not telling Casey earlier the real reason she thought she shouldn't do the show."

Charlotte furrowed her brow in disagreement. "I wouldn't read that much into it," she said. "She's just a really loyal friend and is worried about Casey."

"I'm sure she is," Laurie said, "but it's my understanding she was worried it would come to this. Neither one of us would be in this situation if she'd told us from the beginning she had her doubts about Casey's innocence."

Charlotte looked away, and Laurie realized she'd spoken out of turn. Laurie was bothered that Angela had let Charlotte go to bat for her cousin with Laurie, when apparently she had told her aunt she thought Casey was guilty. But Charlotte had known Angela far longer than Laurie. It wasn't Laurie's place to question their friendship. "Anyway," Laurie said, "thank you for understanding my decision."

"At least I can tell Angela I tried," Charlotte said matter-of-factly. "Speaking of Angela, I better get a move on. She's already down at the warehouse. And speaking of warehouses, you might need one to expand your office. It looks a bit like a serial killer's lair in here." She rose from the sofa and began browsing the various whiteboards Laurie was using to organize her thoughts. "What is all this stuff?"

"It's not as bad as it looks. Most of those printouts were a futile attempt to find out who's been posting negative comments about Casey online. I had a theory it might be the real killer."

"Or it was yet another weirdo writing from his mother's basement," Charlotte said. "You should see the hateful things people post on Ladyform's Instagram account. Everyone's either too fat or too skinny or too old. It's easy to be cruel when you can be anony-

mous. What's the deal with 'and also'?" Charlotte asked, pointing to
the large red block letters that Laurie had circled.

"A phrase our favorite troll tended to use. Anyway, it's not important now. Good luck on your show. I'm sure it'll be amazing."

"Do you want to come?" Charlotte asked.

"Really? I'd love to."

"Cool. I'll put you on the list for Saturday. And good luck on
your show, too. I feel horrible for Angela, but I know this is going to
be a big win for you."

A *big win*, Laurie thought once she was alone. The words reminded
her of something Alex had said when they were first arguing about
Mark Templeton. "You win," he had said. She picked up her cell
phone from her desk, hoping he might have called, but she had no
new messages.

She was tired of waiting. She typed a text message. *Do you have
time to talk?* Her finger hovered over the screen, then hit the send
button.

She waited, filled with anxiety, as she saw dots on the screen, in-
dicating that he was composing a response. *I got your message earlier.
I just need some time to think. I'll call when things have cooled down.*

Cooled down, she wondered. More like, gone cold.

She heard a knock on the door. It was Jerry. "It's been Grand Cen-
tral in here," he said. "You ready to make that punch list of what we
need to do before we can start editing?"

They'd started the list earlier today. An affiliated studio in D.C.
would get footage of the exterior of Casey's childhood home and
high school. Jerry was tracking down yearbook photos and video images of Tufts, where Casey had spent her college years.

Once they were seated at the conference table, Laurie said she still thought they needed to interview someone who knew Casey and Hunter as a couple. "We have Andrew's recollections, but of course he's going to emphasize the negative. Mark Templeton's obviously a no. And Casey's cousin and mother won't be talking to us any time soon. Didn't Casey have any friends?"

"She did, as in past tense. They dropped her like a hot potato once she was arrested."

"What about her friends' boyfriends? Maybe there was a go-to couple for double dates." She was thinking out loud now. "Actually, Sean Murray might be perfect."

It took Jerry a moment to recognize the name of the man who had been Angela's boyfriend fifteen years ago. "I thought he already passed."

"He did, but he wasn't adamant about it. I didn't push, because it didn't seem important." Laurie now realized there was another reason Sean might be helpful. It would be interesting to know if Angela had ever told him that Casey's own family thought she might be guilty. "And I think he was worried how his wife would feel about his crossing paths with Angela again."

"But now that she's not on camera—"

"Let's track down his address. I might have a better shot in person."

58

Thanks to traffic on the Brooklyn Bridge, it took Charlotte's taxi nearly an hour to make the six-mile drive from Laurie's Rockefeller Center office to the Brooklyn warehouse where Ladyform would host its fall show in four days. As she swiped her credit card for the enormous fare, the cabdriver seemed to read her mind. "This time of day, it's better to take the subway over the bridge." Taking the hint, she left an extra tip to get him back into Manhattan, where business would be better.

She found a one-foot gap beneath the warehouse's steel roll-up door. She gave the handle a hard pull until the door rolled up enough for her to slip inside, then pushed it back to its starting place behind her. She'd been here three times previously, enough to know the basic layout of the building. What had been a distribution center for a commercial linen company had been overhauled into a three-story building with huge, arched windows and soaring ceilings. Eventually, the floors would be split into individual condo units, but for now the developer was bringing in revenue by renting out the largely unfinished space for photo shoots and corporate events. After Angela found the listing, Charlotte had immediately agreed that it was perfect for their fall show. They could "bring their vision" and "make the place their own," as the leasing agent said. Plus, it was dirt-cheap.

The first floor would be set up like a cross-fitness gym to feature the workout clothes and bodywear that Ladyform was already famous for. The second floor would be staged like a typical workplace with office cubicles, starring Ladyform's new expansion into business-casual attire for the working woman. And the third floor would have a homey feel to highlight pajamas and weekend loungewear.

"Angela?" she called out. Charlotte's voice echoed through the warehouse. "Angela—where are you?"

The only overhead lighting came from the dim, fluorescent ceiling boxes that buzzed above Charlotte as she worked her way through the first floor. Portable construction floodlights cast shadows as she passed. The stage lights wouldn't arrive until tomorrow, but the set was coming along nicely. A row of treadmills faced a series of Pilates equipment. Visitors would walk between the two as if moving through a gym, with models "exercising" on either side.

Charlotte recognized three large bins of sporting equipment and a box with their soon-to-be-released, long-sleeve workout tops that had been in the hallway outside Angela's office earlier that morning. She used the light from the screen of her cell phone to read a note that had been taped to the side of one of the open bins. *For first floor gym set.*

Having completed a loop through the first floor, she made her way to the elevator at the front of the warehouse. The doors opened, but when she stepped inside and pushed the button for the second floor, nothing happened. She tried hitting 3, but that didn't work either. Spotting the stairwell door in the corner, she took the steps instead. She was disappointed to see that the second floor seemed barely touched, other than more notes that Angela had taped throughout the space.

She was nearly out of breath when she reached the third floor, which seemed slightly more put together than the second. Two faux "rooms"—a living room and bedroom—had been constructed like the soundstage of a television show. A few pieces of furniture were in place. More notes evidenced Angela's presence. Charlotte could only read the one closest to her: *Accent wall. Paint gray.*

"There you are," Charlotte said, spotting her friend sitting cross-legged on an area rug in the fake bedroom. "I may need to work less and work *out* more. Two flights of stairs were a killer."

"They're high ceilings, so it's probably more like four or five." Angela looked up momentarily from the sketch pad she was writing on. "Can you believe what a wreck this is? And, as you probably discovered, the elevator's on the fritz. That's why the second floor's barely touched. It got stuck downstairs in the middle of the day. The agent promised it'll be fixed tomorrow, but trust me, I'm getting a price concession. I should have been here all day riding herd on the crew."

"Your family needed you. That comes first." Charlotte had spent five years in a frenzy of worry about a family member. She couldn't imagine what it would be like to find out that someone you loved like a sister—the way Angela loved Casey—was probably a murderer. "I spoke to Laurie. No luck, I'm afraid."

"Well, maybe it won't be up to her. Paula was talking about hiring a lawyer."

"I doubt it will do any good. I hate to say it, but is it possible your cousin is actually guilty?"

Angela's marker stopped moving. "I honestly don't know what to think anymore," she said quietly. "I'm so sorry I got you involved."

Charlotte was walking through what they were calling the "at home" set, impressed by the details outlined on Angela's notes. *Place light here* in one spot. *And also here* in another. *This chair is too low. And also it looks like it's meant for the second-floor set.*

Charlotte did a double take as she read the note on the chair. "You wrote all these?" she asked.

"Of course, I did. Who else was going to do it?"

59

It was late afternoon, but Laurie decided she had to try to interview Sean Murray. She had his address and went downstairs and hailed a cab. I might have more luck face-to-face than I would on a phone call, she thought.

Sean's Brooklyn Heights brownstone was on a quiet, tree-lined street, where children could ride their bikes on the sidewalk toward Prospect Park, and small purebred dogs roamed free on the occasional fenced front lawn. Laurie had thought many times about moving to give Timmy a larger home and more open space, but he loved his school and his friends and seemed perfectly content in their apartment on the Upper East Side.

From the front stoop, she heard the thunder of rapid footsteps inside the brownstone in response to the doorbell. "Daaa—aaad," a young voice called out. "There's a grown-up at the door. Should I get it?"

A deeper voice gave a response she couldn't make out, and soon she was looking at Sean Murray, the man who had been dating Angela when Hunter was killed. She recognized him from a few of the photographs Casey had provided for a montage. She could tell that Sean recognized her name when she introduced herself. "I wanted to talk to you again about the possibility of helping with our program." She lowered her voice. "As it turns out, Angela won't be participating in the show. I thought that might change the dynamics."

He stepped back so she could enter and walked her into a sitting room at the front of the house. She could hear children's voices and the sound of a television from upstairs. Sean took a seat in the wing chair across from her.

"I know you weren't sure how your wife would feel about the show," Laurie said. "Perhaps we should meet somewhere else?"

Sean let out a small laugh. "I felt silly the second I said my wife would mind. Jenna doesn't have a jealous bone in her body—"

"Then why did you say it was about Jenna?"

"Because I'm a terrible liar," he said, laughing again.

"You just didn't want to talk to me," she surmised. She started to pick up her briefcase, assuming the trip had been futile.

He held up a hand to stop her. "It's not that. It's—Oh, I may as well tell you. Angela asked me to find a reason not to sign on."

Unbelievable, Laurie thought. Angela had made it clear she had concerns about Casey's decision to go on *Under Suspicion*, but now it turned out that she had been actively undermining them.

"Is that because Angela has always believed Casey was guilty?"

Sean's eyes widened. "Absolutely not," he insisted. "Personally, I think Casey did it, but I can't know for sure. But Angela?" He shook his head. "She was a fierce advocate for Casey. Supporting Casey brought out the best in her."

"How so?" Laurie asked.

"I have no idea what Angela's like today, but back then, her whole identity was wrapped up in being a model. But she was losing work, always to younger women. She started to live in the past, as if her best days were behind her. It wasn't easy. Angela could be vain—and bitter. But she was completely unselfish after Hunter was killed. She told anyone who would listen that her cousin was innocent. It was almost like being Casey's most loyal supporter became her new identity."

"So why didn't she want you to talk to the show?"

Laurie could tell that Sean was on the fence about revealing a private conversation. "Fine, I'm telling you, because it's for her own good. She and Casey are practically sisters. They shouldn't have secrets between them. Angela didn't want me talking to you because she never told Casey that she was in love with Hunter."

"She was in *love* with him? She and Casey both told me that it was just a couple of dates. They even joked about it."

"Trust me, I heard that comedy routine, too. No, it was definitely more than that. Casey was so concerned with all those high-society women swooning over Hunter that she never noticed the way her own cousin looked at him. But I did. One day, I caught Angela staring dreamily at his picture in the newspaper, so I confronted her, point-blank: 'Do you have feelings for your cousin's fiancé?' She tried denying it initially, but when I told her that I couldn't continue a relationship with her if she wasn't honest with me, she came clean. She said that at one point she had really loved him. She made me promise never to tell Casey."

"You stayed with her, even after she lied to you?"

"Well, she didn't lie so much as not tell me the whole truth." Laurie couldn't help but think about her own bump in the road with Alex—or was it the end of the road? She forced herself to focus on Sean as he continued to explain. "Ironically, knowing about Angela's past relationship with Hunter made me feel closer to her. Her love for Casey was stronger than anything she ever felt for Hunter. She wanted Casey to be happy and didn't want to do anything to cause a problem in her marriage. I admired her selflessness. But I can't believe she's still hiding this from Casey after all these years. Why does it matter anymore? If anything, it shows how much Casey meant to her. But once she told me, it felt like a wall came down between us."

Laurie pushed away thoughts about her own wall, the one between her and Alex. The one she couldn't seem to drop.

"So why did you break up?"

"Because being a little closer isn't the same as true love. I think Angela really did try to love me, but I wasn't him."

"Hunter, you mean."

He nodded. "I felt horrible when he was killed. To be honest, I used to wish something bad would happen to him, knowing Angela was still carrying a torch for him. I hoped she'd finally be over Hunter and let me into her heart after he was killed. But then one night I was going through her hallway closet, searching for a replacement bulb for her dining room light. I found a box she had kept from her time with Hunter—like a 'memory box' or something. I gave her an ultimatum. I told her she needed to get rid of it if we were going to stay together. She became enraged. I'd never seen her like that before. It scared me, frankly. She taunted me and said that I'd never be as good a man as Hunter."

Laurie could tell that the words still stung all these years later.

"That was the end of our relationship. You just can't get past that."

No, Laurie thought. There are some things you can't get past. She hoped that wasn't the case with Alex.

"It worked out fine, though," Sean said, his voice becoming cheerful. "Met the real thing two years later. I can't imagine life without Jenna and the kids."

Sean's description of Angela was at complete odds with the impression she'd given Laurie. What she described as a few casual dates with Hunter had obviously meant much more than she'd let on. If the relationship had ever been serious, certainly Hunter would have mentioned it to Casey. And neither Hunter's father nor his brother mentioned Hunter ever dating Casey's cousin. Instead, it had been a running joke that Hunter and Angela would have made a terrible couple.

But maybe Angela hadn't agreed. Maybe she was faking the laughter, while she kept a memory box devoted to Hunter in her closet. Laurie pictured Angela, short on modeling work and with no other career plans—removing the contents when she was alone, sitting on her bed and dreaming about a reality where Hunter Raleigh III had chosen her instead of her younger cousin.

"Sean, that box you found. Did it happen to contain a picture of Hunter with the President?"

He smiled. "You guys are good. How did you find out about that picture?"

60

Charlotte and Angela had decided to take a "divide and conquer" approach. Charlotte left her friend to continue working on the "home" set upstairs, while Charlotte circled back downstairs to decide the exact layout of the exercise-themed set on the ground floor.

She unpacked the yoga mats and hand weights from the bins Angela had used to transport them from the office. She was always impressed by Angela's ability to find savings in a budget. They were renting the larger equipment like treadmills and Pilates machines for the show, but Angela was the one who'd raided Ladyform's on-site gym for these smaller items.

Charlotte was trying to decide between two different layouts she'd sketched, but found her mind wandering as she looked at her sketch pad. She paused to read all of the notes that Angela had taped around the first floor for the set builders. She found yet another use of the term *and also*."

She reached into her briefcase for her iPad, opened her email, and searched for archived messages from Angela. As she read through them, certain sentences jumped out at her in a new way. *I confirmed with the light company. And also we need to discuss music. Let's go to Lupa tonight. Best pasta! And also there's a shop two blocks away I want to scope out.*

And also. That was the phrase Laurie had highlighted from many of the negative comments posted about Casey online. Charlotte had never noticed, but Angela seemed to use the phrase, too. Maybe it was common, she thought. On the other hand, she couldn't help but replay Laurie's comments that afternoon. *Angela may have already had suspicions. She was worried it would come to this. Neither one of us would be in this situation if she'd told us from the beginning she had her doubts.*

Maybe Angela had known all along that Casey was guilty but didn't want to tell the police. Casey and her parents had been Angela's only family after her mother died. She could imagine Angela feeling torn about whether to turn on Casey if it meant losing not only her, but her aunt and uncle as well. But to post negative comments anonymously online while pretending to be her most loyal defender? To let Charlotte plead Casey's innocence to Laurie, even as she carried her own doubts?

Charlotte could not believe that Angela would be so deceitful. She was tempted to ask her directly, but in the likely event she was wrong, she didn't want to pile any more stress onto her friend's plate.

Then she realized there might be another way to put her concerns to rest.

61

Laurie called Paula Carter from the sidewalk outside Sean Murray's house. Paula picked up after one ring. "Oh, Laurie. Please say you've changed your mind. Is there any way you'll cancel the show?"

"No, but it may be better than that, Paula. I may have found a lead on the missing picture. But I have to ask you a question. Two nights ago, Casey called me at home, asking me not to mention the details of the photograph missing from Hunter's house. She said that withholding that detail from the show was something she, you, and Angela discussed."

"That's right. Of course, I tried once again to get her to call the whole thing off, but she ignored me as usual."

"But the idea of not mentioning the picture of Hunter and the President: Exactly whose idea was that? Can you remember?"

"Oh, sure. That was Angela's. She said that's how they do it on all the detective shows. Do you want to talk to her about it? She's down in Brooklyn getting ready for Ladyform's fashion show, but I'm sure you can call her cell."

Laurie assured Paula that wasn't necessary and asked her not to mention her call to anyone else for now.

As Laurie hung up the phone, she knew exactly why Angela hadn't wanted Sean Murray to speak to Laurie. She didn't want anyone to know that she was the one who removed that picture from the nightstand after she murdered Hunter and framed the woman he'd chosen over her.

Charlotte had described Angela as panicked about stopping the television show today—*desperate* was the precise word she'd used. But contrary to Charlotte's belief, Angela wasn't desperate to protect her cousin from humiliation. She was desperate to protect herself.

Laurie called Charlotte's cell phone, but the call went directly to voice mail. She tried twice more, with no luck.

She didn't want Charlotte to be caught in the crossfire when Angela realized that she was going to be arrested. She had to warn her. She pulled up her Uber app and requested the nearest driver.

62

At the warehouse, Charlotte was pulling up the most recent print-out from Ladyform's Information Technology Department summarizing Internet usage on the company computers. The monthly list notified her of every single website accessed at Ladyform, ranked with the most commonly used sites first. As usual, Ladyform's own website and social media platforms dominated the top of the list. She hit "Command-F" on her keyboard to access the find function. She typed in the word *Chatter* and hit enter.

She remembered Laurie complaining about the speed with which the *Chatter* blog had broken the news of Casey's release—and in such a negative light.

Seventeen hits in the last month—all from one computer. The users were listed by computer numbers, rather than name.

She pulled out her cell phone to call the IT Department, but couldn't get a signal. She finally found two signal-bars at the front of the warehouse, just inside the rolling steel door. It did not take long for Jamie in IT to confirm that the computer in question belonged to Angela. He also confirmed that she hadn't merely read the blog. She had used her computer to submit comments on the page for "anonymous chatter." Charlotte had a feeling that the time stamps for those entries would line up with the comments Laurie had been tracking.

She sent a quick text to Laurie: *I think I know who's behind those "And also" notes you were curious about. It's complicated. Let's talk tonight.*

Laurie understandably wasn't going to pull her show, but Charlotte might be able to convince her to leave Angela's name out of it. Charlotte could only imagine what a difficult decision it had been for Angela. She loved her cousin, aunt, and uncle, but Casey was a murderer. Those Internet comments about Casey's guilt must have been her way of trying to see that justice was served, without completely losing her only remaining family.

When Charlotte returned to the workout set, Angela was standing, hands on hips, next to the pile of exercise equipment she'd brought from the office. She picked up a pair of hot pink, three-pound hand weights and did a few curls, feigning fatigue. "What do you think? Set all this up in one station, or scatter it around the larger machines?"

"Great minds think alike," Charlotte said, reaching for the two alternative sketches she'd been contemplating. "I couldn't decide either. Maybe we should flip a coin. In the meantime, can we talk about something?"

"Sure.

"So this is awkward, but you know you can tell me anything, right?"

"Of course. What's up?"

"I know about *The Chatter*. And RIP_Hunter. I know it was your way of trying to tell the world Casey was guilty."

"But how did you—"

"We monitor Internet use at the office. I noticed a pattern in the last month." She saw no need to tell Angela that she'd specifically looked for one. "I'm just confused. You've always told me how close the two of you are. You said she was innocent."

"I can explain, but, honestly, I was looking forward to finally getting my mind off Casey today. Let's figure out this set first, and then I'll tell you way more than you want to know about my cousin and me. Deal?"

"Deal."

"Hand me that mat over there?"

Charlotte turned around and bent over to reach for a blue yoga mat. The thud of the three-pound hand weight against her head knocked her to the ground, where a blanket of darkness covered her.

63

Laurie was waiting outside Sean Murray's brownstone for the Uber car that was supposed to have arrived three minutes earlier when a new text message appeared on her screen. It was from Charlotte: *I think I know who's behind those "And also" notes you were curious about. It's complicated. Let's talk tonight.*

She immediately tried calling Charlotte, but got her voice-mail message again. She pulled up Charlotte's contact information and tried her office number instead. Her assistant answered. "Sorry, Laurie, she's at the warehouse with Angela, but she must have her phone on. She just had me connect her to someone in IT a few minutes ago."

That phone call must have been around the same time Charlotte sent the text about RIP_Hunter. "Do you know what she was calling them about?" Laurie asked.

"She had a question about Internet usage—who was looking at what from their company computers. You wouldn't believe the garbage people look at during work. No common sense."

Laurie asked her for the address of the warehouse, and then thanked her for the information and ended the call. Charlotte had been looking at the RIP_Hunter comments when she was in Laurie's office. Something about them must have sparked her curiosity.

If she had figured out that Angela was behind the posts, she was in real danger.

Laurie was dialing 911 when she spotted a black SUV with an Uber sticker in the window. She nearly jumped in front of the car to make sure the driver didn't pass her.

"911, what's your emergency?" the dispatcher asked.

Laurie blurted out the address of the warehouse as she climbed into the backseat of the SUV. "Please hurry," she said to the driver.

"Is that your location, ma'am? I need you to tell me what's going on."

"Sorry, no, I'm not there. Not yet. But my friend is. She's in danger."

The dispatcher was all business. "Did your friend call you? What kind of danger are we talking about?"

"She's in a warehouse with a woman we suspect of murder. She texted me because she figured out something very critical, and now she's not answering her phone."

"Ma'am, I really am trying to understand you, but you're not making any sense." Laurie saw the Uber driver eyeing her suspiciously in the rearview mirror. She realized she sounded insane. She forced herself to slow down and explained to the dispatcher that she was the producer of Under Suspicion and that a woman named Angela Hart was likely guilty of committing a murder for which someone else had already been convicted. "She knows we're on to her. I'm very worried about my friend. Her name's Charlotte Pierce. Please, it's a matter of life and death."

She saw the driver roll his eyes and shake his head. To him, she was just another crazy New Yorker.

"Okay, ma'am. I understand you're concerned, but you haven't told me of any violence, threats of violence, or any other concrete danger to your friend. I'm putting in a request for a welfare check, but it may take a while. We've got two major call-outs in that same precinct."

As the daughter of a police officer Laurie knew that a welfare check was a low priority. She could be waiting for hours. She tried again, but could tell her urgent pleas were falling on deaf ears. The clock was ticking. She hung up and called her father's cell phone. On the fourth ring, she heard his voice mail inviting her to leave a message.

"Dad, there's an emergency." She didn't have time to explain the entire story. "Casey's cousin Angela is the killer. And now I think Charlotte's in danger at a warehouse in DUMBO. The address is 101 Fulton Street in Brooklyn. I called 911, but the dispatcher entered it as a welfare check. Charlotte's not answering her phone. I'm headed there now."

As she ended the call, with a sinking heart she realized why Leo hadn't picked up. He had been asked to consult on a new antiterrorism task force. The first meeting was at the mayor's office this afternoon.

He might notice a text, she thought, and began tapping on her phone: *EMERGENCY. CHECK MY VM MESSAGE. CALL ME.*

64

"No, no, no, no." Angela was standing over Charlotte's prone body, her hands pressed together tightly to control the energy pulsing through her own veins. "What did I do? *What* did I do?"

She crouched to her knees and reached a tentative hand for Charlotte's throat. Charlotte didn't flinch from Angela's touch, and her skin was warm. Angela placed two fingers on her carotid artery. She felt a pulse. She leaned over Charlotte's face. She was still breathing.

Charlotte was alive. What am I going to do now? Angela agonized. Maybe I can still make this work. I have to think and be careful, just like that night at Hunter's house. Charlotte has to die, here, right now, and it has to look like an accident. If I can push her down the elevator shaft from the third floor, it will certainly kill her. They'll think that the bruise on the back of her head was caused by the fall.

Feeling more confident now that she had a plan, she looked around and then rushed to the pile of tools the builders had left with the construction materials, not even knowing what she was looking for until she stumbled onto a packet of zip ties and a box cutter. She slipped the knife in her pocket.

She was about to slip the zip tie around Charlotte's wrist when she stopped. Looking at the thin, wiry bands, she wondered if these would leave marks on her wrists and ankles, marks that could not be explained by a fall down an elevator shaft. There had to be something she could use that wouldn't—

Angela almost smiled at the irony of her solution. After checking Charlotte to assure that she was not yet regaining consciousness, she hurried over to one of the cardboard boxes and retrieved two stretchy super-soft Ladyform workout tops.

She cinched Charlotte's wrists together behind her back and was working on her ankles when she heard Charlotte begin to moan softly. She needed to work faster.

"There," she said, stepping back to admire her handiwork. Charlotte might regain consciousness, but she wouldn't be going anywhere.

Angela's thoughts were racing. She wanted to stop time and travel backwards to a parallel universe ten minutes in the past. If she could have hit the pause button at that exact moment, she would have seen that the situation wasn't as dire as it felt. All Charlotte knew for certain was that she had clicked on a few websites from work. Depending on how closely Ladyform monitored employees' computers, Charlotte might even know that she leaked information to Mindy Sampson and posted negative comments about Casey online. At that instant in time, if she had been thinking straight, she could have talked her way out of this. But of course she wasn't thinking straight, because she'd been panicked about that stupid television show ever since she heard Laurie Moran's name.

"Maybe I shouldn't feel so bad about what's going to happen to you after all," she said bitterly as she stared at Charlotte. "Your family's connection to *Under Suspicion* is what helped persuade Laurie Moran to work with Casey in the first place."

All these years, she had led Charlotte—and everyone else—to believe that she was Casey's most loyal friend and advocate. She was the one who regularly visited Casey in prison. How many times had Angela been told, *You're such a good friend. You're such a good person. Casey's so lucky to have you.*

Was there any way she could hold on to that now?

At first, she was merely annoyed at the thought of Casey on television, claiming to be innocent. Once again, at least in some eyes, she'd be the sweetheart who could do no wrong. But then Casey told her she'd noticed a picture was missing from Hunter's nightstand after the murder. Worse, Casey had told Laurie about it. In that moment, Angela believed that the truth was finally going to come out.

But then she realized how much time had passed since she killed Hunter Raleigh. The human mind is fragile. Memories blur and fade. She was certain that Sean would remember the fight that ended their relationship. He'd recall that it was about Hunter. He might even call to mind the box of mementos he discovered in her closet. But would he have memorized the exact contents of the box? Would he conjure up the one specific photograph of Hunter and the President? Maybe not. In fact, *probably* not, or so Angela had struggled to convince herself. And of course she had disposed of the box's contents the very next day, as much as it had pained her.

Charlotte began to move. She let out a low groan of pain. It was guttural.

Angela had taken a chance by phoning Sean after Casey suggested that Laurie interview him for the show. "After all these years, I think it would be hard if the two of us were to cross paths again. You're happily married. I'm still alone. Why didn't we end up together? I'd prefer that not to be an issue. Does that make sense?" He agreed that it did, even though it didn't, because people were so quick to assume that a single woman her age would not be happy alone.

But now Charlotte was starting to wiggle, not understanding why she couldn't move her limbs. "Angela?" she asked, in a faltering voice.

Angela tried to slow her mind down. Even though I persuaded Sean to decline Laurie's show, I didn't dare ask directly about the memory box he'd found in my closet. Any mention of it could have triggered his recollection or made him wonder why I was asking him about that. I had to cross my fingers that he wouldn't think back on that night. I had to hope that maybe he wouldn't even see the show. I could picture his wife saying, "Why are you watching that? Is it because you're curious about Angela?" If he didn't watch, no problem. If he didn't remember the picture of Hunter and the President, no problem. And even if he put two and two together, I could have said Sean was confused. He may have seen a different photograph. Or he had held a grudge against me all these years. I could have said I admired the photo and Hunter had given me a copy. There was no way to convict me of murder beyond a reasonable doubt based on an ex-boyfriend's ancient memory of a framed picture in a storage box in my closet.

But now look what I have done. I have no choice. I have to kill her and make it look like an accident.

Charlotte was regaining consciousness. Angela reached for the weapon she'd been carrying in her purse as a precaution since the day Casey signed the papers to appear on *Under Suspicion*. She could tell from Charlotte's terrified expression that she was awake enough to see the gun in Angela's hand.

"Okay, boss," Angela said, "you need to get up on your feet. Let's go."

65

Laurie's Uber driver came to a halt in front of the address she'd gotten from Charlotte's secretary. She offered a weak thank-you to the driver. "Sorry, it probably sounded like you were driving into a war zone."

The driver was already checking his phone to connect to his next customer. "No offense, lady, but you've got a wild imagination. If you ask me, you should take a walk around the block. Maybe learn a bit about meditation. It's the only way I make it through the day."

He drove away, leaving Laurie alone in front of the warehouse. She heard a dog bark in the distance. The streets were surprisingly quiet.

She called Leo again, but his cell phone went straight to voice mail. She tried her own apartment next.

"Hey, Mom." One of Timmy's video games played in the background.

"Is Grandpa back from his meeting?" she asked, trying to keep her voice from sounding stressed.

"Not yet. Kara and I are playing Angry Birds."

Whenever his favorite babysitter was there, Timmy was perfectly happy to have Laurie and Leo stay out late.

Her father had to be on the subway.

She tried Charlotte's cell phone again. There was no answer.

At the front of the warehouse, she spotted a foot-wide crack beneath the steel roll-up door. Am I already too late? Did Angela realize that Charlotte was on to her . . . ?

She couldn't wait any longer. She slid her back beneath the gate, pressed her belly to the ground, and shimmied inside.

66

Leo was deep in thought as he exited the lower Manhattan office building. He missed the excitement of police work, but did not want to jump back in full-time. The opportunity to work on this task force was perfect. It would be several evenings each month, and he could do a lot of his work from home. He could continue to look after Timmy and be around to help Laurie.

As he walked the three blocks to the subway, he spotted a cab discharging passengers and changed his mind. After they got out, he jumped in the back and gave the cabbie Laurie's address. He reached for his cell phone to check for messages. He then remembered that he had turned it off to avoid interruptions during the meeting.

His heart raced as he saw Laurie's text and then listened to her voice mail. The building Charlotte and Laurie were in was less than two miles away. "Change of plans," he shouted to the cabbie. "Go to 101 Fulton Street in Brooklyn and step on it!"

He yanked open his wallet and held up his police credentials so the driver could see them in the rearview mirror. "I'm a cop. You won't get a ticket. Move!"

His first call was to the police commissioner's office. He was promised that squad cars would be immediately dispatched to the Brooklyn address.

•   •   •

As the cabbie wove through the narrow streets causing loud horn blares from angry motorists, Leo called Laurie's cell phone. His heart sank when it went to her voice mail.

67

Her head hurt. Barely conscious, Charlotte felt herself being half-pushed, half-carried up the stairs. Why couldn't she move her arms? Her legs were so hard to move. Something was tugging against them.

What happened?

She heard Angela's voice.

"You need to keep moving. Come on, Charlotte."

Angela's voice. *And also. And also.* Angela had sent those terrible emails. Why? Charlotte felt a hard jab against her back.

"I started carrying a gun when your dear friend decided to investigate Casey's conviction." It was Angela's voice, but it was a different-sounding voice. It had a desperate, hysterical quality.

They had reached the second floor. Charlotte felt her knees buckle, but Angela shoved her forward. "Keep going up, damn you.

"Charlotte, don't worry. When something happens to you, the show will go on." She began to giggle. "Maybe your family would even like me to offer a dedication to you. Better yet, they might offer me your job."

Once they reached the third floor, Charlotte collapsed to the ground. "You don't . . . have . . . to do this," she pleaded.

"I do, Charlotte," Angela said grimly, her voice rising. "I have no choice. But we're friends. I promise it will be quick. You won't suffer a bit."

Charlotte yelped in pain as Angela yanked on the wrists tied behind her back, dragged her to her feet, and started pushing her toward the elevator shaft.

68

I can't take the elevator, Laurie thought frantically. I can't let Angela know I'm in the building.

She heard a voice scream from upstairs. "I promise it will be quick. You won't suffer a bit."

Her father would have warned her against entering the warehouse alone, but she hadn't had a choice. She dropped her bag down on the floor, pulled out her cell phone, and made sure the volume was off. If she had any chance to save Charlotte, she needed to remain silent. Kicking off her shoes, she made her way to the stairwell.

69

Charlotte was pulling against Angela's grasp as Angela guided her toward the broken elevator.

"I didn't tell you," Angela was saying in that same giggly voice. "The elevator's stuck on the first floor, but the doors will still open on this floor. It's a fifty-foot drop."

She let Charlotte, whose breathing was labored, collapse against the wall next to the elevator.

"I don't understand," Charlotte gasped. "Why are you doing this?"

Angela tucked her handgun into the waist of her suit pants and slipped the box cutter from her jacket pocket. Charlotte flinched when she saw the blade. "No!"

"I'm not going to hurt you," Angela said. "Not with this anyway." She cut the workout top from her ankles first. In a reflexive action, Charlotte began to wiggle each foot once her legs were freed.

Angela pushed the call button for the elevator. The doors eased open, but there was no sound of the car moving up from the first floor. Angela was reaching for Charlotte's wrists to drag her toward the shaft when Charlotte jerked away. Steeling herself against the dizziness, she fought for time. The words could barely escape her lips. "Please, before I die, tell me the truth. You killed Hunter, didn't you?"

70

From the top of the stairwell, Laurie could see Angela and Charlotte next to the warehouse elevator. Angela's back was to Laurie, and she was pulling some type of cloth from around Charlotte's lower legs. Charlotte was facing out, leaning against the wall.

"I'm not going to hurt you," she heard Angela say. "Not with this anyway."

Laurie saw her opportunity. She stepped out from the dark stairwell and into the room, and waved both arms. Please let her see me, she prayed. Please let her see me.

The warehouse room was cavernous and dimly lit. Charlotte would only notice her here if she was looking in this direction. She fumbled with her cell phone to pull up the flashlight function.

She found another chance when Angela moved toward the elevator. She waved the beam of the phone quickly in Charlotte's direction and then immediately turned it off.

Did she see me? There was no way to know.

Then she heard Charlotte's voice. "Angela, explain something to me. How did you manage to kill Hunter and frame Casey?"

Laurie felt herself breathe again. Her plan may have worked. Charlotte was trying to buy some time. Hopefully she knows I'm here.

But she couldn't help Charlotte from here. She began moving slowly across the room, searching for the darkest shadows as she made her way toward her friend.

71

Charlotte thought she heard a sound in the distance, and then saw a quick flash of light. Was someone there, someone who might help her? It was her only hope. Charlotte could see the darkness awaiting her behind the open elevator doors. And she knew she didn't have the strength to stop Angela from pushing her into it.

A blinding headache started to engulf her mind.

Angela is a murderer. Angela is trying to kill me, she thought. She had to find a way to save herself, to buy time. She had to get Angela to start talking. If someone is there, help me please, she prayed.

"At least tell me the truth," she pleaded. "You killed Hunter, didn't you?"

Charlotte felt a moment of relief when Angela took a step backwards and placed the box cutter in her pocket. But then she substituted the gun from the back of her waistband.

Angela's voice was rapid and approaching hysteria.

"Oh, Charlotte, you were so kind to let me leave early all those Fridays to see Casey. No one knew the joy I took watching her age in that horrible place. It was wonderful and great fun. My little cousin, my *sister*—always smarter, more loved—ends up in prison. Then she was despised. Loathed for killing Hunter. When we were young, no one ever thought I'd amount to anything special. I was the one with the single mother. I never got the grades Casey got, or did all the school activities. I was the one who skipped college to be the model, the party girl. No one ever thought I'd have a career, or could marry someone like Hunter Raleigh. But Casey's parents always acted like she walked on water."

"But why kill Hunter? Why kill me?" Now Charlotte's voice was a whisper.

"I don't want you to die," Angela said, "just like I didn't want Hunter to die. I was stupid to think your friend's show might find enough to convict me. Now look what I've done."

She began to sob. "You'll tell everyone what happened, what I told you."

"But why did you kill him?" Charlotte gasped.

"That wasn't supposed to happen. It was all Hunter's fault."

Charlotte couldn't make sense of Angela's disconnected thoughts.

"He was dating Casey, just like he dated me, and others. But then he proposed, as if she were special, as if they were in some kind of fairy tale. Casey told me all about how he'd broken down, crying about the pain of watching his mother die of breast cancer. She had the audacity to say they had *bonded* about a common loss." Her voice was now raised to the point of screaming. "But that loss wasn't Casey's; it was *mine*. Don't you get it? It was *mine*. She may have lost an aunt, but I lost my mother, just like Hunter. But, no, Casey was the one he shared that with.

"They were planning the wedding. It was absurd. Casey was pretending to be Miss Perfect, but Hunter needed to see Casey for her true self. He'd forgiven her after a few of her rants, but he needed to see that she'd be an embarrassment to him. I bought some Rohypnol on the black market and slipped it into her second glass of wine." Now Angela laughed. "Needless to say, it didn't take long."

"I still don't understand," Charlotte whispered, hoping to prolong the story. Help me, she thought. Somebody help me. I was wrong about the light. Nobody's here.

Now it was as though Angela were talking to herself. "I left the gala early, just as planned, because I had a photo shoot the next day. But I didn't go home. I drove to Hunter's house. I parked down the road. When they got there, I waited a few minutes. I went to the house. The door wasn't completely closed so I pushed it open. Casey was lying on the couch. Hunter was bending over her saying, 'Casey, Casey, come on, wake up.' When he saw me, I told him I was so worried about Casey that I followed them up. I pointed to her and said, 'Hunter, look at her. Do you really want to marry this drunk?'

"He told me to shut up and get out."

Over Angela's shoulder, Charlotte could see someone, *Laurie*, working her way through the half-built sets. She had no idea how long she could keep Angela talking. When she's finished, she thought, she'll push me into the shaft.

"Hunter ran into the bedroom. I followed him. I tried to tell him that I was only trying to help him, to keep him from making a mistake. But he wasn't even paying attention to me. That was when I decided that if I couldn't have him, neither would Casey. I knew he kept a gun in the nightstand."

Laurie had stopped behind the "living room's" sofa, the last spot of cover on her path toward them. Charlotte gave the slightest nod in her direction to signal that she could see her. Laurie's here, Laurie's here, she thought. Keep stalling!

"He rushed into the bathroom. I could hear the water running in the sink. I grabbed the gun while he was still in there. I knew how to use it, too. Casey wasn't the only woman Hunter had taken to the range. He came out of the bathroom with a wet cloth in his hand. I guess he was planning to put it on dear Casey's forehead. But he didn't get the chance."

Angela smirked. "He looked so confused when he saw me pointing the gun at him. The next thing I knew, he was lying on the bed, bleeding, dying. I knew I had to get out of there. But first I had to think. It had to look like Casey had shot him.

"Hunter had dropped the damp cloth on the floor. I picked it up. Fingerprints. Did I leave any? I wiped the drawer of the nightstand.

"I fired a shot at the wall.

"I went into the living room."

Charlotte could see that Angela was reliving the night of the murder. Her voice sounded as if she were in a trance.

"Casey had to be the last one to use the gun. I wiped it off. I put it in her hand. Put her finger on the trigger. Fired another shot at the wall. Held the gun with the cloth. Hid the gun under the sofa.

"Sleeping Beauty never stirred. Thought about the pills. If the police test Casey's blood, they'll know she's drugged. What if she drugged herself? Took the other Rohypnol pills out of my purse. Wiped the bag the pills were in. Pressed Casey's fingers on the bag. Put it in her purse. Wasn't I smart?"

"How could you have done that to Casey?" Charlotte asked as she watched Laurie moving closer to them.

The question snapped Angela out of her rambling.

"I'm done talking." Angela shifted the gun to her left hand and pulled out the box cutter from her pocket. "Turn around," she told Charlotte.

This was Charlotte's only shot. She had to take it. She turned slightly so Angela could cut the workout top from her wrists. Then she twisted into a low crouch and rocketed up, slamming the top of her head against Angela's chin. Searing pain shot through her body. She heard the echo of metal against concrete as Angela's gun fell to the warehouse floor.

72

Laurie rushed forward when she saw Angela careening backwards, she and her gun tumbling to the floor. Laurie lunged toward the weapon. Too late. She saw it slide into the elevator shaft, and then heard a clang from the first floor as the gun hit the metal cage two floors below.

Charlotte was bent over, her hands still tied behind her. Angela had regained her footing and was advancing toward Charlotte. Laurie saw the glimmer of a small silver blade.

"Get away!" Laurie called out as she rushed toward them. "She has a knife."

Charlotte stumbled forward, fell, and curled her body into a ball. She tried to protect her face by pressing it against the floor.

Laurie ran toward Angela, then leapt on her back with all the force she could muster. They both fell to the ground. Angela was on her hands and knees, but her right fist was still clenched around the knife. All Laurie could think about was the blade of the box cutter. She could not let Angela get back up again, not while she had that blade.

She grabbed Angela's right bicep and tugged it, trying to shake her grip on the knife.

Charlotte was no longer in a fetal position, but was still on the floor, kicking at Angela's arms. Laurie managed to stagger back onto her feet. She stepped hard on Angela's wrist, careful not to let her bare skin near the shimmering blade. She dug her weight hard against Angela's bones until she saw her grip loosen. "Get the knife," Laurie yelled. "Get it!"

Charlotte kicked the knife away from Angela's hand, and Laurie lunged across the floor to grab it. "I got it," she cried. She rushed toward Charlotte and cut her wrists free.

Angela had scrambled to her feet and was rushing toward them. She stopped when Laurie held up the box cutter. "Don't make me do it, Angela!"

Angela's shoulders slumped, as the reality of what had happened set in. She was out of options. Laurie heard the shriek of approaching sirens. When she turned to look out the window, Angela began running toward the staircase. She was halfway across the room when Leo, gun in hand, raced out from the staircase.

"Freeze. Down on the ground. Put your hands behind your head," he shouted as he advanced toward Angela.

Moments later, there was a pounding on the stairs as several police officers rushed up and into the room. Leo held up his shield. "I'm Deputy Commissioner Farley." He pointed at Angela. "Cuff her!"

73

When Paula had returned to the hotel and told Casey that Laurie was going forward with the show, she finished with the anguished cry "I begged you not to do this to yourself, do this to us. I warned you not to do this. I told you—"

"ALL RIGHT! Stop it. Don't you think I know I made a mistake? Now everybody will think that even though I served fifteen years in prison, I got off easy. I should be serving a life sentence. And that's probably what you think."

They drove back to Connecticut in stony silence. Paula's few attempts at conversation went nowhere. It was six o'clock. She went into the living room and turned on the news. She heard the anchor say, "This just in. There has been a stunning new development in the case of the fifteen-year-old murder of philanthropist Hunter Raleigh. We're going to our reporter on the scene, Jaclyn Kimball."

Oh God, Paula thought. What now?

Stunned, she watched as Angela was led out of the warehouse in handcuffs, a police officer on each arm.

"Casey," she shrieked. "Come here. Come here."

Casey rushed in. "What's going on?"

Then she heard Angela's voice. Her eyes froze on the screen.

Reporters were pushing microphones toward Angela as she was

hustled toward a squad car. One could be heard shouting, "Angela, why did you kill Hunter Raleigh?"

Angela's face was twisted with rage. "Because he deserved it," she snarled. "He was supposed to be mine and Casey stole him. She deserved to go to prison." A police officer pushed her into the backseat of a squad car and slammed the door shut.

Several seconds passed before either of them could speak.

"How could she have done this to you?" Paula cried. "Oh, Casey, I'm sorry. I'm so sorry for not believing you." Tears streaming down her face, she turned to her daughter. "Can you ever, ever forgive me?"

As Casey felt an immense burden fall from her shoulders, she reached out and enveloped her mother in her arms. "Even if you didn't believe me, you always stood by me. Yes, I forgive you. It's over. It's over for both of us."

74

At two o'clock the next day Laurie stood on the stoop outside General James Raleigh's townhouse and rang the bell. She was surprised when the General himself answered the door immediately.

He led her up to the library. She sat in the same chair she had used when she interviewed Andrew two and a half weeks earlier.

"Ms. Moran, as you can imagine, I'm stunned. The woman who my son loved so dearly spent fifteen years in prison for a murder she did not commit. I turned a deaf ear to all her protestations of innocence. After she was convicted, I introduced Jason Gardner to my publisher. I wanted him to write a book that would further destroy her.

"I made a promise to appear on your television show, and then broke that promise.

"I have been wrong from the very beginning. I tried to convince my son to break his engagement to Casey Carter. Then after she served all those years in prison, I was pleased to see that even after she was released, her torment would continue.

"Now, if you will have me, I would like to appear on your program and offer my profound apology to her on national television.

"I want to tie off a loose end you were interested in. Hunter was concerned that my assistant, Mary Jane, had been fired from her previous position. Here's what happened. She was the executive assistant to the husband of her best friend. When she inadvertently stumbled across his travel plans with his mistress, he fired her. He told her he would make her life miserable and ruin her own reputation if she breathed a word of it. In these twenty years with me, she has been a superb employee and confidante."

"General, all this has been so terrible for you. Please know that I understand that."

"I phoned Casey this morning." He choked back a sob. "I told her that I was sorry I hadn't welcomed her into our family with open arms. She was remarkably forgiving. I understand now what my son saw in her."

A few minutes later General Raleigh walked Laurie to the front door. "I want to thank you again for everything your program has done. Nothing can bring back Hunter. But it has made me think. In the years I have remaining, I am going to try to be a better father to Andrew."

Laurie kissed his cheek and wordlessly went down the steps. She stepped into the waiting car and gave Alex's address.

75

Alex answered the door himself. She saw no sign of Ramon. He gave her a quick hug but it felt chilly.

"Thanks for seeing me," she said.

"Of course," he said briskly, leading the way to the living room. "Can I get you something?"

She shook her head and took a seat on the sofa, leaving a spot next to her. He sat on a chair across from her instead.

"Alex, I know you said you needed time to think, but the silence is driving me crazy. They say never go to sleep angry. We haven't spoken in two days."

"They say that about couples who are married, Laurie. We're far from that, aren't we?"

She swallowed. This was going to be even harder than she'd expected. "No, but I thought—"

"You thought that I'd wait for you, however long it took. That's what I thought, too. But when I needed time—just a few days to think about how you and I might fit together, with our work, with our lives—you couldn't let me have it. Instead, you're here, demanding something I'm not sure you even want."

"I'm not demanding anything, Alex. I'm sorry I pressed so hard about Mark Templeton. You're right; I should have trusted you when you said to leave it alone. I just want things to go back to how they were before this case."

"To how they were? And how exactly was that? Where were we, Laurie? What are we now that I'm no longer your host? I'm your dad's sports buddy, your son's pal. But what am I to *you*?"

"You're—you're Alex. You're the only man I've met since Greg died who actually makes me wish I could move on."

"I know this sounds cold, Laurie, but it's been six years."

"Please understand that for five of those, I woke up every day in limbo. To even have dinner with another man without knowing who killed Greg would have felt like a betrayal. That's the space I lived in when you first met me. I'm still learning how to move out of it. But I will, I know I will. I feel myself waking up again. And you're the one—the *only* one—who makes me want to do that."

Time seemed to stop while he looked at her in silence. She couldn't read his expression. She forced herself to breathe.

"I wanted to think it was just a matter of time, Laurie. I really did."

She couldn't help but notice that he was using the past tense. No, she thought, please don't let this happen.

"I was willing to wait as long as it took. But this . . . *thing* that happened with your show is troubling. I just can't ignore it. We've both been telling ourselves that it's all going to work out in time, but maybe the problem is that you just don't trust me."

"I said I'm sorry. It's not going to happen again."

"But you can't control your own heart, Laurie. Greg was a hero. He saved lives in an emergency room. You were his one true love. Then you had Timmy to make you a family. And I've seen how you worship your father, too, who's also one of the good guys. He fights crime and helps victims. And that's what you do now with your show. But who am I? Just some lonely bachelor who makes a living as a hired gun, defending the guilty."

"That's not true—"

He shook his head. "I certainly don't think so, but you do. Admit it, Laurie: you'll never admire me, not like Greg. So you can keep telling yourself you're trying to move on. But you won't. Not until you find the right person, and then it will just happen. It will be effortless. But this?" He gestured between the two of them. "This has been nothing but effort."

"What are you saying?"

"I care for you deeply. I loved you deeply. I probably still do. But I can't wait in the wings forever. Now I think it's time for us to stop trying. I'm letting you go."

"But I don't want that."

Alex let out a sad laugh. "That's not how the whole 'if you love someone, set them free' thing works, Laurie. You don't get a say in this. If you ever feel like you're truly ready to be with me, let me know and maybe we'll go from there. But that's not going to be today, or tomorrow, or next week."

In other words, he was done waiting.

When he hugged her at the door, it felt like good-bye.

No, Laurie thought, as she stepped into the elevator. This is not the end of this story. I'm ready to live again—not in limbo, but freely and happily, the way Greg would want me to. Alex is the one I want to share my life with, and I'll find a way to prove that to him.

Alex was about to pour gin into a metal shaker when Ramon emerged from his room. Shooing Alex out of the way, he stepped in to take over.

"Your martinis are always better than mine," Alex said gratefully.

"I couldn't help but notice that you were smiling," Ramon observed. "Did everything go well?"

Alex knew that causing Laurie pain now was the price to be paid for the future.

"This has been a tough case, Ramon," Alex said, as he reached for the glass Ramon set in front of him. "But I just gave a good summation, and I believe the jury's going to decide in our favor."

He leaned back and began to sip the martini.

Mary Higgins Clark & Alafair Burke

The Cinderella Murder

Television producer Laurie Moran is elated when
the pilot for her reality drama, *Under Suspicion*, is a success.
Each episode revisits a cold case, and the very first episode
helped to solve an infamous murder.

Now Laurie has the ideal case to feature in the next
instalment of *Under Suspicion*: the Cinderella Murder. When
Susan Dempsey, a beautiful and multi-talented UCLA student,
was found dead, her murder left numerous questions. Had she
ever shown up for the acting audition she was due to attend
at the home of an up-and-coming director? Why does Susan's
boyfriend want to avoid questions about their relationship?
And why was Susan missing one of her shoes
when her body was discovered?

With the help of lawyer and *Under Suspicion* host Alex Buckley,
Laurie knows the case will make a great program, especially
when the former suspects include Hollywood's elite and tech
billionaires. The suspense and drama are perfect for the silver
screen – but is Cinderella's murderer ready for a close-up?

Paperback ISBN 978-1-4711-3849-2
eBook ISBN 978-1-4711-3851-5

Mary Higgins Clark & Alafair Burke

All Dressed in White

Five years ago Amanda Pierce was excitedly preparing
to marry her college sweetheart. She and Jeffrey had already
battled through sickness and health, although their lives were
certainly more richer than poorer as Amanda was set to inherit
her father's successful garment company.

Then Amanda disappeared the night of her bachelorette party.

In present-day New York City, Laurie Moran realizes a
missing bride is the perfect cold case for her *Under Suspicion*
television series to investigate. By recreating the night of the
disappearance at the wedding's Florida resort with Amanda's
friends and family, Laurie hopes to find the same success
solving the cases featured in the series' first episodes.

But Laurie and *Under Suspicion* host Alex Buckley
quickly discover everyone has their own theory about
why Amanda disappeared into thin air . . .

Paperback ISBN 978-1-4711-4870-5
eBook ISBN 978-1-4711-4871-2